DRAGON

STEVEN BRUST

DRAGON

TOR®

A TOM DOHERTY ASSOCIATES BOOK

NEW YORK

DRAGON

Copyright © 1998 by Steven Brust

This book is printed on acid-free paper.

Edited by Patrick and Teresa Nielsen Hayden

Design by Basha Durand

A Tor Book
Published by Tom Doherty Associates, Inc.
175 Fifth Avenue
New York, NY 10010

Tor Books on the World Wide Web:
http://www.tor.com

Tor® is a registered trademark of Tom Doherty Associates, Inc.

Library of Congress Cataloging-in-Publication Data

Brust, Steven
    Dragon / Steven Brust. — 1st ed.
      p. cm.
    "A Tom Doherty Associates book."
    ISBN 0-312-86692-5 (acid free paper)
    I. Title.
  PS3552.R84D73   1998
  813'.54—dc21   98-23558
                                CIP

First Edition: November 1998

Printed in the United States of America

0 9 8 7 6 5 4 3 2 1

This book was written for my dear friend, Geri Sullivan, who rocked the whole album cover situation.

Acknowledgments

Thanks to the following people who were of great help with research: Corwin Brust, Gail Catherine, Paul Knappenberger, Beki Oshiro, and Gypsy.

Thanks also to Emma Bull, Raphael Carter, Pamela Dean, and Will Shetterly for helpful suggestions and general Scribblification; to Fred A. Levy Haskell for last-minute proofing; to Liz, Beki, Cyndi, and Tesla for chocolate, first reactions, and Stuff; and to Patrick and Teresa for many things, but especially for the Staten Island Ferry.

It's high time I acknowledged and thanked Steve Bond, Reen Brust, John Robey, and John Stanley: You Know Who You Are.

Always and ever, my thanks to Adrian Morgan, whose fingerprints are on every page of every book I've written about Dragaera.

And special thanks to Stephen Jones of Wembly, England, who first suggested this one.

When all is in harmony the army can withstand
natural attacks and those that appear to be supernatural.
                                    SUN TZU, *The Art of War*

DRAGON

1

MEMORY IS LIKE A WATCHACALLIT

No shit, there I was. . . .

We'd been cut up so many ways and so many times we hardly had a skirmish line, and the enemy kept getting reinforced. I, like the rest of the outfit, was exhausted and terrified from swords buzzing past my ear and various sorts of sorceries going "whoosh" over my head, or maybe it was the other way around; and there were dead people moaning and writhing on the ground, and wounded people lying still, and that was almost certainly the other way around, but I'm giving it to you as I remember it, though I know my memory sometimes plays tricks on me.

More on that in a second.

First, I have to ask you to excuse me for starting in the middle, but that's more or less where it starts.

So there I was, in a full-scale battle; that is, in a place where no self-respecting assassin ought to be. Worse, in a full-scale battle with the keen sense that I was on the losing side, at least in this part of the engagement. I stood on Dorian's Hill, with the Wall about two hundred yards behind me, and the Tomb (which is not a tomb, and never was, and ought not to be called that) about a quarter of a mile to my left. I wanted to teleport out, or at least run, but I couldn't because, well, I just couldn't. I had a sword, and I carried enough other weaponry to outfit half of Cropper Company (my unit, hurrah hurrah). In front of us was The Enemy, getting closer with each step, and looking like this time they meant to stay. There were so many of them, and all I could think of was, "If they want this damned hill so badly, let them have it," but I knew that was wrong, and certainly my messmates would have argued with the sentiment; we'd worked hard enough to take it away from them the first time. (And we had failed. So why did we now occupy the hill? I don't know; they don't explain these things to foot soldiers.)

Then, as if that wasn't bad enough, I heard the rip of the juice-drum playing "Time To Be Alive," which meant to form up for a charge. I guessed the Captain had decided we weren't strong enough to defend, or else he wanted to go out in a blaze of glory. I don't know: it seemed to me that if you already had the high ground, why waste it by charging? I wanted to call him an idiot but I knew he wasn't.

I relaxed my grip on my sword and took the requisite Three Deep Breaths as he positioned himself in front of us. I found myself right next to Dunn, the alternate bannerman, which put my life expectancy at just marginally above his, and his was just about the same as the bannerman, and *hers* was mathematically almost indistinguishable from zero. Well, they had both wanted the job; now they had it.

The Captain gave no speeches this time; I guess he'd said everything he had to say over the last couple of days. He gave the signal that started us moving forward.

As before, I discovered that I was moving, although I don't remember ever deciding to; I wondered, as I had several times before, if there was some sort of subtle magic involved, but I don't think so. I recall that I really, really, *really* wanted to bolt, but I still couldn't, so of course I did the only thing I could: I started praying. It was far too late for that, however, and nothing happened.

Or maybe something did; I'm not sure.

Oh yeah, I was going to talk about memory. Maybe memory is where it starts. I don't know where it starts; that's part of why I'm doing this, hoping to put it together and make some kind of sense out of the whole thing. Of course, the gold ingots are a bigger part of why I'm doing this. Where was I? Right, memory.

I woke up one morning remembering something I'd forgotten the day before. I'd been having a one-sided conversation with a metal box, much as I'm doing now, in exchange for a good sum of raw gold and various useful oddities and trinkets, and I'd felt like I'd fulfilled my part of the bargain, but then, the morning after I finished, I realized what I'd forgotten, and my first thought was that someone had been playing with my memories. My second thought was that, if this were true, I was going to hurt someone. My third thought was to consider, if someone *was* repressing my memories, who that someone had to be. This was chilling, and it brought me fully awake, which led to one of those irritating sessions of "How much was a dream?" After several minutes I had it sorted out in my head so I got up.

Loiosh, my familiar, was just stirring. He gave his bat-like wings one lazy flap, hissed at me sleepily, and said, *"How 'bout something to eat?"* into my mind.

I said, *"Do you remember Deathgate Falls?"*

"No. I'm senile. Of course I remember—"

"As you approach the Falls, do you remember there being a large statue?"

"Sure, Boss. Where Morrolan performed that embarrassing ritual. What about it?"

"Nothing." Right. The ritual. I had forgotten that, too. I hate having disturbing thoughts before breakfast. I hate having thoughts before breakfast.

"Is it important, Boss?"

"Let it go, Loiosh."

That was then, and it illustrates what a tricky thing memory is: I had forgotten something important that had happened just days before, yet now, more than three years later, I remember waking up and talking to Loiosh about it. Interesting, isn't it?

But here, I've left you, you odd, shiny contraption with presumed ears at both ends, confused about who and what I am, and generally what I'm on about. Okay. I'll let you stay confused a little longer, and if you don't trust me to clear everything up, then you can go hang. I've been paid.

I whipped up a quick omelet, ate it, and washed up, considering whether to ask someone about my odd memory lapse. I'd made two acquaintances recently who might know, but I felt loath to ask them; something about expressing weakness, I suppose. But it bothered me. I was still thinking about it when I finished donning my Jhereg colors (grey and black, if you're taking notes) and making sure my various weapons were in place; after which I stepped out onto the street I all but owned.

I don't usually travel with a bodyguard. For one thing, it would be hard to find anyone who could give me more warning of danger than Loiosh; for another, I'm not important enough to be a real threat to anyone; and for yet another, it's humiliating. I know that to some in the Organization the number of bodyguards is a status symbol, but to me they are only an irritation.

But I'm different. I wasn't born into the Organization. I wasn't even born into House Jhereg. In fact, I wasn't born a citizen; I'm human. They aren't. This is enough of a difference that it can explain all others.

So you can look around as I did. See the Teckla running around like the small rodents they are named for, doing things they think are important, selecting fruits at the fruit stands or pieces of fabric from the weavers, laying a bet with the local bookmaker, rushing to work in a garden or at a weaver's, and, directly or indirectly, feeding me. See the Chreotha or the Jhegaala, with titles of the nobility but lives of the bourgeois selling the fabric or the fruit or buying brain-drugs or trying to get a bargain from the local fence and, directly or indirectly, feeding me. And, rarest of all, see the nobles themselves, strutting about like Issola in spring, scattering pennies to the paupers, having servants buy select wines and the more exotic brain-drugs, and, directly or indirectly, feeding me.

It's surprising that I stay so thin.

None of them gave me any special regard as I strolled by for another day of extracting from them everything I could. I like it that way.

The walk from flat to office was short, yet it was enough time for me to get a feel for what was going on in the neighborhood; on that day there was nothing worth noting—not the least clue, as it were, of the events that had already been set in motion. I arrived, as I recall, early that day. The Jhereg operates all day, but the real action is mostly at night, so things get started correspondingly late; I rarely see my office before noon. That day I arrived before my secretary, hung my cloak on the cloak-rack, set my rapier against the wall, and sat down at my desk to see what, if any, correspondence had arrived during the morning.

There was one item: a piece of expensive parchment sat in the middle of my desk; on it, in a neat, elegant hand, was written, "V. Taltos, Baronet." I picked it up and inspected the back, which showed a Dragonshead seal.

I set it down again and considered before opening it. I may have been a bit afraid of what it would say. No, I most certainly was afraid of what it would say. I picked it up and broke the seal before Loiosh could start on me.

> Baronet—
>
> It would give me great pleasure to see you again. It may also prove profitable for you. If you would like assistance in transportation, you may inquire of Baron Lokran e'Terics at the House of the Dragon. Arrive today between noon and the tenth hour, and I will take the time to see you at once.
>
> I Remain, my dear sir,
> Cordially
> Morrolan e'Drien
> P.S.: You expressed a preference for a formal invita-

tion over our last method of asking for your help; I hope
this meets with your approval—M.

I set the letter down again and thought about many things.
As always when dealing with Morrolan, I didn't quite know
how to take him. He calls his home Castle Black, which is either
pretentious to the point of being silly, or a just and reasonable statement of his power; take your pick. He was unusual—
perhaps "unique" would be a better word—in that he was a
Dragaeran, and a Dragonlord no less, who studied Eastern
witchcraft, which either showed that he did not share his compatriots' attitude toward humans, or showed that he was so con-
temptuous of us that he could offhandedly learn our secret arts;
take your pick. The "last method" he referred to had been offensive enough that we had almost killed each other over it, so
this reference was either a nasty cut or a peace offering; take
your pick.

However, it never occurred to me not to accept his invitation.

"We're going to Castle Black, Loiosh."

"I can hardly wait, Boss. When?"

I consulted the Imperial Orb through my psychic link. It was
less than an hour before noon.

"Now," I told him.

I strapped my rapier back on, not terribly reassured by its
weight hanging at my side and the scabbard's tapping against my
leg. Melestav, my secretary, was just arriving. He seemed startled
to see me. I said, "I have an errand. If you never see me again,
blame Morrolan of the House of the Dragon. See you."

I stepped back out onto the street—the first steps, as it were,
that began the journey that led me toward war and death. I
hired a cabriolet to cut down on the number of actual steps involved. I gave the runner no particular attention, but I tipped
him well. This is probably significant of something.

The House of the Dragon faces the Imperial Palace, just a bit west of north, and is marked by a forty-foot-high marble likeness of Kieron the Conqueror holding his greatsword in one hand, its point off to the East; seeing it makes my arm tired. There is no discernible expression on Kieron's face, at least from below. There are (surprise surprise) seventeen steps up to the doors, which were standing open when I arrived, a bit footsore, just about noon.

When you enter the House of the Dragon, you are in the Great Hall, a vast, huge, booming, echoing place with murals on the walls depicting violence, skinny windows that don't let much light in, a marble floor, a single, very wide stairway planted in the middle of the Hall and running up out of sight, and many tiny hanging lamps way, way up on the ceiling where they do no good at all and probably require levitation to service; yet there is sufficient light to see the murals, begging the question of how they actually illuminate the place.

I didn't much care for it.

I hadn't been surrounded by so many Dragonlords since I was arrested after the death of my previous boss, and I didn't like this a lot more than I liked that. They were standing in groups and were all of them armed. They were talking quietly, I suppose, but the place echoed horribly so it seemed awash with noise. There was grey bunting draped here and there, which meant that someone had died. I stood there like an idiot for a long, long time—say half a minute—with Loiosh on my shoulder, and then noticed a pair of sentries, on either of side the door—that is, either side of me—and observed that they were staring at me with decidedly unfriendly expressions. This made me feel much more comfortable, because I'd rather be hated than ignored.

I approached the man because the height of the woman would have put my eyes at breast-level and this didn't seem to be the right time for that. I put some jaunt into my step because Dragonlords, like many wild animals, can smell fear. He looked down at me (my eyes were level with his collar bone) and kept his eyes away from Loiosh; he probably thought I'd get too much satisfaction out of seeing him react to the Jhereg on my shoulder, and he was right. I said, "I seek Baron Lokran."

The Dragonlord swallowed, clenched his jaw, and said, "Who are you?"

I thought about making an issue of the question, but I didn't know the protocol and I didn't like the odds. "Vladimir Taltos of House Jhereg, on an errand for Lord Morrolan e'Drien." That should shut him up.

It did. "Up the stairs, straight back, last door on the left. Clap and enter."

I sketched a bow, resisting the temptation to make it over-elaborate.

"What are you afraid of, Boss?"

"Shut up, Loiosh."

The steps were set too high for my comfort, making it a challenge to climb casually with, I assumed, the eyes of the two Dragonlords on my back. I managed as best I could. My footsteps echoed, and the stairway went on for much too long. When I finally reached the top I walked straight back to the end of a hallway longer than the building that houses my entire operation. It ended in a large door which I ignored; instead stopping at the one to my left, as directed. One clap and I entered.

Lokran turned; he had, apparently, been staring out the window. He was young, with bright eyes, and had a faded white scar above his brows—the scar obviously had some sort of sentimental value for him or he'd have had it removed. His hair was dark, straight, and brushed back in almost a Jhereg-cut. He had rings on four fingers of each hand, and the rings all had jewels in them. The room held four stuffed chairs, a sofa, and no desk; a plain grey banner hung above the window. Three or four short, black staves were leaning against the far wall, and a heavy sword in a black sheath stood next to them.

His eyes narrowed briefly when I entered, then he said, "Taltos?" pronouncing it correctly.

I bowed and said, "Lokran?"

He nodded. "Come a little closer."

I did.

He gestured casually in my direction, as if he were brushing away an insect, and my bowels twisted, and I was in the courtyard of Castle Black, standing, as far as I could tell, on thin air that felt like a hard surface, say flagstones, but looked like nothing was holding me up. Just like that. He could have bloody warned me.

I've given a lot of thought to the question of why teleports upset my stomach; why they seem to have that effect on all Easterners, but not on Dragaerans. In between teleports, I've often decided it is all in the imagination of the Easterner, but right after a teleport I've found that answer unsatisfying. The explanation that sprang to mind as I stood before Morrolan's castle, surrounded by his walls, towers, and guards, is that teleports also upset the Dragaeran stomach, but Dragaerans just won't admit it; how can having your innards flop around so violently that you can *feel* them sloshing *not* make you queasy? Could natural selection account for it? I don't buy it; I just don't think that nature had it in mind for people to get from one place to another without passing through the intervening area.

These thoughts, I should explain, were one way I occupied my mind while I gave my stomach time to settle down. Another way was to observe that the sentries in the towers were watching me, although they didn't seem especially surprised. Okay, so I was expected. Over one tower floated a single banner, all of grey.

Eventually I risked a look down. There were trees below me that looked like miniature bushes, and the two roads and one stream were lines of brown and blue respectively, meeting and crossing and running almost parallel to form a design that, if I tried, I could convince myself was a mark in some runic alphabet. Maybe it was a symbol that told the castle, "Don't fall down." That was a comforting thought.

I adjusted my cloak, ran a hand through my hair, and approached the double doors of Castle Black. They swung open as I approached, which I should have been expecting, because they'd done the same thing last time. I cursed under my breath but kept a small smile on my lips and didn't break stride—there were Dragonlords watching.

I hadn't noticed it the last time, but one reason that it is so effective to see Lady Teldra appear when the doors open is that she is all you can see—the entryway is unlit, and except for her you might be entering the void that one imagines as the land of the dead. (The land of the dead, however, is not a void—it's worse. But never mind.)

"My Lord Taltos," said Teldra. "Thank you for gracing our home. The Lord awaits you. Please, enter and be welcome."

I felt welcome in spite of my more cynical side whispering, "Whatever."

I crossed the threshold. Lady Teldra did not offer to take my cloak this time. She guided me into the hall with all the paintings, through it, up the wide, curving stairway, and eventually to the library. It was big and full of stuffed chairs and thick books; three of the books, sitting just beyond the entrance, were massive jewel-encrusted objects each chained to a pedestal; I wondered but resolved not to ask. As I entered, Morrolan set a book down and stood up, giving me a small bow.

He opened his mouth, probably to make some sort of ironic courtesy, as a counterpoint to Teldra's sincere one, but I said, "Who died?" before he could get the words out. He shut his mouth, glanced at Loiosh, and nodded toward a chair next to his. I sat down.

He said, "Baritt."

I said, "Oh."

Morrolan seemed to want me to say something, so eventually I said, "You know, the first time I met him I had the feeling he wouldn't be—"

"Do not joke about it, Vlad."

"All right. What do you want me to say? I didn't get the impression he was a friend of yours."

"He wasn't."

"Well?"

Lady Teldra appeared with refreshment—a white wine that would have been too sweet except that it was served over chunks of ice. I sipped it to be polite the first time, and then discovered I liked it. The Issola glided from the room. There was no table on which to set the goblet down, but the chair had wide, flat arms. Very convenient.

"Well?" I repeated.

"In the second place," said Morrolan, "he was an important man. And in the first place—"

"He was a Dragon," I concluded. "Yeah, I know."

Morrolan nodded. I drank some more wine. The sensation of cold helps reduce the sensation of sweetness. I bet you didn't know that.

"So, what happened to the poor bastard?"

Morrolan started to answer, then paused, then said, "It is unimportant."

"All right," I agreed. "It is unimportant to me, in any case." I had met Baritt, or, more properly, his shade, in the Paths of the Dead. He had taken an instant dislike to Morrolan because Morrolan had the bad taste to be traveling with me, which should give you an idea of how Baritt and I had hit it off.

I continued, "I assume it isn't a request for sympathy that led to your invitation."

"You are correct."

"Well?"

He turned his head to the side and looked at me quizzically. "What is it you gave me, Vlad?"

I laughed. "Is that it? Is that what this is all about?"

"Actually, no. I'm just curious."

"Oh. Well, remain curious." I had, in fact, injected him with the blood of a goddess for reasons too complicated to explain now, and, at the time, I was in no condition to explain any-thing.

"As you wish. Baritt, as I say, died. In going through his possessions—"

"What? Already? He can't have been brought to Death-gate yet."

"And—?"

"Well, that seems awful quick for you long-lived types."

"There are reasons."

"You're just full of information, aren't you?"

"Were I to tell you matters pertaining to the internal politics of the House of the Dragon I should only weary you. And I should then have to kill you for knowing. So my thought was not to trouble you with such information."

"A good thought," I said.

Loiosh shifted on my shoulder, evidently getting restless. "As I was saying, in going through his possessions, certain items were discovered."

He stopped. I waited. He resumed.

"He had a large collection of Morganti weapons. A *large* col-lection. Hundreds of them."

I repressed a shiver. "I suppose the reason he had them is none of my business, too."

"That is correct. And, in any case, I don't know."

"Well then, what about them?"

"I spent a good portion of yesterday inspecting them. I have an interest in such things."

"Figures."

His eyes narrowed for a moment, then he evidently decided to ignore it. "Such weapons," he went on, "represent power. Some covet power, some are threatened by others coveting power."

"Which are you?"

"The former."

"I knew that," I said. "I didn't expect you to admit it."

"Why not?"

I couldn't answer that so I didn't. "Go on," I said. "Who's the enemy?"

"You are perspicacious."

"Yeah, but my physicker says it can be treated."

"He means you're perceptive, Boss."

"I know that, Loiosh."

"Yes," said Morrolan. "I believe that I am likely to come into conflict with someone over possession of these weapons."

"Who might that be?"

"I don't know. There are several possibilities. The likeliest is—well, it doesn't matter."

"That's helpful."

"For what I want from you, you don't need to know."

"That's fortunate. Well, what do you want then?"

"I want you to arrange for the stolen weapons to be traced."

"Some weapons have been stolen?"

"Not yet," he said.

"I see. How certain are you?"

"Reasonably."

"Why?"

"That, too, is unimportant. I will be protecting them, as will various others. Whoever wishes to steal one or more will have to hire an expert thief, and that means the Jhereg, and that means—"

"I might be able to find out what's become of it. I see."

"Boss, this could get you into trouble."

"I know."

I sat back and looked at Morrolan. He held my gaze. After a moment I said, "That isn't at all the sort of thing I'm any good at, Morrolan. And, to tell you the truth, if I did find out, I don't believe I could bring myself to tell you. It's a Jhereg thing, you know?"

"I believe I do, yes." He frowned and seemed to be considering. "On the other hand," he said, "if I understand how you—

that is, how the Jhereg—work, whoever did the stealing would be unlikely to be more than a tool, hired by someone else, is that correct?"

"Yes," I said, not terribly happy about where this was going.

"Well then, could you find out—"

"Maybe," I admitted.

"What would it take?"

"Money. A lot of it."

"I have money."

"I still want to think about it. It could put me into a situation I'm not certain I'd like."

"I understand. Do think about it, though. I can offer you—"

"Don't tell me. I'd rather not be tempted. I'll let you know."

He nodded and didn't press the issue, which earned him some points with me.

"There's another matter," he said.

I bit back irony and waited.

"The circumstances of Baritt's death—"

"Which are none of my business."

"—have, among other things, made me aware of the vulnerability of Castle Black."

"I beg your pardon?"

"The circumstances of—"

"I heard you, I just don't understand. How is a castle floating half a mile or more in the air vulnerable? Other than to falling down, of course."

"That isn't likely."

"I'm glad to hear it. Which reminds me, why don't my ears pop when I teleport up?"

He looked smug but didn't tell me. "Obviously," he said, "the castle can be penetrated by anyone who can teleport and conceal himself from my guards."

"You don't have any security precautions?"

"Some, but not enough. It seems to me you could be of some assistance in telling me where to improve them."

I thought it over, and realized that I knew exactly how to go about it. "Yes, I can do that." I considered asking about payment, but on reflection calculated that it would be more profitable to do a good job and allow him to display his generosity. He frowned for a moment, and seemed lost in thought.

"*Psychic communication, Boss.*"

"*I knew that, Loiosh.*"

"*You're a liar, Boss.*"

"*Well, yeah.*"

At about that time, a Dragonlord entered the room and bowed to Morrolan. He was short and rather stocky for a Dragaeran, with short, light-brown hair and pale eyes; he didn't strike me as a fighter, but he wore a blade, which meant he was on duty in some capacity.

Morrolan said, "Fentor, this is Baronet Vladimir Taltos. I know you are willing to work with Easterners, but are you willing to take orders from a Jhereg?"

Fentor said, "My lord?"

Loiosh said, "*What did he say?*"

I said, "Errgh?"

Morrolan said, "I've just hired Lord Taltos as a security consultant. That puts you in his charge, under certain circumstances."

I felt my mouth open and close. Morrolan had what? And when had he done this?

Fentor said, "That will not be a problem, my lord."

"Good," said Morrolan.

"Excuse me," I said.

"Yes?"

"I . . ."

"Yes?"

"Never mind. A pleasure, Fentor."

"The same, my lord."

"*Boss, you've just been hired.*"

"*Well, yeah. Recruited, actually.*"

"You should tell him to never use this power in the service of evil."

"I'll be sure to."

It occurred to me, also, that it was going to be harder, now that I was more or less working for him, to avoid trying to get the information he was after. Of course, maybe I'd get lucky, and no one would steal any of the weapons. Something made me doubt this.

Fentor bowed cordially to us both and made his exit.

I said, "Morrolan, what aren't you telling me?"

"Many things."

"In particular. I get the feeling that you aren't just generally worried about someone stealing some random Morganti weapon."

"You should trust your feelings; they seem to be reliable."

"Thank you so much."

He stood abruptly and said, "Come with me, Vlad. I'll show you around and introduce you to a few people."

"I can hardly wait," I said.

I got up and followed him.

2

CROSSING LINES

Do you know what a battlefield smells like? If so, you have my sympathy; if not, you still won't, because I have no intention of dwelling on it except to say that people don't smell so good on the inside.

We stepped over the piles of dirt (I can't call it a "bulwark" with a straight face) that we'd spent so much time and sweat creating, and moved forward at a steady pace; not too fast, not too slow. No, come to think of it, *much* too fast. A slow crawl would have been much too fast.

I adjusted my uniform sash, which was the only mark I carried to show which side I was on, since I'd lost my cute little cap somewhere during the last couple of attacks. About half of the company had lost their cute little caps, and many of the enemy had, too. But we all had sashes, which identified the side we were on, like the ribbons that identify sandball teams. I never played sandball. I'd seen Dragons playing sandball in West Side Park, alongside of Teckla, though never in the same game at the same time, and certainly not on the same team. Make of that what you will.

"Have you thought about getting up in the air and away from this?" I asked my familiar for the fifth time.

"I've thought about it," he answered for the fourth (the first time he hadn't made any response at all, so I'd had to repeat the question; we'd only sustained three attacks hitherto). And,

"*How did we get into this, anyway?*" I'd lost count of how many times he'd asked me that; not as many as I'd asked myself.

We moved forward.

How *did* we get ourselves into this?

I asked Sethra, not long ago, why she ordered us to hold that position, which never looked terribly important from where I sat—except to me, of course, for personal reasons that I'll go into later. She said, "For the same reason I had Gutrin's spear phalanx attack that little dale to your left. By holding that spot, you threatened an entire flank, and I needed to freeze a portion of the enemy's reserves. As long as you kept threatening that position, he had to either reinforce it or remain ready to reinforce it. That way I could wait for the right time and place to commit *my* reserves, which I did when—"

"All right, all right," I said. "Never mind."

I hadn't wanted a technical answer, I'd wanted her to say "It was vital to the entire campaign." I wanted to have had a more important role. We were one piece on the board, and only as important as any other. All the pieces wish to be, if not a player, at least the piece the players are most concerned with.

Not being a player was one of the things that bothered me. I was, I suppose, only a piece and not a player when I would carry out the order of one of my Jhereg superiors, but I had been running my own territory for a short while at that point, and had already become used to it. That was part of the problem: In the Jhereg, I was, if not a commander-in-chief, at least a high ranking field officer. Here, I was, well, I guess I was a number of things, but put them all together and they still didn't amount to much.

But how *did* we get ourselves into this? There were no great principles involved. I mean, you judge a war according to who is in the right as long as you have no interest in the outcome; if you're one of the participants, or if the result is going to have a major effect on you, then you have to create the moral principles that put you in the right—that's nothing new, everyone knows it. But this one was so *raw*. No one could even come up with a good mask to put over it. It was over land, and power, and who got to expand where, without even the thinnest veneer of anything else.

Those veneers can be important when you're marching down toward rows of nasty pointy things.

Baritt died, that's what started it all. And Morrolan convinced me to set up a trap to find out who would be likely to steal what I preferred not to come anywhere near. Kragar, my lieutenant in the organization, looked worried when I told him about it, but I'm sure even he, who knew Dragons better than I ever would, had no clue how it would end up.

"What if someone does steal one, and you find out who," he said, "and it turns out to be someone you don't want to mess with?"

"That, of course, is the question. But it seems unlikely to be a Jhereg behind it."

"No, Vlad, it will be a Dragon. That's the problem."

Well, he was a Dragon; he should know. No, he wasn't a Dragon, he was a Jhereg, but he should still know. He had once been a Dragon, which meant—what?

I studied Kragar. I knew him better than I knew anyone I didn't know at all. We'd worked together as enforcers when I first entered the Jhereg, and we'd been working together ever since. He was the only Dragaeran I didn't hate, except maybe Kiera. Come to think of it, I didn't understand her, either.

Kragar was courageous, and timid, warmhearted, and vicious, and easygoing, and dedicated, and friendly, and utterly ruthless; as well as having the strange ability, or shortcoming, to blend into the woodwork so completely one could be staring right at him without realizing he was there.

I couldn't remember a single idea of mine that he hadn't thrown cold water on, nor a single one that he hadn't backed me on to the hilt—literally, in some cases.

"What is it?" he said.

"I was ruminating."

"Shouldn't you do that in private?"

"Oh, is someone here?"

"You're a riot, Vlad."

"In any case," I said, picking up the conversation from where it was lying in the middle of the floor, "there's a lot of money in it."

Kragar made a sound I won't attempt to describe. I could sense Loiosh holding back several remarks. It seems I surround myself with people who think I'm an idiot, which probably says something deep and profound about me.

"So," I said, "who do we put on it?"

"I don't know. We should probably go over there ourselves and look things over."

"I was afraid you'd say that."

He gave me a puzzled glance that went away quickly. There are matters on which Dragaerans and humans will never understand one another, and soul-killing weapons are, evidently, one of those. I mean, they hate them as much as or more than we do; but Dragaerans don't usually have the sort of overwhelming dread that such weapons inspire in a human. I don't know why that is.

"How do we get there?"

"I'll hire a coach."

Baritt had lived in a square, grey stone building on the outskirts of Adrilankha, in the hills to the west. He probably called it a castle. I could call my tunic a chair if I wanted to. It had three stories, a large front door, a couple of servants' entrances, a few glass windows, and a sharply sloped roof. His estate struck me as too rocky, and the soil too sandy, to be good for much. There was peasant activity, but not a great deal. There were a pair of guards in front of the main door, in the livery of the House of the Dragon. As Kragar and I approached, I saw one was wearing the same emblem that Morrolan's people sported; the other had a badge I didn't recognize.

I rehearsed the conversation I was about to have with them. I won't share it with you because the actual conversation disrupted my plans.

"Baronet Taltos?" said the one wearing Morrolan's badge.

I nodded.

"Please enter."

Trust me: The conversation I'd been prepared for would have been much more fun to relate. But there was compensation. The guard said, "Wait—who is he?" noticing Kragar for the first time.

"My associate," I said, keeping my chuckle on the inside.

"Very well," he said.

I glanced at the other guard, who was busy being expressionless. I wondered who he worked for.

Kragar and I passed within.

Rarely upon crossing a threshold have I been struck by such a sensation of entering a different world—I mean it felt as if between one step and another I had left Dragaera and entered a place at least as foreign as my Eastern ancestral homeland. The first surprise was that, after passing by the stone entryway of the stone house, you reached a foyer that was full of blown glass— vases, candelabra, empty decanters, and other glasswork were displayed on dark wooden pedestals or in cabinets. The walls were painted some color that managed to squeak in between white and yellow where no color ought to live, making everything seem bright and cheery and entirely at odds with any Dragonlord I'd ever met or heard of—and certainly with the Baritt I'd met in the Paths of the Dead.

My reverie was interrupted by Kragar saying, "Uh . . . Boss? Where are we going?"

"Good question." Most sorcerers would work either in a basement, where it's most reasonable to put any heavy objects they might need, or up in a tower, where there is less risk of wiping out the whole house if something goes wrong. In Baritt's case, probably some random room in a random place because it was convenient.

Loiosh moved nervously on my shoulder. We left the foyer and entered a sitting room of some sort, with more blown glass and decanters just like the others except full. On the wall to my left was a large oil of Baritt, looking imposing and dignified. There was a small door at the far end that should have led to the kitchen, and hallways heading off to the right and the left; one would presumably lead up a set of stairs to the bedchambers, the other to the rest of this floor. We took the one to the right and found a wide, straight stairway of polished white stone. We went back and tried the other hall, which looked more promising.

"*Hey, Boss.*"

"*Yeah, Loiosh?*"

"*There's something funny. I'm getting a feeling. It's like—*"

"We're being watched, Vlad," said Kragar.

"Not really surprising," I said.

"*I noticed first.*"

"*Shut up.*"

"Ignore it, I think," I told Kragar. "It would be odd if no one had any surveillance spells. Should we try that door?"

"The big ironbound one with the rune carved on it, barred by a pair of Dragonlords with spears crossed in front of it? Why should it be that one?"

"You're funny, Kragar. Shut up, Kragar."

"Who are you, and what is your business?" said one of the guards, standing like a statue, her spear not moving from its position in front of the door.

"You know both answers," I told her.

She twitched a smile, which made me like her. "Yeah, but I have to ask. And you have to answer. Or you could leave. Or I could kill you."

"Baronet Taltos, House Jhereg, on an errand from Lord Morrolan, and for a minute there I liked you."

"I'm crushed," she said. Her spear snapped to her side; her companion's also moved, and the way was clear. She said, "Be informed that there is a teleport block in place around the house in general, and that it has been strengthened for that room."

"Is that a polite way of telling me not to try to steal anything?"

"I hadn't intended to be polite," she said.

I said, "Let's go."

"After you," said Kragar. Both guards twitched and then looked at him, as if they hadn't noticed him before, which they probably hadn't. Then they pretended they'd seen him all along, because to do anything else would have been undignified.

There didn't seem to be any way out of it, so I pulled back the bolt and opened the door.

There's a story, probably apocryphal but who cares, about Lishni, the inventor of the fire-ram. It seems he invented it out of desperation, having no other way for his flotilla of six cutters to escape a fleet of eight brigs and two ships of the line that had cut him off during what started as a minor action in one of the wars with Elde. As the story goes, after arming his cutters with his new invention, he went out, sank seven of the ten ships and damaged the other three, then, in another moment of inspiration, took his crews ashore, captured the Palace, and forced an unconditional surrender that ended the war right there. As he walked out of the Palace with the signed surrender in his hand, one of his subordinates supposedly asked him how he felt. "Fine," he said.

As I say, I very much doubt it happened like that, but it's a good story. I bring it up because, if someone had asked me how I felt when I walked into a room full of more Morganti weapons than I had thought existed in the world, I'd have said, in the same way, "Poorly."

"Boss . . ."

"I know, Loiosh."

The weapons were piled everywhere. It was like stepping into a room full of yellowsnakes. I could feel the two Dragonlords behind me, and even the knowledge that I was showing fear in front of them couldn't propel me forward.

"This is pretty ugly, Vlad."

"Tell me about it, Kragar."

"I wonder what he wanted them for."

"I wonder why the Serioli invented them in the first place."

"You don't know, Vlad?"

"No. Do you?"

"Sure. Well, I know what they say, at least."

"What do they say?"

"Back before the beginning of the Empire they were invented by a Serioli smith in order to make war so horrible no one would fight anymore."

I snorted. "You're kidding. Do you believe they could be that stupid?"

"Oh, but it worked."

"Huh?"

"Among the Serioli."

"Oh."

"Shall we go in?"

"I don't think I can."

"That's a problem."

"Yes."

We stood there like idiots for a little longer.

"Should we leave, then?" he asked.

"No, dammit."

"All right."

Hours and hours went by. All right, maybe a minute. The worst part was knowing those Dragonlords were right behind me. Showing fear in front of a Jhereg is bad business; showing fear in front of a Dragon hurts my pride.

Kragar said, "I have an idea."

"Good," I said. "I accept. An excellent idea. Whatever it is."

"This will take a couple of minutes."

"Even better. You think I'm in a hurry?"

Kragar's brow wrinkled. I suspected psychic contact.

"All right," he said. "He'll be here."

"Who?"

"Someone who can help. I met him some years ago when I was—it doesn't matter."

He might as well have completed the sentence. Kragar wasn't born into the Jhereg—he'd once been a Dragonlord himself—and whatever reasons he had for not being one anymore were his own business.

"What's his name?"

"Daymar. He's a Hawklord."

"All right. How can he help?"

"Psychics."

"What about them?"

"He's very good. He can do things with the powers of his mind that skilled sorcerers can't do using the power of the Orb. He—just a minute." He stepped out of the room for a moment and spoke quietly with the guards. When he returned, there was a thin, sharp-featured Dragaeran with him, all in black, with a sort of dreamy, vague expression on his face that was quite at odds with his features and with other Hawklords I'd known.

"Hello, Kragar," he said in a low, quiet voice.

"Hello, Daymar. This is my boss, Vlad."

He bowed politely, which also set him apart from others of his House. "Pleased to meet you," he said.

"And you," I told him.

He studied the room. "Very impressive," he said. "I've never seen so many at once."

"I was thinking much the same thing," I said.

Kragar said, "Can you, uh, tone them down a little? Vlad is a bit sensitive to their aura."

He turned to me with a look of curiosity. "Really? That's interesting. I wonder why?"

I refrained from saying, "Because I'm an Easterner with a su-
perstitious dread of the damned things"; instead I just shrugged.

"Mind if I find out what it is about you that—"

"Yes," I said.

"All right," he said, appearing to be a little hurt. Then he
looked around the room again. "Well," he said, "it shouldn't be
difficult," and, just like that, I felt better. Not *good*, mind you,
but better—it was as if they were still out there, and still hungry, but much farther away.

"How did you do that?" I said.

Daymar frowned and pursed his lips. "Well," he said, "if we
consider the aura emitted by each weapon as a spherical field
of uni—"

"Psychics," said Kragar.

I walked into the room as if there was nothing to it, and began
looking around. Kragar and Daymar stayed behind me.

The weapons were a bit more arranged than I'd first
thought—they were stacked, rather than just lying around, and
they were all in sheaths or scabbards—I tried not to think of how
it would feel if they'd been naked. I couldn't, however, discern
exactly what the order or arrangement was.

"The most powerful are at this end," said Daymar conversationally, "and the weakest are down there. That's a Jhereg on
your shoulder, isn't it?"

"Psychics," I said. "And a keen eye for detail as well," I added.

"Excuse me? Oh, that was irony, wasn't it?"

"Sorry. I'm a bit jumpy."

"Oh? Why?"

I glanced at Kragar, who, it appeared, was gallantly attempting not to smile. I left the question hanging and tried to look like
I was studying the weapons, while simultaneously not really
looking at them. This isn't easy, and it didn't work—they kept
assaulting my mind, Daymar's psychic ability notwithstanding.

"How do you link to it?"

"Excuse me?"

"The Jhereg. You must have some sort of psychic link to it. How—"

"Witchcraft," I said.

"I see. Does it involve—?"

"I don't care to discuss it."

"All right," said Daymar, looking puzzled and maybe a little hurt once more. I wasn't used to running into Dragaerans who had sensitive feelings.

"So," said Kragar. "Any ideas on how to go about this?"

I glanced at him again, and he flushed a little—whoever this Daymar was, I wasn't prepared to discuss my business in front of him, and Kragar ought to have known that.

"What are you trying to do?" said Daymar.

"It's hard to explain," I said.

"Oh, well then—" he said, and, as I was still looking at Kragar, I saw a startled look spread over his features.

I said, "What—"

"*Mind probe, Boss. A really, really, good one. And fast. That guy—*"

I picked up the weapon closest to me, a dagger, and pulled it from its sheath. I crossed the room, stopping in front of Daymar, about four feet away. I stared up at him, holding the weapon casually in front of me. I was no longer frightened of the thing; it was as if something had taken control of me, and that something was red and burning. I said, "Look, I appreciate your help, but if you ever mind-probe one of my people again, it'll be the last thing you ever do, in this life or any other. Is that clear?"

He seemed a little startled but not at all frightened. "Sorry," he said. "I won't do it again."

I turned away, took a deep breath, and sheathed the weapon. I never know what to say after I've intimidated someone; I ought to keep a list of tough-guy remarks.

"I do have a suggestion, however."

I turned around and stared at him, not quite sure what I was hearing.

"*Boss, either you're losing your touch or this guy is really stupid.*"

"Well," continued Daymar, "since I know anyway . . ."

I gave Kragar a "What should I do about this?" look, and he returned a "Don't ask me" shrug.

I sighed. "All right, Daymar. Let's hear it."

"Well, Morrolan thinks someone is going to try to steal these weapons, right? And you—"

"Do you know Morrolan?" I said.

"Certainly. Why?"

"I just wondered. Go on."

"You want to trap whoever it is."

"Trap? Maybe. At least find the culprit, if there is one."

"I can set up a psychic trace that will let us identify anyone who steps in here."

"Sounds too easy," I said.

"No one guards against psychics."

"What about Kiera?"

"Who?"

"Never mind," I said. "If something is missing and we don't know how, Kiera took it."

"Then what?" put in Kragar.

"That's easy. We give up and report failure, which I should have done already."

"Sounds reasonable."

"Well?" said Daymar.

"All right," I said. "Do whatever you have to do."

"It's done," he said.

"I—"

"*I believe him, Boss. Something happened.*"

I graced Kragar with another look. In case I've failed to communicate it, I wasn't entirely comfortable with how things had worked themselves out, and Kragar presented an easy and not unreasonable target; he accepted the role with good grace.

Loiosh said, "*Don't worry, Boss; it'll all work perfectly. No, really.*"

I turned to Daymar. "How does it work?"

"If any of those weapons are moved from this room, I'll receive a psychic impression of whoever moved it."

"Then what?"

"Whatever you want. I can put you in touch with him, or get a location—"

"You can? *You* can?"

"Why, yes," he said, looking slightly startled. "Is something amiss?"

I don't know why I should have thought we'd be done with him. Wishful thinking, I suppose.

"All right," I said. "I think we can say we've done all we have to here. Let's go."

"Where are we going?" asked Daymar.

I started to answer, bit it off, gave Kragar a pleading look, and made my escape. Whatever Kragar said must have worked; at least Daymar didn't follow us back to the office.

That day, I was prepared to call even that a victory.

3

On Stolen Swords and Borrowed Books

We had closed a good share of the distance between us before they broke into a run. I'd thought (insofar, that is, as I'd been thinking at all) that they were going to stop, take a defensive position, and wait for our attack, as we'd done when they'd charged us, and on reflection, they probably should have. They had spears, and if they'd just held steady and stuck them out, it would have been ugly for us. But that wasn't how they played it—they came right at us, maybe hoping we'd back down, turn, and run. Strategically a bad move, psychologically sound. Or, to put it another way, seeing them coming at us scared the shit out of me, a feeling mitigated only by the nasty pleasure of knowing how it felt to charge up a hill.

But there was no way we could stop, you see; the juice-drum was rattling around us, we were already moving, and we'd become a juggernaut, plowing forward, bristling with points, and at a certain stage I stopped feeling fear. I stopped feeling anything. I just went ahead and did it because there was nothing else to do. Even my own mission, my private plans and intentions, went out of my head, and the means became the end: I was advancing because my company was advancing, and when we met them we'd destroy them because that was what we did. It was never *my* job, but for a while, as I said, that didn't occur to me.

It was all different. I don't mean this battle in particular, but battle in general. I still wasn't used to it. Did anyone ever get used to it? If so, how? Except someone like Napper, and he was nuts.

I'd known battle would be different from assassination, and even different from the street brawls I'd been forced into from time to time, but knowing it and living it are not the same. I'm used to cold, but battle is hot; I'm used to precision, but war is chaos; I'm used to trying to kill, but this kind of fighting involved trying to stay alive.

The sound of footsteps, my own and my comrades', blended with the juice-drum, then overpowered it and became a rhythm that I picked up in my head to the echo of "Why? Why? Why? Why?" which was far too philosophical for the moment. We hardened soldiers, you see, are philosophical in camp, but very practical in the field. That was something else I learned. In camp, you have to be philosophical, or crazy, or funny, or nasty, or something, just to keep yourself from going out of your head while you're waiting for another chance to be a hero. It's a means of passing the time. That is one similarity between Dragons and Jhereg I can't deny: we know how to wait.

Another is that we don't like waiting. For my part, if something is going to happen, I'd just as soon that it happened quickly. With that in mind, I suppose you could say I got lucky way back at the beginning of all this, when I tried to carry out Morrolan's mission: I didn't have to wait. We heard from Daymar the very morning after we set the psychic trap.

I was just settling into my chair and enjoying the rare pleasure of an empty desk; if there's something on the desk, it usually means there is something I ought to be doing. I was about to have my secretary bring me some klava when Kragar, whom I had not noticed enter my office, said, "Someone stole one of the weapons, Vlad."

"Melestav!" I called. "Please bring me some klava."

"Right away, Boss," he answered from the next room.

Kragar began again, "Vlad—"

"I heard you. I'm going to pretend I didn't. I'm going to have some klava. Then you can tell me about it."

"If you want it directly, I could have Daymar—"

"No."

"Let me see if I understand. Do I take it you *don't* want Daymar to—"

"Kragar, shut up and let me drink my klava. Then you can be funny. If you try to be funny before I've had my klava, I will probably have to kill you, and then I'll be sad."

"Ah. Well. I wouldn't want you to be sad."

I squeezed my eyes tightly shut. When I opened them Kragar was gone. A little later Melestav tiptoed in, set a steaming cup in front of me, and tiptoed out again.

"Well, we're in some kind of mood today, aren't we, Boss?"

"I was fine when I got here."

I drank my klava slowly. There is a perfect way to position the lips on the cup to take in just the right amount of klava to avoid burning yourself. Everything comes with practice. I reflected on practice and on annoyance and I drank my klava and then I called for Kragar.

"Okay," I said. "Let's have it."

"I got word from Daymar this morning that his psychic alarm had been tripped sometime last night. He says it failed to wake him, for which he sends his apologies—"

"Apologies? I didn't think he did that."

"—and suggests that the thief must be quite accomplished."

"All right. We'd best head over and see what was taken."

"He knows what was taken: one greatsword, very large, not terribly potent. Plain cross-guard with brass knobs, leather grips, sharp on one edge and part of the other, enough of a point for stabbing."

I tried to call up a memory of that weapon, failed, but Loiosh managed—he put the picture into my mind. I saw it leaning against a wall along with several cousins. I hadn't noticed it; it had been utterly undistinctive and, for a Morganti blade, not even very well constructed.

"So, just as a guess, Kragar, I'd say it was a test, rather than that blade they were after. What do you think?"

"Possible. Or there's something about it we don't know. History, enchantments, something like that."

"Could be that, too. Any suggestions about what we do next?"

"You could always hire Kiera to steal it back."

"Letting whoever it is know that we know, for which we'd get a probably useless weapon. Any useful suggestions?"

"Whatever we do, we have to find whoever it was who took it. I presume Daymar will be able to find out."

"Right. See to it."

"Me?"

"Yes. I designate you Speaker to Daymar."

"Thank you so much."

"I pride myself on knowing my subordinates and matching tasks to their skills."

"Don't start, Vlad."

There was actually a bit of truth in that remark—though only a bit. Since I'd been in control of the area, one of the things I was learning was what I could delegate and what I had to do myself. In fact, a little later I ran into a situation where—but never mind. That's another story.

Kragar left; I stared off into space. Loiosh said, "You worried, Boss?"

"I'm a worrier, chum."

Unfortunately, there was nothing much to do that day, so I got to be pensive. I wanted to get up and pace, wander around the office, sit back down, and do all the things one does when one is nervous. But it's just no damn good letting your subordinates think you're easy to shake, so I sat at my desk, cooked some meals in my mind, remembered past lovers, and exchanged banter with Loiosh.

Lunchtime was a relief. I went to an Eastern place run by a

woman named Tserchi and had roasted duckling in a sour cherry sauce garnished with celery root and served with a pan-fried garlic bread that wasn't as good as Noish-pa made but was perfectly edible. I tried to linger over the food, which of course made me eat faster. Tserchi joined me after the meal. I had a sorbet for dessert along with an orange liqueur and the pleasure of hearing her complain about how much she had to pay for ice. I was glad she was there, because I don't like eating alone. I made it back to the office and Kragar was waiting for me.

I noticed his cloak when I returned, so I knew he was there. I sat down at my desk and tried not to look like I was waiting for him.

If you're getting the impression that I'd built this thing up into something far more important than it probably was, well, I told myself the same thing. The fact that I turned out to be right might make me seem prescient. I don't know. I've been wrong about such things, too, but those occasions don't make for interesting stories.

"Okay, Vlad, I've got it," Kragar told me.

"Took you long enough," I said, just because I was irritated.

"Uh huh. And suppose I just walked in and gave you a name. What would you say?"

I'd have told him to go find out about the guy, of course, and probably have made some sarcastic remark about his failure to have already done so. Sometimes you have to admit defeat.

"Okay," I said. "Good work."

"Thanks."

"Sit down and let's hear it."

Melestav stuck his head in right then and said, "Kragar? I found that map."

"Thanks. Bring it in, please."

We're always polite to each other around the office.

I bit back any questions that Kragar would feel smug about answering, and waited. I shuffled paperweights and writing gear off to the side of my desk while Kragar unrolled a map that almost covered it. The map seemed fairly recent, and had the peculiar mix of sharp and fuzzy areas that denotes a psiprint; most of it, however, was very clean and distinct, indicating a skilled and careful artist. I recognized the region at once because Dzur Mountain was marked near the left-hand border, and I recognized the Barnsnake River two-thirds of the way toward the right, which meant the markings on the right border were the foothills of the Eastern Mountains.

Kragar pointed to an area a little above and to the right of Dzur Mountain. "Fornia County," he said, tracing an area that ran almost all the way to the edge of the map.

"Never heard of it."

"Oh, well, never mind, then."

"Get on with it."

"Melestav is looking for a more detailed map, just in case we need it. But that's where the weapon went."

"And what do you know of Fornia? Count or Countess?"

"Count. Fornia e'Lanya. Dragonlord, of course. And a neighbor of Sethra Lavode."

"I wonder who borrows sugar from whom?"

"Huh?"

"Never mind. Eastern custom."

"The name 'Fornia' comes from the old language of the House of the Dragon and means 'patience.' There's probably a story there but I don't know it. Fornia is old; over two thousand. A sorcerer of some repute. Battle magic, mostly. He also keeps a staff of sorcerers to assist him. No discoveries, but they have a good reputation in the House."

I grunted.

Kragar continued. "He did a fair bit of expanding before the Interregnum, and he's been at it again during the last hundred years or so. Maintains a standing army of about six hundred, but also hires as needed, including Easterners. He—"

"Easterners? I don't understand."

"He's been known to hire Eastern mercenaries for certain actions."

"Eastern mercenaries?"

"Yes."

"I didn't know—I've never heard of—"

"Neither did I and I haven't either."

"Are you sure about it?"

"Yes," said Kragar.

"From where in the East?"

"Not your part. Farther south, as I understand it. Some foot
soldiers, but a lot of horsemen. He's known to keep a strong
cavalry and to use it well."

"What do you mean, my part?"

"The part of the East your family came from."

"How do you know which part of the East my family came
from?"

"Vlad—"

"Yes?"

"Did you think I would be willing to work for you without
finding out anything about you?"

"Uh . . . what else did you find out?"

"You don't really want to know, do you?"

"Hmmm. All right. Go on."

"That's very strange, Boss."

*"How much Kragar knows about me? Or the business with the
Eastern mercenaries?"*

"Well, both, but I was thinking about the Eastern mercenaries."

"Yeah, it's strange."

"Did you find out why he'd have stolen the weapon?"

"No, but I have a theory: the same reason anyone else would
have; they represent power. If you want things like that, they're
the sorts of things you'd want."

I digested that and failed to find a suitable response. "You
said he keeps trying to expand his area. What does the Empress
have to say about it?"

"He's been going after other Dragonlords; the Empress has pretty much the same attitude about that as about Jhereg wars: Let them have at each other as long as it doesn't interfere with the workings of the Empire."

"Interesting parallel; I wonder what Morrolan would think about it?"

Kragar smiled. I think, as a one-time Dragonlord, he took special joy in remarks like that. Of course, it also made him a good source of information about matters military.

"All right," I said. "Let me summarize. What we have is a matter of Dragons acting like Dragons. This Fornia is after more land and power, so he steals a Morganti weapon, and Morrolan is after the same, so he doesn't want him to, and we can tell Morrolan who this guy is, and then we're done, and there's nothing more to it. Right? Heh. So, what haven't you told me?"

"The main thing is: Dragonlords don't steal."

"I see. And therefore?"

"One possibility is that he wanted it really, really badly. Another is that he intended to be outraged."

"Excuse me?"

Kragar paused and stared at the ceiling as if to formulate a complicated thought. "He steals the thing, Morrolan accuses him of stealing the thing, he gets outraged."

"Oh. Is he a Dragon or a Yendi?"

"They aren't all that different, Vlad." I started to speak, but Kragar quickly said, "I should qualify that. Yendi are like that all the time, but a Dragon on a campaign is capable of subtlety when necessary."

"Okay, I get it."

"So," said Kragar, "there's likely more going on than we know about."

"Well, okay, fine. How does it concern us?"

"I don't know. Maybe, if we're lucky, not at all."

I sighed. "Okay. I'll report what I've found out—"

"What *who* has found out?"

"—to Morrolan and see what he says. But I'm *not* going to go steal that thing back." Then I asked hopefully, "Is there anything that needs attention around here before I go put myself in the Dragon's maw?"

" 'Fraid not."

"All right. Thanks. Good work."

You don't, Sethra explained to me after it was all over, get to pick and choose your resources when you begin a campaign. In other words, the object is to make the best use of what you have and to find a way to pit your strengths against the enemy's weaknesses. She used a complicated example I didn't follow involving pitting cavalry against sorcery, and long, fast marches against an enemy entrenched in a long line. Her point being that the first thing you do when starting a campaign is assess your own strengths and weaknesses and your opponent's in light of your goals.

As I say, I didn't follow the analogy, but now, looking back on it, when I can, if I want, see everything I did in military terms, I suppose you could say that it was somewhere in there that I began to take stock of my own forces, as if this were a campaign I had decided to enter on. The fact is, it wasn't until a day or two later that I became committed to it, but even as I sat there in my office contemplating what Kragar had told me and preparing another visit to Castle Black, I was, even if I didn't know it, embarking on a campaign, and somewhere in the back of my head I was assessing the forces I had to work with and preparing myself for what was to come.

I just didn't think I was going to give my report to Morrolan and be finished with it, even though I couldn't have told you why I had that feeling.

But my campaign had no goal, at least at that point, which made the preparation a bit tricky. And it was all unconscious, which made it trickier. And the fact is, I still think I'd have been done with the whole thing if Fornia hadn't . . . but no, we'll leave that to its proper place.

This time I had one of my own sorcerers do the teleport: a guy named Temek who had been with me all along. He was competent as a sorcerer, though his main skill was, let's say, elsewhere. He did a good enough job.

When I reached Castle Black, I made a point of noting landmarks—most of them way below me—in case I had to teleport myself there one of these days. I achieved only limited success, but I'm never excited about performing a teleport; I'm not that good at it. The stream was very thin below me, and details were hard to pick out, but there was certainly some sort of footbridge over it, partially hidden by a pair of trees at one end. The trees themselves, and those nearby, seemed from above to be oddly shaped; perhaps shiptrees bred millennia earlier for designs no longer used. Then again, perhaps my eyes and the altitude were conspiring to trick me.

When I felt ready, I moved toward the doors of Castle Black; I even managed a jaunty salute toward a pair of guards who watched me from the wall. They didn't appear to notice. Again the doors swung open and again Lady Teldra greeted me. She was tall and lithe and managed to achieve beauty without sexuality—that is, I enjoyed looking at her but felt no desire. This is unusual for me, and I wondered if it was a calculated effect.

"The Lord Morrolan," she said, "will join you in the library directly. Would you care for refreshment?"

"Please."

She escorted me up the long winding stairway to the library, left me for a moment, and returned with a glass of a red wine that had too much tannin for my taste and was too warm, but which was good anyway. I'd been in that library on several occasions; this time, while I waited, I looked at some of his books. Most of them seemed, predictably, to be either history or sorcery. There were some books about the East that aroused my interest, in particular one called *Customs and Superstitions in the Eastern Mountains*, and another called *The Wars for Independence in the Mountain States*, both published in the East, and both written by someone called Fekete Szüszí, which I knew to be a Fenarian name. I wasn't sure what I thought about Morrolan having such books.

Loiosh informed me of his approach just before he said, "You may borrow them, if you wish," so I could avoid letting him startle me.

"I'd like that very much."

"I should warn you, however, that I have several volumes devoted to curses for people who don't return books."

"I'd like to borrow those, too."

"What brings you here?"

"I have the name you're after."

"Ah. So soon?"

"If you're going to employ Easterners, you'll have to adjust to things happening quickly."

"Boss, do you think he really has books full of curses for people who—"

"It wouldn't surprise me a bit, Loiosh."

"All right, then," said Morrolan. "Who is it?"

I gave him the name and watched his face. I might as well have been watching his rows of books.

"Very well," he said.

"Is that all?"

"No."

"Well, Boss, did you think—"

"Shut up."

"What else, then?"

"The weapon must be retrieved."

"Yeah. I know some thieves. If you want it stolen back I'll give you a name or two."

"They wouldn't work for me. Besides—"

"I know. Dragonlords don't steal. And that isn't what you want anyway."

Morrolan nodded, but his thoughts seemed elsewhere. "More important, however, is that the Count of Fornia be taught a lesson."

"A lesson? I hope you aren't going to ask me to kill him, because—"

Morrolan's nostrils flared and he started in on a glare which died on the vine. "You are jesting, I presume. Please do not make such jests in the future."

I shrugged. I hadn't been, but there was no reason to tell him that. I was relieved he wasn't going to ask me to put a shine on a Dragonlord anyway.

"No, I think I must go to war with him."

I looked at Morrolan and blinked. "Well, of course. Certainly. That's obvious. What else can one do? But how does that concern me?"

"It doesn't, directly."

"Well, that's a relief, anyway."

"*Too bad, Boss. I was hoping for a commission.*"

"*Shut up, Loiosh.*"

"*Lieutenant Loiosh . . . has a nice sound, don't you think?*"

"*Shut* up, *Loiosh.*"

"*Attention, First Jhereg Lancers, forward at a march—*"

"*Shut the fuck up, Loiosh.*"

"*Yes sir, Colonel. Aye aye. Shutting up, sir.*"

"I don't suppose you have any experience in military reconnaissance?"

"I assure you, in the small fishing village I come from it forms the sole topic of conversation."

"I hadn't thought so. Still, you may prove useful. In the meantime, I appreciate what you've done. I'll have payment sent over by messenger."

"Payment is always appreciated. But I'm not entirely happy with the 'you may prove useful' business. I don't suppose you could tell me what you have in mind?"

"If it were a Jhereg matter, would you tell me?"

"Of course. Openness and Honesty is my credo."

He twitched me a smile.

I said, "Just out of curiosity, how does this work? Are you going to declare war on him, or what?"

"A formal declaration of war isn't called for in an action of this type. I'll just send him a message demanding the return of the sword, or accusing him of stealing it, and that will accomplish the same thing. But there are preparations to be made first."

"Like gathering an army?"

"Yes, and planning a campaign, and, above all, hiring a general."

"Hiring a general?" That time I was actually startled. "You're not going to lead the army yourself?"

"Would you assassinate someone yourself if you could get Mario to do it?"

Actually, I probably would, but— "I see your point. And who is this military genius who is the moral equivalent of Mario? Wait, no, don't tell me. Sethra Lavode."

"Good guess."

"I've always been bright for my age." Then, "Wait a minute. How do you know about Mario?"

He looked smug again. I must stop giving him occasion to look smug.

I said, "You think Sethra will do it?"

"I know she will."

"Because she's a friend?"

"For that, yes, and other reasons."

"Hmmmph."

"Boss, there's a lot going on here that we don't know about."

"You think so? Really? Next you'll tell me that a Dzur in the wild can be dangerous."

"How 'bout if you do the killing and I do the irony?"

That, in any case, concluded the interview with Morrolan. I picked up the books I was borrowing and made my way down the stairs toward the front doors, where a sorcerer was prepared to make me sick again. I stopped at the landing and studied the painting there up close. It was ideally viewed from the floor below or above, but up close I could see the texturing that went into the detail work, and, though it strained my neck, I could study the head of the wounded Dragon. Even in a painting, there was something powerful and intriguing about the way those tentacle-like appendages around its neck seemed to wave and flutter—apparently at random, yet there was purpose in it. And the expression on the Dragon's face spoke of necessity, but of a certain joy as well. The wound in its side, which was closest to me, was skillfully rendered to evoke pity but not disgust, and even in the young Dragon there was a certain hint that, though requiring protection, it was still a Dragon and thus not to be trifled with either.

My eye kept returning to those tentacles, however, as if they were a puzzle that might be solved, revealing—what?

"*Dragons are more complex than they seem, aren't they, Boss?*"

"*I was just thinking the same thing.*"

"*Especially Morrolan.*"

"*Yes.*"

"*Did you notice what he didn't ask about?*"

"*Yes. He never asked about the weapon that was stolen.*"

"*You're not as stupid as they say, Boss.*"

"*Save it, Loiosh. Instead, tell me what it means.*"

"*That he already knew about the theft. Which means when we were setting that trap, we weren't doing what we thought we were. Although what we were doing I couldn't guess.*"

"*Yeah. Maybe. Or it might mean something else entirely.*"

"*What else?*"

I studied those tentacles again—random patterns that, somehow, made a kind of sense.

"*That he knew there was a particular weapon that would be stolen, which means the theft wasn't just a test or trial, but accomplished what it was supposed to, and there's more to that weapon than we'd thought there was. Which would make sense, of course. Or Kragar's*" idea: It didn't matter what was stolen; the idea was to annoy Morrolan enough to start a war, just because he wanted a war. In fact, we were probably wrong about everything and, no doubt, still are. Whenever we come to a conclusion, we should just assume we're wrong and go from there."

Loiosh was silent for a moment. Then he said, "I like the artist."

"So do I," I said. "Come on. Let's go home."

I turned my back on the wounded Dragon and walked out of Castle Black.

4

CALL TO WAR

Sethra Lavode once gave me a brief history of battle-magic, but I don't remember a whole lot of it; it wasn't important at the time, and my acquaintance with her was new enough that I was thinking less about what she said than the fact that she was saying it. I do remember bits and pieces, however. Between what she said and what I subsequently learned from Morrolan and Aliera, I can give you a very rough overview. It goes something like this:

The earliest practical spells were reconnaissance and illusion; both very powerful, but easily countered. Later there were means developed of creating mass destruction, and all sorts of effort went into protecting one's army. Defense eventually outstripped offense to the point where a soldier could usually consider himself safe from any direct sorcerous attack as long as he wasn't carrying too much metal. It was somewhere in here that armor went by the board, except that some used (and still use) wooden armor, and wooden shields are still common, and warriors in the House of the Lyorn still wear copper or bronze vambraces to prove that they are fearless or stupid—two conditions I've never been able to tell apart.

Various methods were created for allowing the foot soldier to carry pre-prepared offensive spells into battle, and these, too, got stronger and more sophisticated, until some big battle, the name and date of which I didn't pay much attention to, where some sorcerer found a means of making every one of the enemy's "flashstones" blow up in his hand—which added a whole new level of spell and counter-spell, and made the common foot soldier leery about having anything to do with sorcery.

Offensive spells, after that, got bigger, more powerful, more sophisticated again, and often involved sorcerers working together to send huge, powerful spells capable of wreaking havoc on an entire force, and so, again, countermeasures were developed until battle became more a test of the skills of sorcerers than of soldiers and generals. This reached its peak just before the Interregnum with a Dragonlord named Adron, about whom the less said the better.

The Interregnum threw all of that out, and war returned to the proper mayhem of soldiers slaughtering each other like gentlemen, and since the end of the Interregnum the sciences of mass destruction have slowly been building up again, with the difference that, sorcery being now so much more powerful, it is hard to find a soldier incapable of some sort of sorcerous attack, and almost impossible to find one incapable of defending himself against sorcery. But the concentration required to cast a spell, or to defend against one, is concentration that isn't being used to avoid the sharp thing someone is likely swinging at you. All of which means that, for the most part, sorcery is beside the point. At least for now. Check back again in twenty or two hundred or two thousand years and you're likely to find a different answer.

To put it another way: In the early days of the Empire, when sorcery was simple and weak, it had little effect on battle; now, in the latter days of the Empire, when sorcery is powerful and sophisticated, it has little effect on battle.

Except, of course, against Easterners, who are helpless against it.

This, at any rate, was how Sethra had explained it before I began my brief military career. In the battle, her words seemed more important and far less accurate; the enemy kept sending nasty spells at us, and sometimes they'd kill someone, and several times they almost killed me.

I hated that.

I would not have needed the lecture to understand what it all meant to the common foot soldier: It meant that, every once in a while one of your comrades would fall over, dead and twitching, with no visible sign of what had happened; that rather more frequently someone would go down, killed or wounded, after being hit by what looked like nothing more than a faint reddish light; and that, even while engaged in hand-to-hand fighting, you had to be aware that someone could be targeting you for something unhealthy.

At least, since the enemy was charging us, they couldn't throw javelins at us, and the spells became fewer as we clashed. The first few seconds after the lines meet is the most intense time of the battle; it is more intense, to the warrior, that is, than the inevitable crisis point where the battle is decided. The first few seconds are when you don't have to do any thinking; later the action gradually slows down, or seems to, until eventually you have time to let your fear catch up to you. As I said, I remember little of that first clash, but the thing I remember most is the sound of ten thousand steel swords thudding into ten thousand wooden shields, and the occasional clang and scrape of sword against spearhead. No, it wasn't really that many, it just sounded like it. Loiosh probably made some smart remarks. It is often a blessing to forget.

I remember noticing that Aelburr was somehow on his feet again, wounds notwithstanding, and swinging away with a will; and I caught a glimpse of Napper, being happy about the only time he ever was, which irony was lost on me because I'd grown used to it. It's amazing what you can grow used to with sufficient provocation, but irony, an old friend of mine, is just no good except at a distance. I wasn't catching any irony at the time, though now I can realize how ironic it is that, in spite of all my worry, and in spite of Kragar's comments, and in spite of Morrolan's hints, I almost certainly would have been done with the whole business when the messenger arrived with my payment the day after I made my report to Morrolan.

I would have been, if.

They showed up at my flat shortly after I returned from the office after speaking with Morrolan. I opened the door in answer to an imperious clap. There were three of them, all men, all Dragonlords, and two of them were armed. The third said, "Your name is Taltos." He pronounced it as if he'd seen it written but never heard it, from which I could draw conclusions that were, no doubt, useful for something.

"More or less," I told him. Loiosh flew over and landed on my shoulder. I was worried, and even a bit frightened. I don't worry much about opening my door, because the Jhereg considers one's home sacrosanct; but who knows what Dragons think?

"My name is Ori. My Lord the Count of Fornia requests and requires you not to interfere in any way in his concerns. This is the only warning you will receive. Is that understood?"

I took a moment to work that through. Fornia knew that I was involved. Okay. And he was warning me to stay out of the way. What did he imagine I was going to do? And why was he even bothering to threaten me?

It was puzzling as well as annoying, but the annoyance predominated. Three Dragonlords—*three*, for the love of Verra, and one of them clearly a sorcerer, come into my home and tell me what to do? Even the Jhereg doesn't do that. Even the Phoenix Guard, when they're harassing the Jhereg, doesn't do that. If a Jhereg or a representative of the Empire wanted to threaten or intimidate me, they'd have the courtesy to call on me in one of my workplaces—say the office, or a restaurant, or an alley. This business of having my home invaded set me off, but I resolved to be diplomatic about the whole thing. I said, "What if I request and require the Count of Fornia to kiss my ruddy bum?"

Both of the Dragonlords drew their swords as best they could in the confined space of my entryway; at the same time they moved forward. An instant later they fell backward; one because there was a Jhereg in his face, the other because I'd thrown a knife into his shoulder.

Ori raised his hand, but I knew very well what it means when a Dragonlord isn't carrying a sword. At the same time as I'd thrown the knife (a boot knife, one of only four knives I was still carrying after disarming myself when I'd gotten home), I let Spellbreaker, about eighteen inches of gold chain, fall into my left hand. I set it spinning to intercept whatever he was about to throw at me.

Ori turned out to be pretty fast; some part of his spell got past, and I felt weak, dizzy, and I couldn't move the right side of my body. I let myself fall over and started rolling away from the door.

The effects of the spell were short-lived; I was able to stand and come up with another knife—this one a stiletto, not well suited to throwing—and start Spellbreaker spinning again. If Ori threw something else at me, the chain got all of it, and Loiosh was keeping the one Dragon pretty busy, but the other one, my knife still sticking out of his shoulder, had picked up his sword with his left hand and was charging me.

This was cause for some concern.

There was no way to parry his sword with my stiletto, so I did the only thing I could, which was to move in at him and hope to get past his attack.

I felt my knife strike home, and, at the same time, something hit me in the side, and then I felt the floor against my face. I did some calculations as I was lying there: Loiosh could handle the one, and, with luck, I had disabled the other at the same time as he'd gotten me, but there was still the sorcerer to worry about. I tried to roll over, and noticed that Spellbreaker was no longer in my hand; this is where I got really worried. I tried again to roll over, and I figured I must have succeeded because I was looking at the ceiling; that was a start. Only the ceiling was wrong, somehow. I tried to get up, wondering when the pain was going to hit me. Someone said, "Lie still, Vlad."

A woman's voice. Whose? I knew it, but I couldn't place it. But I was like Hell going to lie still. I tried to sit up again.

"Lie still. It's all right."

All right? What—?

Aliera e'Kieron came into view overhead.

"You're at Castle Black, Boss."

"Castle Black? How did I get here?"

"Morrolan came and got you."

"How did he—?"

"I told him."

"How could you—?"

"I wasn't sure I could."

"Am I ever going to be able to complete a—"

"How do you feel?" asked Aliera.

"Angry," I said. "Very, very angry. I would badly like to kill someone. I—"

"I mean, how do you feel physically?"

That was a tougher question, so I took some time to consider it. "All right," I finally said. "My side is a little stiff. What happened?"

"Someone cut you."

"Bad?"

"Fairly deep," she said judiciously. "No organs were damaged. Two ribs were cracked."

"I see. Considering all of that, I feel great. Thanks."

"Any pain?"

"Some."

"It'll get worse."

"All right."

"Would you like something for the pain?"

"Pain doesn't bother me," I told Aliera.

She didn't choose to be impressed.

I'd first run into Aliera in a wizard's laboratory, trapped inside
a piece of wood, which had hindered our ability to get to know
one another. Later, when she was breathing and talking and
such, we'd been too busy for much chatting. I'd picked up that
she was related to Morrolan—which wasn't surprising, because
I imagine most Dragons are related to most others, one way or
another. As far as I knew then (I learned more later, but that
doesn't come into this story), she was fairly typical for a Dragonlord, except shorter. Evidently she had some abilities as a
physicker.

"Who was it?" she asked.

"A Dragon," I said.

She nodded. "So Morrolan informs me. I meant more specif-
ically."

"Someone in the employ of Fornia. There was a sorcerer
named Ori; I didn't get the names of the blademen."

"What did they want?"

"They wanted me to stay out of their business."

She nodded as if it made perfect sense that this request involved attempting to cut me in half crosswise. I suppose it makes
sense to me, too. And it might even have seemed reasonable if
they hadn't walked into my home to do it. Maybe that doesn't
make sense to you, and maybe it is even irrational, but I'd been
in the Jhereg for several years, and to us, well, you just don't do
that.

"Will you?" she said.

"Stay out of his business? Not anymore," I told her.

She laughed a little. Her eyes were light brown. "You sound
like a Dragon."

"I'd challenge you to a duel, but that would just confirm your
opinion, so I'll pass."

"Good thinking," she said.

I kept my anger under a lid because it works better that way,
because I can use it that way. It was a very cold anger, and I

knew that it would sustain me for quite some time—for long enough, at least, to track down this Fornia and do unto him.

But not now. Now I had to stay cool and recover. I took a deep breath and let my vision wander. The ceiling was of some very dark hardwood; my own was a textured plaster of some kind and much lower—the trained eye picks up these details almost instantly. There were other subtle things that had made me feel I might be in the wrong place when I first became conscious—like, my entire flat would nearly have fit into the room, and every item of furniture—three chairs, a desk, a table, and a sofa—cost more than I made for killing a man.

I said, "What do you know of this weapon Fornia had stolen?"

"Why?"

"It seems to be the cause of all this unpleasantness; either the weapon, or the fact that he stole it, or . . ."

She waited. "Yes? Or?"

"Or something entirely different that I have no clue about. I always have to include that as one of the possibilities."

She looked at me. "Well, you seem to be out of danger, and I have better ways to spend my time than to be interrogated by a Jhereg, so you'll have to excuse me."

"Hugs and kisses to you, too."

She gave me a glance and floated out of the room. I carefully sat up, discovered that doing so hurt, and began looking around for my clothing.

"*On the little table at the foot of the bed, Boss. You're going to need a new shirt, and your trousers have some bloodstains.*"

"*All right. Feel like shopping?*"

"*Going to buy me something?*"

"*Like what?*"

"*Catnip.*"

"*Catnip? Does catnip affect you? When did you—?*"

"*Probably not. But I don't want to eat it myself.*"

"*Then why—?*"

"*Bait*," said Loiosh.

"*Funny, Loiosh. No, but maybe I'll buy you a set of opposable thumbs.*"

"*Heh.*"

I was starting to lose count of the teleports to and from Castle Black over the last couple of days; but I had another done for me, and then went to South Adrilankha, the Easterners' quarter, where I replaced a few items of clothing and supped. I stopped by my grandfather's for a visit, but he was out. I returned to my own area, found a sorcery supply store that was still open, and started to buy a mild painkiller, but then changed my mind and bought a strong one. I also picked up an enchanted dagger because the spells on my own were wearing thin and you never know when you might need a spell in a hurry. The guy at the store explained that the enchantments on the blade were so powerful that three people I'd never heard of had been in awe of it, and so on until I shut him up and bought the thing for half of what he had first asked.

Then I went home, took the painkiller, and started cleaning up the damage to my flat. There were no bodies there, but there were some bloodstains. I resent bloodstains in my home, especially when some of the blood is mine. I became angry all over again. I got rid of the stains by covering them with a rug, then I picked up some furniture that I don't remember being overturned, and may have done a bit more before the painkillers hit and, apparently, I made it to the bed before falling asleep.

A day in the life.

I woke up sore, moody, and in need of klava. If I ever get really rich, I'm going to hire a servant just to bring me klava in the morning. I managed to rise, make the coffee, and brew a fairly effective pot of klava, into which I poured some cow's milk and the last of the honey. I made a note to order more ice, no matter how expensive it was. I should really learn to make my own; cooling and heating spells are supposed to be pretty simple.

I was dressed and working up the energy to leave when someone clapped outside my door. Twice in two days would be stretching the laws of probability, so I wasn't worried; or, at least, I told myself I wasn't worried as I picked up a dagger and opened the door.

I didn't recognize the visitor, but she wore the colors of the House of the Dragon. I might have struck immediately if I hadn't noticed that she wore Morrolan's emblem on her shoulder, and if I hadn't been too stiff to move quickly. She said, "You are—?"

"Baronet Vladimir Taltos, House of the Jhereg."

"Then this is for you," she said, handing me a small bag that jingled. "If you'd be so kind as to touch this ring."

I touched the ring, took the bag, and shut the door as she turned away. I'd forgotten that Morrolan owed me money. I counted it and was pleased.

I thought about treating myself to a cabriolet ride to the office, but I'd be seen, and people would wonder why, and some of them might guess right. I also thought about taking more pain-killers, but even a little would make me woozy, and that just won't do in this business; I had to be as stoic as I'd pretended to be to Aliera the day before.

Bugger.

I took the walk to the office slowly, not noticing much going on around me; when you hurt, too much of your attention is focused in to have much to spare for the rest of the world. I made it to the office, and Melestav greeted me with the words "You okay, Boss?"

"Yeah," I said. "Anything new?"

"A couple of requests for credit extensions, a request for a meeting from someone named Koth, nothing else."

I grunted. "Any idea what Koth wants?"

"To hire you."

"Thank him and put him off. I'm busy for the next week, maybe two. I'll look at the requests later."

"All right."

"And tell Kragar I want to see him."

I hung up my cloak and eased myself into my chair. Then I leaned back and closed my eyes, and Kragar said, "You all right, Boss?"

"Fine," I said. "All things considered."

"All right. What things need consideration?"

"I got jumped."

I opened my eyes. I looked around the room for Kragar, then found him sitting in the chair opposite me. He was staring at me intently, suspecting, I suppose, that we were about to be involved in some affair within the Jhereg—like someone trying to make a move on my territory. I said, "I got jumped by three Dragonlords."

"Phoenix Guards?"

"No. The business wasn't connected with the Organization in any way. They were Dragonlords doing business as Dragonlords, and their business was jumping me."

He leaned back, and his expression altered from worry to surprise.

"Really? My, my. Now, that isn't something every Jhereg can say. Where did it happen?"

"Right in my own Verra-be-damned flat."

"Hmmm," he said. "Want to tell me about it?"

I did. He said, "To a Dragon, it's different—"

"I know. I'm not a Dragon."

"Ah." He studied me. "So now you've decided to go after Fornia?"

"Yes."

"Has it occurred to you that you may have been attacked in order to get you to go after him?"

"Yes. It has occurred to me. It is even possible. But do you think it likely?"

"I have no idea. But when we were talking before, you were saying—"

"I know. But it's one thing to be aware of complex strategies and lies that might be going on around you. It's another to let yourself become so worried about deception that you become paralyzed."

"Profound, Boss."

"Shut up, Loiosh."

Kragar shrugged. "All right. If you write that down, I'll save it for your epitaph."

"In the meantime, what do we do about Fornia?"

Kragar caught my eye. "There's always the obvious."

"Yes. I'd been thinking about that."

"And?"

"What do you think?"

"It'll be tricky."

"I know. You can't just put down a Dragonlord as if he were a nine-copper hustler. It'll get ugly. People will talk. But I want to."

"I can start doing some checking."

"That would be good."

"But you should be aware that Morrolan will be, uh, pretty unhappy."

I said, "Not that I care all that much, but why?"

"People will think he had it done."

"Oh. That isn't my problem."

"Are you sure?"

I considered. "Just *how* unhappy is Morrolan likely to be?"

"Very," said Kragar. "From everything I know, he'll set out to make your life either miserable or short. You'll probably have to fight him."

"Great," I said. "Well, is there anything we can do to Fornia short of killing him that wouldn't set Morrolan on my ass?"

"Hmmmm. Maybe."

"Yeah?"

"Well, I know what would really get to him: losing."

"Losing? Like, in battle?"

"Yeah."

"Great. Well, Morrolan is going to attack him. I could always enlist in the army. But somehow I can't imagine myself in uniform, marching off to battle." I really said that. Funny, isn't it?

Kragar said, "There are other ways."

"Oh? Keep talking."

He studied his right thumb. "I'm not sure I have anything definite yet. We don't know enough. But if Morrolan is really going to attack him—"

"He is. He plans to sign Sethra Lavode on as his general-in-chief."

Kragar gave an I-am-impressed look and said, "Then you could probably do something nasty to him to help Morrolan. There are a number of possibilities. An army is a great deal more delicate than you'd think. Just destroy a list of supplies he needs and you've created enough confusion to give him headaches. Or sneak in and burn a map or two. Or have someone impersonate an officer and send a company marching the wrong way. Or—"

"I think I get the idea."

He nodded. "Once we know more we can be more specific."

I shook my head. "I'm trying to imagine myself as some sort of—I don't know—saboteur."

"I'm trying to imagine it, too. And I'm trying not to laugh."

"Thank you so much."

He shrugged. "Well, so he got you mad, and you want to get him back. You're stuck. If you can come up with something better, let me know."

"I can still kill him."

"Yeah, there's that."

I said, "If you come up with a way to turn a profit on this, let *me* know."

"Oh, that's easy. Morrolan will probably pay you for it."

"Do you think so?"

"Yep."

"Well, that's something."

He shook his head. "Hasn't anyone ever told you that revenge is wrong?"

"No, Kragar," I said. "That got left out of my education."

"Too late now," he said.

5

MOURNING IN THE AFTERNOON

The next thing I remember doing is dodging around, trying to stay alert and not get killed. The first clash was over, and there were a lot of dead and wounded around, but things had broken up a bit. I didn't see Virt or Aelburr anymore, but I caught a glimpse of Napper about twenty yards to my left, flailing about in fine style; I was sure he, at any rate, was enjoying himself. Our colors were still waving, but I didn't recognize the woman holding them; Dunn was either dead or wounded. I hoped he was happy; he'd gotten what he wanted.

There was nothing like a line of battle, but there were clumps of fighting here and there, and many of us, on both sides, who were either looking for someone to fight or hoping not to find someone. This is, I suppose, where spirit of battle really matters: If we'd had more of it, I'd have been trying harder to kill someone. If they'd had more of it, I wouldn't have been able to hang around the fringes of the fighting. At some point in there, I noticed fresh blood on my sword, and I wondered how it got there.

The trouble was: My comrades were fighting for each other. In part, to keep each other alive, and in part because they knew each other, had trained together, and none wanted to be the only one to bug out. I'd been through enough with them to know that that was the thing that kept them going; but I *hadn't* trained with them, and I didn't know them, and even by then I wasn't quite sure why I hadn't bugged out. I still didn't know what had kept me there the first time the enemy had come at us over hastily thrown-up earthworks.

There was a short breathing space, and I relished it—hell, I gloried in it. Strange, huh? I was in as much danger, perhaps, as I'd ever been in, and I remember how delighted I was that there were spaces of time when no one was trying to kill me. Long spaces of time—seconds on end.

Then Loiosh said, "*Remember why we're here, Boss?*"

"Damn you anyway."

"*Boss—*"

"No, no. You're right. I have a job to do."

"*But how—*"

"Oh, I know how." There was a little hillock, really just a rise in the ground, before me—just down the hill and up another. "*I just have to get over that hill and spot their command post, which will be protected by the best warriors I've ever met and more sorcerous ability than you can find outside of Dzur Mountain. Then I have to finish up what I came here for. No problem.*"

"*I know that. I meant how. Too bad we don't know any invisibility spells that will stand up.*"

"*Too bad I'm not Kragar.*"

Someone stumbled in front of me. An enemy. He looked at me, and I looked at him. He had lost his shield somewhere, but held most of a spear. I don't think he'd been coming after me, the force of battle had just placed him there. He probably would just as soon have run away, and I'd just as soon he did, but, of course, neither of us could trust the other to be sensible. He whipped the remains of his spear toward me. I moved in, knocked his weapon aside with the strong of my blade, and cut him in the neck. He went down and I moved on. I don't know if I killed him. I hope I didn't.

I looked around, and I was as alone as I could be, under the circumstances.

I started down the hill at a trot.

"*Quick-march now, Boss.*"

"*Oh, shut up.*"

I thought about how comfortable my office was. I thought about how pleasant it would be to be sitting there. I remember—now, I didn't think about it then—how Kragar left me alone in the office to think over the idea of working with Morrolan's army as some sort of spy or saboteur; I couldn't quite wrap my head around the idea, but at the time, I was angry enough not to care. I needed to sort all that out so I yelled out that I didn't want to be bothered for a while.

"Okay, Boss!" yelled Melestav. "Anyone wants to come in and kill you, I tell them to wait, right?"

"Yeah," I yelled back. "Unless they're Dragons. Any Dragons who want to kill me can come right in."

He didn't say anything. I had gotten in the last word on Melestav; that had to be a good sign.

I closed my eyes and thought about Morrolan. I pictured him, tall, thin, rather dark, a very slight hook in the nose, eyes deep and rather close together, a bit of slant to his forehead, and I imagined his voice, a smooth baritone, mellow, and forming words with an assumed elegance—

"*Who is it?*"

"*Vlad.*"

"*Yes?*"

"*Am I reaching you at a bad time?*"

"*Not as bad as ten minutes later would have been. Which reminds me: Do you prefer the blood of a reptile or a mammal when you want to set up a room so you know if it's been violated?*"

"*Your own blood is best for anything of that type, because you want it to come back to you. But you only need a drop; it's symbolic.*"

"*Thank you. What is it you wish of me?*"

"*I want to know if I can be useful to you.*"

"*You just were.*"

"*Other than that.*"

"Exactly what do you mean?"

"Against Fornia. Could your army use someone able to sneak in and out of the enemy camp, cause annoyance, disruption—"

"You're taking this rather personally, aren't you, Vlad?"

"Yes."

"Are you certain you want to do this?"

"Well, no. Not entirely. I'm just considering it."

"I see. We should talk."

"I suppose so."

"Are you busy later this afternoon? Say, in a few hours?"

"I could get free."

"Then meet me . . . no offense, Vlad, but are you able to receive a teleport position?"

"Yeah, just barely, if you give me a lot of time to fix it."

"Then I'll give you one. Are you ready?"

"Yeah, go ahead."

"Here."

Okay, I knew how to do this; I'd even done it once or twice before. I made an effort to drop those little controls we always keep on our thoughts. I mentally framed a picture—in my head, I always have big elegant gold frames—then thought of the space within as black. I held onto it and moved it around until it was mentally facing *out*, facing the imaginary direction of my psychic link with Morrolan. It gradually acquired color that I hadn't put into it, and details formed, until, in only a minute or two, I was seeing a place: the bottom of what appeared to be a cliff, a small stream before it, a few evergreens nearby. I couldn't tell how high the cliff was from what Morrolan was showing me, but it seemed to be large, and I certainly would have no desire to attempt to scale it: It seemed perfectly sheer, and grey, and, if you'll permit me, ominous. The ground was rocky and brown, with a few sparse bits of grass sticking up here and there; the stream, as far as I could tell, was little more than a trickle of water.

I concentrated; as I'd told Morrolan, I wasn't all that good at fixing locations for a teleport, but at last I felt reasonably certain I wasn't likely to send myself off to the middle of the ocean or forty feet under the ground. I said, "Got it."

"The seventh hour."

"Why there?"

"There will be an event taking place that you may wish to witness."

I thought about interrogating him some more, but decided it was pointless. "I'll be there," I told him.

"What do you suppose that was about, Boss?"

"I imagine I'll find out."

"Do you trust him?"

"Within limits. I doubt he wants to have me killed."

"Oh, good. Nothing to worry about, then."

I handled a few things around the office, then went down into what I called the "lab" and performed a very minor and easy ritual to help along the healing in my side—just a few instructions to the damaged parts suggesting they go ahead and heal; the indication of success was how hungry I was after, so I went over to the Garden House and had a big plate of egg noodles with squid and leeks to help the process along. Then I headed to Turningham's and looked for a book, found a historical romance by Munnis that I hadn't read, bought it, went home, read the first page, and set it aside for later. I discovered I was hungry again, and that my side was itching and feeling better, all of which meant my spell really was working. I've performed spells of that type, oh, I don't know, maybe a score of times, yet I still get a little thrill, almost of surprise, when I see evidence of it working; like I'm putting one over on nature.

I ate some bread and cheese, took a nap, and Loiosh woke me up a few minutes before the seventh hour.

I managed the teleport myself, without too much difficulty, and arrived right at the appointed hour. The spot at which Morrolan had me appear was a quarter of a mile away from a mass of humanity, all gathered together directly in front of the sheer cliff, which stretched up until its top was lost in the overcast. It was much bigger than I had guessed. I studied it until my neck hurt, then, as my gaze returned to what appeared to be a gathering of several hundred people, at which I could see new arrivals teleporting in at an alarming rate, Loiosh made a squeaking sound and dived into my cloak.

"What—?"

"Didn't you see them, Boss?"

"No, I was looking at—"

"Giant Jhereg, just like at Deathgate Falls."

"We can't be anywhere near there."

"Tell them that."

I looked up again, and, yeah, there were a few shapes that occasionally dipped out of the overcast, circled, and vanished again.

"They're very graceful, Loiosh. You should watch."

"You should drown in a chamberpot, Boss."

"Greetings, Vlad."

I jumped a little, then turned around and said, "Hello, Morrolan. What's the occasion?"

"A ceremony to honor Baritt's passing over Deathgate Falls."

"What? We're near there?"

"No. But his tomb will be here."

"His tomb? I don't . . . how can he have a tomb if his body is going over the Falls?"

"Well, it's not a tomb exactly. Call it a cenotaph. Or a monument. But this mountain has been selected as the place to be consecrated to his memory."

"He gets a whole mountain?"

"He earned it."

"What do I have to do to earn a mountain?"

Morrolan chose not to answer. He said, "I should appear at the ceremony. Would you like to come along?"

"Is that a joke? As what?"

"My retainer. I have the right to have anyone I choose in my suite."

"An Easterner? A Jhereg?"

"Certainly."

"You have something in mind, don't you?"

"Of course."

"Want to let me in on it, in my capacity as the device to be exploited?"

"I'd rather surprise you."

"I'm not all that fond of surprises."

"I understood that you wanted to exact payment from our friend Fornia for what he did to you."

"Yeah."

"Well then, come along and let's do so."

I sighed. "All right, lead on. But . . . skip it."

He led the way. As we approached, I spotted Aliera off to one side; she stood out as the shortest individual in the crowd. She spotted us and waved. A few others noticed us; I caught some double takes, and suspected I was now the object of a great deal of conversation among a few score Dragonlords. I had mixed feelings about this, but it wasn't all unpleasant. Morrolan, who had brought me, after all, was wearing the dexter half of a smile.

I said, "You enjoy being talked about, don't you?"

He smirked outright, but gave no other answer.

We reached Aliera, who nodded to me and looked a question at Morrolan, who said, "He is considering joining our cause."

"Against Fornia?" I nodded, and she said, "You're taking this a little personally, aren't you?"

"I think I will soon begin to take personally everyone telling me I'm taking things personally."

"Do that," she said. Then, to Morrolan, "But why bring him here?"

"I have reasons, my dear cousin. A little patience and you will know."

I could see Aliera deciding whether to take offense; eventually she gave a hint of a shrug and turned away. I was standing in quite a crowd of Dragons, many of whom were giving me looks; more of whom were glancing at Morrolan. He appeared to be enjoying the attention. I spotted a familiar figure: Ori. He was looking at me.

"Vlad!" said Morrolan sharply.

"What?"

"This isn't the place."

I almost asked "For what?" before I realized that my hand was on my sword hilt. It took a deliberate effort to drop my arm back to my side. Ori was standing next to a very old Dragonlord, who had dressed himself in the simplest military fashion: black everything with buttons and hems of silver. His face was wrinkled as a prune, and his slitted eyes were studying me.

I said, "Fornia?"

"Yes," said Morrolan.

I studied the man, then turned once more to Morrolan. "Well, here you both are."

"Yes?"

I shrugged. "Why don't you just kill him?"

He graced me with a scaled-down smile. "There are more reasons than I have time to expound upon."

"Name three."

"All right. One: We are at a ceremony where violence would be improper. Two: If I initiated violence at this ceremony, everyone would take his side and we'd be outnumbered about three hundred to one. Three: I want to see what happens if he's left alone."

I grunted. The second answer seemed convincing enough. And what happened was that Fornia and Ori approached us. Morrolan bowed deeply, Fornia acknowledged; I assume the difference in the bows had to do with respective age. Fornia looked me over and said to Morrolan, "What is *he* doing here?"

"Taking your measure, Lord Fornia. He seems to have developed a grudge against you, and I permitted him to accompany me so that he might get a good look at you. For later," he added.

"I've just explained to him why he ought not to do anything improper just at the moment."

This seemed to be my cue, so I gave Fornia a big smile.

Fornia turned his head and spat.

I said, "In the desert culture of my people, to spit in a man's presence is to demonstrate loyalty. Am I to assume that you are my vassal?"

"*You're making that up, aren't you, Boss?*"

"*What do you think, Loiosh?*"

Ori said conversationally, "I should have killed you."

"Yes," I said promptly. "You should have. Your mistake. You won't be permitted another."

He took a step closer, so that he could look down on me. "Are you threatening me, Easterner?"

I grinned up at him. "Yes, but not as an Easterner; as a Jhereg. That's an entirely different matter, isn't it?" At that point Loiosh, who has always had a gift for theater, emerged from my cloak and climbed up to my shoulder.

Ori jumped, startled, in spite of himself, then he scowled. He said, "I will rip your soul from your body and bind it to an iron kettle so I can contemplate how your arse burns when I cook my stew."

"Good thinking," I said. "I know some excellent stew recipes if you need them. Adding a little fennel, for example, will—"

"That's enough, Vlad," said Morrolan.

"If you say so," I told him. "But I tell you, you Dragaerans don't know how to cook."

"Vlad—"

"Except for the occasional Lyorn, who seem—"

"Vlad!"

I shrugged and gave Fornia and Ori another big grin.

Fornia said, "I am not worried. You would not countenance assassination, Lord Morrolan."

"Of course not," said Morrolan. "And I assure your lordship I've been trying to talk my associate out of doing anything rash."

"Your veiled threats," said Fornia, "are as empty and absurd as your pet Easterner's coarse ones."

"Exactly," said Morrolan with a bow.

"If you want what is mine," said Fornia, "you may attempt to take it from me."

"Yours by right of theft, my lord?"

Fornia laughed. "You stand with a Jhereg at your heel and speak to me of theft?"

"You stand with a thug at your elbow and speak to me of Jhereg?"

"This is pointless," said Fornia, and turned away.

"So, as I understand it, is the weapon you've taken."

Fornia turned back, gave Morrolan a smile over his shoulder, then walked away, Ori trailing after him.

"And that, my dear Vlad," said Morrolan as soon as Fornia was out of earshot, "is what we came for."

"To bait him?"

"No, to see that smile."

"Oh. And what did you learn?"

"That whatever he was after, he got it."

"Excuse me?"

"The sword he took was what he was after, not a test, and not a failed effort at something else."

"But then, what is it?"

"I don't know."

"Morrolan, it was a very weak, very large, Morganti greatsword."

"No, it was more than that. Exactly what it is I still don't know, but more than that. I now know at least that much for certain."

"Because of that smile?"

"Because of that smile."

"If you say so. And, I take it, I was here to provide a basis for the sparring match?"

"That, yes, and to make him think. And maybe to worry him a little."

"If you worry him too much, he may decide you really do intend to have him assassinated, and he might beat you to the punch."

"He'd no more hire an assassin than I would."

"But Morrolan, you have."

"You know what I mean."

"Sure. But does he?"

"We've made our point here, Vlad. I must stay for the service, but you can return home if you wish. Or stay; it's up to you."

"What's going to happen?"

"Aliera will go forward and deliver a benediction, asking the Gods to receive Baritt's soul, and then his deeds will be related, and those who knew him will tell all manner of lies about what a fine fellow he was, and a bullock will be sacrificed to whoever his patron deity was—Barlen, if I'm not mistaken—and Aliera will perform another benediction, and then we'll all go home. It should take about ten hours."

"Ten hours?"

"More or less."

"Why Aliera?"

"It is her right and her duty."

"Why is that?"

"I assure you, Vlad, you don't need to know details of the internal politics of the House of the Dragon, nor would I be justified in telling you."

"All right. I guess I can skip the services."

"Very well. I'll be in touch."

"I imagine you will."

I walked away so I could perform my slow and clumsy teleport out of the sight of all those Dragonlords.

"Do you think he was telling the truth, Boss?"

"Who?"

"Morrolan."

"About what?"

"About why he brought you along."

"Oh. I imagine so. Why?"

"I think he was telling half the truth."

"All right. What's the other half?"

"He wanted you committed to helping him against Fornia."

I thought that over. "You're probably right," I said at length.

"It worked, didn't it, Boss?"

"Yeah, it worked."

Eventually we reached a large rock that I could step behind to perform the teleport. I never saw the services for Baritt. I hope they went well; I assume Aliera did a good job of whatever she was supposed to do. Actually, now that I think about it, I know why it is that it was Aliera's right and duty, but never mind; you don't need to know details of the internal politics of the House of the Dragon.

"What it comes down to, Loiosh, is that I just don't like the guy."

"Is that any reason to—"

"Of course it is. And if you say I'm taking this personally, I'll trade you in for a mockman and use its tail for a door-clapper."

"Heh."

I walked to the front of my flat, passed the bed, and opened the shutters on the window that looked down into the street. It was late evening, and as I watched the passersby I had the feeling that I was giving up the security of what I knew for a world in which I was ignorant and helpless as a newborn.

"Loiosh, no one's messed with my head, right?"

"I'm afraid not, Boss. This is all you."

"Just checking."

"You may want to visit your grandfather, Boss."

I felt a touch of annoyance, then sat on it. "You're right, chum. I will, before I actually do anything. But—"

"I know, Boss. You're committed."

"I hate being pushed around, that's all."

"But you don't mind being manipulated?"

"You talking about Morrolan?"

"Yes."

"Yeah, I mind. But he didn't have me beaten."

Loiosh fell silent, leaving me to think about it. I watched the people in the streets below me and thought about going out for a drink, then thought better of it. I touched my side, which was still a little sore, but getting better. In a day or two there would be nothing left of the beating I'd gotten except the memory.

"I'm going to take this guy down, Loiosh."

"I know you are, Boss."

I pulled the shutters closed.

6

Assault on Helpless Wood

There are, according to Sethra Lavode, in a brief conversation I got to listen to before I marched off to war, two basic schools of thought in terms of generalship: lead from the front, or lead from the rear. The former is better for morale but can have unfortunate consequences if your officer gets killed. The latter has many advantages in terms of communication and observation, but soldiers don't fight quite so well for a leader who is playing it safe. Sethra says that, really, it depends on circumstances, and a good general ought to be willing to lead either way when appropriate. In the case of our enemies, the officers in charge of brigades—a brigade being about three thousand strong, according to Sethra's intelligence reports—led from the front. The brigade size made sense, she explained, because that was about the largest number of soldiers who could hear the officer shouting orders. The other officers were in back, along with the chief of the sorcerers corps and whatever aides might be appropriate. The brigadier, as a compromise with safety considerations, tended to be surrounded by some elite group of warriors, dedicated to protecting him during the course of the battle. The higher ranking officers received similar protection, but they didn't need it as much—I suppose it was a status symbol the way having a lot of bodyguards is in the Jhereg.

The placing of sorcerers in battle also varies according to tastes of the general and needs of the situation, but, more often than not, sorcerers were attached to a brigade and hung around next to the brigadier. Thus, not only were the sorcerers able to receive orders quickly, but they could do a lot to protect the officer directing that part of the engagement.

Got all that?

I mention it because it flashed through my mind as I went over that hillock, behind the front line my company was engaged with, to seek out the command staff.

In other words, I was going to have to go up against an elite force of warriors as well as some number of sorcerers in order to accomplish my goal.

What was I doing here again? Oh yeah, I lost my temper and talked myself (I can't blame anyone else) into offering Morrolan my services, and he was rude enough to accept, that's what happened. And now—

And now things were moving, which is just what I'd wanted back then when everything came to a standstill. I got what I wanted; isn't that grand?

Still, as I said earlier, I don't enjoy waiting, and, especially after I've made a tough or questionable decision, I want things to be moving, and as usual when I want things to be moving, everything slowed down.

Nothing surprising there: Once you've determined to do something time is needed to make plans, gather materials, and put your plans into motion, all of which causes events to unfold too slowly; it's when you are forced into action before making a decision that things happen too quickly. Watching Morrolan and Sethra taught me that this is true in military matters, and I've always known it was true in my own life.

Or else it's just the universe being perverse; that's the other possibility.

Whichever, I spent several days having fruitless and aimless conversations with Morrolan, who agreed that I could be useful but was infuriatingly vague on the specifics. He seemed to understand without my saying it that I had become committed to helping him. This, in turn, increased my suspicion that the beating had been a setup on Morrolan's part to recruit me, and I retained that suspicion for some time, but I won't keep you in suspense: I eventually learned that Morrolan had nothing to do with it; the attack was just what it seemed. Every once in while, a Dragon will do something obvious and direct that is no more than it appears to be. I think they do it to throw you off.

I met with Morrolan, Sethra, Aliera, and a pale Dragonlord I didn't recognize. Morrolan didn't perform any introductions. I didn't say anything, because I didn't know what to say and because I was still a bit intimidated to be in the presence of Sethra Lavode.

She spread out a map, pointed to a spot, and said, "We strike here, wait for a counterattack, and retreat this way, toward the Eastern Mountains."

There were nods around the table. I'd been there for about half a minute and I was already confused.

She went on, "Of course, if there is no counterattack, we continue this way, hit here, and here, and here, until there is one, then retreat as planned. If he should allow us all the way to here, we can lay a siege, but I can't imagine it playing out that way."

"What will be the organization?" said Morrolan.

"Divisions. Three of them. I want each self-contained, with its own infantry, cavalry, sorcerers, and engineers. The First Division will be mine, and will make the attack. The others will guard our flank and cover the retreat."

"Marching in column, then?" said Aliera.

"There are plenty of good roads leading into and out of the place; once we near the mountains we'll come back together to bivouac. Here." She pointed to another spot. "We can arrange for provender from the area along this route; we'll need to make arrangements if we're west of the Flatstone River, or north of Turtle. Who's doing logistics?"

"I will take personal charge," said Morrolan.

Sethra nodded. "Sorcery," she said.

The pale woman spoke. Her hair was very black, and her voice soft. "His lead sorcerer is named Ori—"

"Ori!" I heard myself say.

"What is it, Vlad?" said Morrolan.

"Nothing," I said, embarrassed. "Never mind."

The woman looked at me, or, rather, through me, then continued. "He is adept at reconnaissance spells; especially eavesdropping on councils. I have protected this meeting. We must always be careful to do so, and to avoid discussing our plans without protection. In battle he is unlikely to come up with anything we can't counter, but he'll keep throwing spells our way to keep our own sorcerers too busy to concoct anything big."

Sethra nodded. "Anything else?"

"Yes," said Aliera. "Why is he here?" She was looking at me.

Sethra turned to Morrolan, who said, "Because I wish it."

Aliera started to speak, then changed her mind and was silent.

The meeting broke up; Aliera and the Dragonlord I didn't know left, Morrolan and Sethra spoke together quietly about details of supply, occasionally venturing off into matters of military theory that I cared about as little as I understood them, and I sat there staring at the map. It was a psiprint, like the one Melestav had shown me, but was more detailed and even cleaner.

Eventually Morrolan noticed that I was still there. "What is it, Vlad?" he said.

"Huh? Oh, nothing. I'm just looking at the map. I like maps."

"Very well. You have no questions?"

"Oh, I have a lot of questions, but I don't know if you feel like answering them."

"Like what?"

"Like why plan for a retreat?"

Morrolan looked expectantly at Sethra. She said, "I prefer a defensive fight when possible, especially when the numbers are close, and these will be. We might, in fact, be outnumbered overall."

"I see. Well, actually, I don't. What are we trying to do?"

This time Sethra looked expectantly at Morrolan. He said, "We need to curb his ambitions. This can best be done by handing his army a severe defeat. Sethra feels she can best do this by convincing him to attack us. We have an edge in our engineering corps—that is, we can construct quick and effective defenses better than he can. So we're going to invade, and invite him to attack, and then beat him."

"All right. I think I get it. And then, what, you expect him to return the sword he stole?"

"Maybe. We may have to negotiate after that."

"What's so special about that sword?"

"The fact that he wanted it."

"But, of all the weapons in that room, why did he take that one?"

Morrolan nodded. "That's what I want to know. I trust we'll find out eventually."

"I see." I considered. "Is there any more you can tell me about Baritt?"

"What do you want to know?"

"For starters, what were the circumstances of his death?"

"I'm afraid I can't tell you that."

"Great."

"If your task were to be easy," said Morrolan, "you wouldn't be earning such a large fee for it."

"Don't play games, Morrolan."

"It's not a game," he snapped, and looked at me through narrowed eyes; I suppose the look was intended to intimidate me. It worked. He started to say more, then, I guess, decided that he'd cowed me enough and didn't have to.

To change the subject, I said, "Who was the pale woman?"

"The Necromancer," he said. "She will be in overall charge of our sorcerers."

" 'The Necromancer,' " I said. "I've heard of her. Heck of a name. Will she raise the dead for us?"

"If necessary," said Morrolan. "But I could do that. If circumstances call for it, she can open a gateway for us that will bring us to a place where eternities pass in an instant, and where life and death have no meaning, and where space can only be measured by the twisting of one's soul. An effective escape, if things go wrong."

I was sorry I'd asked. "Could have used her in the Paths of the Dead," I suggested.

He didn't consider that worth a response.

I said, "I wish I knew what this was all about."

"War," he said.

"Yeah. Over what?"

"In part, whether he's going to keep pushing boundaries."

"Is he pushing yours?"

"Not yet. But he will, if he thinks he can get away with it."

"I see. What else?"

He hesitated. "All right, I'll tell you part of it. Baritt was feared as a sorcerer. He had a great deal of influence within the House and within the Empire. He was very good at getting what he wanted. Before the Interregnum, he was Imperial Sorcerer for a few hundred years. He defended himself against various attacks from various sources with amazing success. He . . . well, he was very good."

"All right, I'm with you so far."

"He was too good."

"Excuse me?"

"He did things he ought not to have been able to do. He stood off armies on his own. At one point he defied the Imperium and made it stick. Things like that."

"Sounds like you."

"Yes."

"Well?"

"I've been wondering for years how he did it. I've come to the conclusion that he had help."

"What sort of help?"

"That's the question, isn't it? Either the aid of a deity or some-thing else."

"Such as?"

"Such as he possessed something. Something powerful. Per-haps an object of some kind—"

"Say, a sword?"

"Perhaps."

"Say, a Great Weapon?"

"That's my guess," said Morrolan. "Based on the fact that it was stolen."

I nodded. "And so, you go to war to get it, because you want it, and you don't want Fornia to have it." I thought, but didn't say, *all of which is why you let him steal it in the first place.*

"Yes," he said.

"And I go to war because he irritated me."

"Yes."

"I guess that makes sense. You think this, whatever it is, will give you any problems?"

"Fornia isn't stupid. I was protecting Baritt's household, and he violated it. He must have expected reprisals. He knows he is likely to be facing Sethra Lavode, Aliera e'Kieron, the Necro-mancer, and, if you'll excuse me, myself. He's a fool if he isn't worried about what we can do. That means he thinks he's up to facing us. He must have some reason for thinking so."

"Uh . . . I see your point. What do you think? Could he be right?"

"Maybe. Still interested?"

"Do you know the Jhereg saying about wizards and knives?"

"Yes. Do you know the Dragon saying about trying to drown water?"

"No, and I'd as soon not. It might be too subtle for me."

Morrolan looked inscrutable and said nothing.

I went back to my flat and, in spite of the stiffness in my side, threw knives at a piece of wood.

No one taught me how to throw knives. I remain convinced that there is a better way to learn. But what I did, a few years ago when I decided it was a good thing to know how to do, was this: I set up a piece of wood against a wall, and I bought a bunch of identical knives and positioned myself exactly nine paces away from the target—just about all I had room for at the time. And I just started throwing them as hard as I could. From the beginning my aim was pretty good; there wasn't much damage to the wall. But I must have thrown four hundred of the things, varying my grip slightly each time, until I got one to hit point first. Then I suppose I threw another couple of hundred until I got it to happen again. And so on.

I have no idea how many thousands of knives I threw at how many pieces of wood before I could regularly stick one in the thing—from exactly nine paces. Loiosh, of course, would periodically make helpful suggestions about how I could convince an enemy to position himself properly.

How long did it take me to learn to hit a target from any reasonable distance? That's easy: I still can't do it reliably. It's a lot harder than you'd think to get the damn thing to go in point first. And even if you manage, it's hard to nail him so well that he's going to be taken out of the action; all of which might make it seem wasted effort.

On the other hand, if you throw a knife at a guy, he's going to duck. Besides, you might get lucky. Anything that may give you an edge when your life is on the line is worth putting some work into, don't you think? And another reason, just as important, is the satisfaction one gets from learning a skill—from learning how to do something you couldn't do before. It is a good feeling any time you're dissatisfied with life. And aside from all that, there's something relaxing about the ritual: deep breath, drop your shoulders, focus on the target, let fly.

So I went home and threw a bunch of knives at a defenseless piece of wood.

The next day I put in a real day at the office for the first time that week. It felt a little odd. I handled a few loan requests, checked on my various interests, sent one of my boys to jog the memory of a forgetful debtor, and had a pleasant lunch at a nearby inn called the Crow's Feet. Then I had a heart-to-heart talk with one of my people who was starting to use a little heavily and might become unreliable, kidded around with Kragar and Melestav, and got caught up reading the local scandal sheets, none of which had any interesting news. And no one tried to kill me all day. Not even any mild threats. It was refreshing.

The next day was Endweek, and most of the soreness was gone from my side; Aliera apparently did good work. I said as much to Loiosh, who suggested I hire her.

Whether I go in to the office on Endweek depends on how much I have going on; that day there wasn't much, so I figured to take the day off, and, that evening, maybe treat myself to a dinner at Valabar's. I mentally went through a list of possible dinner companions and came up with several options. The idea of spending the day finding a nice Eastern girl to share wonderful food with was entertaining. With luck, I figured, maybe I could even forget about this silly situation I'd gotten myself into.

It was about then that Morrolan made contact with me.

"*What the fuck do you want?*" I said pleasantly, as soon as I realized who had invaded my mind.

"*Have I had the misfortune to interrupt something?*"

"*You have interrupted nothing; that's why I'm so irritated. What do you want?*"

"*If you are available, I should appreciate your company on a short journey.*"

"Grand. I assume it's dangerous."

"No," he said.

"You're kidding."

"Are you disappointed?"

"No, just startled."

"If you will meet me here—"

"Can you give me a couple of hours? I want breakfast, and to give it time to settle in before I teleport."

"Very well," he said, and the contact was broken.

I made myself an omelet with sausage, onions, teriano mushrooms, and red peppers. I lingered over it. Loiosh cleaned my plate while I cleaned the frying pan. Then I buckled on my sword, secreted little surprises in their appropriate places in spite of Morrolan's assurance, and donned my cloak—a lightweight one, because the breeze coming in through the kitchen window promised a warm day. Morrolan, most likely, was going to take us someplace cold, but if I'd taken the heavy cloak he'd take us someplace hot and I didn't feel like attempting psychic contact with him in order to ask what I should wear.

I didn't want to call up one of my own sorcerers, so I returned to the House of the Dragon, which turned out to be a mistake; Baron Lokran wasn't there so I had to waste a lot of time finding someone else who would and could teleport me to Castle Black; the worst part being that I had to reach Morrolan to ask him. But eventually I made it there, and I didn't lose my breakfast.

Lady Teldra gave me her warm Lady Teldra smile and, after a pleasant greeting, did not say, "The Lord Morrolan will join you in the library." Instead she said, "If you will be kind enough to accompany me, I will take you to where the Lord Morrolan awaits." Variation. Something different.

"Goodness, Boss. What does it all mean?"

"Glad to," I told Lady Teldra.

We went up the main stairway, as usual, but continued past the library all the way down the long and very wide hallway. It ended in a door, which brought us to another flight of stairs; these were straight and wide, and reached a landing that swept back in an elegant curve before straightening again. At the top was another hallway; this one I'd never seen before. It was also wide, and it curved gently. Teldra opened a door and gestured for me to precede her. I stepped onto a very narrow circular stairway; the stairs were made of iron and they went up a long way. The door closed behind me. I looked back. Teldra had not followed.

"Maybe it's a trap," said Loiosh.

"That isn't as funny as you think it is."

The stairwell was so narrow I nearly had to ascend sideways, and my shoulder kept rubbing against stonework. The metal rail was cold against my hand. There were a lot of stairs. It flashed through my mind that we were getting pretty high up, and then I almost laughed when I realized that we'd started about a mile up in the air, so this climb didn't change much.

At last we reached the top, where there was a thick, black door. I stood outside it like an idiot for a minute, trying to decide what to do, then I clapped.

"Come in," said Morrolan.

I opened the door. It creaked melodramatically. I wouldn't put it past Morrolan to have purposely installed a door that would creak melodramatically.

I was in a round room—about as big around as my flat. The lighting was provided by a pair of half-shuttered lanterns, which gave less light than whatever had lit the staircase on the way up, which meant that I wouldn't be able to see much until my eyes adjusted. I suddenly remembered, from the courtyard, seeing a single tower atop Castle Black. That must be where we were.

"Brilliant, Boss."

"Shut up, Loiosh."

"Notice the window, Boss?"

"It's the only thing I can see."

"How come it's night out past the window, and day when we walked up here?"

"*I've been wondering the same thing.*"

"*That's creepy.*"

"*Yes, it is.*"

My eyes began to adjust. There wasn't much to see, just a low table and a couple of wooden chests. There were curtains all around the tower, and a set of curtains pulled aside from the window; hence there were windows all around the tower, several of them. At least six. Fewer than seventeen, which was both a relief and oddly disconcerting.

"*Boss, when we saw the tower from below, were there any windows?*"

"No."

"*I hadn't thought so.*"

I also noticed that Morrolan was wearing his sword. Since Morrolan wasn't accustomed to walking around his home armed, there had to be an explanation. I wasn't looking forward to it. Especially because "armed" in this case meant Blackwand, one of the seventeen Great Weapons. Its presence did nothing to make me feel better.

He said, "Welcome to the Tower, Vlad."

"Thank you."

"There are very few permitted up here."

"Okay. Would you mind explaining the window?"

"I don't believe you have had the training necessary to understand."

"You're probably right."

"What is important, however, is that I can sometimes make the windows look upon what I wish, and that I can then travel to those places. This can be useful in bringing me to places where I do not have a sufficient mental grasp to teleport, or to a place which lies beyond the confines of what we consider 'the world.' "

"Handy thing to have around. Do you know any place that sells them?"

"And, of course, I can bring anyone I wish with me."

"Uh . . . I'm not sure I like where this conversation is heading."

"I have been attempting to solve the problem of determining exactly what Fornia took from that room, and the related problem of why I failed to notice anything significant about it."

"That's good, Morrolan. A nice mental puzzle will distract you from—"

"Regard the window, Vlad."

"Do I have to?"

But I did, and it was no longer quite black, but had become somewhat grey. A closer look revealed a certain reddish hue amid the grey. And then, near the top, I noticed a bit of orange-red color that seemed a great deal like the sky. The grey had taken on a texture, and suddenly, instead of looking at something mysterious and terrifying, I realized that I was looking at a mountain, with a bit of sky beyond it. Of course, there was no mountain that close to Castle Black, which made it mysterious and terrifying, but you can't have everything.

"Where or what is it?" I said.

"We are looking at Hawk Mountain, in the Kanefthali chain." Something in his voice made me look at him; he was exerting a great deal of effort, more than I'd ever seen from him before.

His left hand was clenched into a fist, turned up, and held stiffly out in front of him at about chin height, the elbow bent. His right hand and arm were moving, going through various gyrations while the fingers extended, contracted, wiggled, twitched, and generally appeared to have a life of their own. Morrolan's eyes were narrowed to slits, and he was breathing loudly, through opened lips, creating a very slight whistling sound through his clenched teeth.

The thought *Earth, water, fire, and air* came into my mind as I compared left hand, right hand, eyes, and mouth; but I strongly suspect it wasn't anything that simple. I've seen sorcery, and I've seen witchcraft, and this didn't look like either one. I wasn't at all certain I wanted to know what it was.

I looked back through the window, and it seemed to be moving—or, more accurately, it seemed as if we were moving.

My knees suddenly felt wobbly and I didn't like it. I looked at Morrolan again, and he was still staring intently through the window. He was making aimless gestures with his hands, and there were beads of sweat on his forehead.

The mountain appeared to rush at us, and I actually felt a falling sensation. I stepped backward and looked for something to brace against. Then it slowed and stopped, and just outside the window, so close I could touch it, was a dirt path leading to a cave that looked to be about forty feet away.

My heart was still racing. I glanced at Morrolan, who now seemed entirely relaxed; only his breathing showed that he had recently exerted himself.

"What's going on?" I managed.

"We're going to ask—"

"We?"

"—our questions of someone who might know the answers."

"Why 'we'? What am I doing here?"

"Just in case."

"I thought you said there'd be no danger."

"I don't expect there will be."

He stepped through the window, and just like leaving an ordinary window of an ordinary house, he stood on the ground outside, on a rocky path, about forty feet from the entrance to a cave. I sent a suspicious look at the cave. I've never been that fond of caves at the best of times.

"But," continued Morrolan, "it never hurts to have an extra blade along just in case. They can be unpredictable."

"Who is they?"

"The Serioli," he said. "Come on."

"Wonderful," I muttered, and stepped through the window.

Interlude: Maneuvers

Some things you do, you never seem to be done with; years later they come back and remind you, slap you, beat you up. Here I am telling a story of what happened years ago, trying to remember how I felt back then, and—well, forgive the digression, but it belongs here.

Just today, Sethra the Younger returned from exile (Sethra Lavode exiled her off the world a few weeks ago in punishment for, well, never mind what for) and sent word asking me to wait upon her. I don't like her, she doesn't like me, and I couldn't imagine how this could be anything good. And there would be no reason for me to go if I had steered clear of Dragonlords and their business, but since Baritt died I've surrounded myself with them, and now I'm in love with a woman who used to associate with Norathar, who is Dragon Heir to the throne. All of which made it difficult to decline the invitation.

Sorry for the confusion—but that's what happens when you start in the past and the present comes up and bites you. And it's what happens when you hang around with Dragonlords. I'd always thought of Dragons, above all, as simple and straightforward—if something gets in your way, you draw and charge and keep hacking until either it's gone or you are. This is another thing I was wrong about. Watching Sethra put together her campaign, arranging for supplies to be where they were needed, anticipating movements and preparing possible countermarches, guiding her intelligence services—well, okay, war is more complex than I'd thought, so I suppose recounting it has to be complex as well.

"*What in blazes could Sethra the Younger want of me, other than my life, which I'm not prepared to part with?*"

"*Couldn't say, Boss. But you know you're going to go find out, so why not admit it?*"

There wasn't much answer to that, so I went ahead and made the arrangements, responding through proper channels, and arrived at Castle Black, where she is staying. We met in one of Morrolan's sitting rooms. She is odd; her features remind me quite a bit of Sethra Lavode's but all done in pastels, and Sethra the Younger was without the terrifying sense of agelessness and power; nevertheless, she has her own aura—a ruthlessness and lust for power that one might expect in a Jhereg.

She tried not to be obvious about how much she disliked me, but casual conversation was beyond her.

"The sword," she began abruptly.

"What sword?" I asked.

"You know damned well—" She stopped, swallowed, and began again. "The sword that was recovered at the Wall of Baritt's Tomb."

I admired the way she put that. "Was recovered." Whatever it was she wanted, it wasn't enough to make her admit . . . oh, skip it.

"What about it?" I said.

"I have it," she said.

"I know," I told her. "I didn't realize it at the time because I didn't know you. But I figured out who you were later. It's funny you should bring this up just now—"

"If you please, Lord Taltos," she said, as if addressing me by title made her lips hurt.

"Yes?"

She looked at Loiosh, riding complacently on my shoulder, then looked away. I heard Loiosh chuckling within my mind.

I thought about baiting her some more, just because this conversation was so obviously distasteful to her, but I refrained, mostly because I was curious. "All right," I said. "What does this have to do with me?"

"I want you to act as intermediary for me with the Lady Aliera."

"You want me . . . wait a minute." I couldn't decide which question to ask first. I settled on, "Why me?"

"Aliera doesn't care for me much."

"Well, come to that, neither do I. So?"

"Negotiations should be handled by a third party."

"Then why not Morrolan? Or Sethra?"

"As for Sethra Lavode, I believe she is still sufficiently vexed with me that I cannot ask her for a favor. And Aliera's relationship with Morrolan is such that she will automatically react with hostility to anything he suggests."

That much was true. But—"What makes you think I have any interest in doing you a service?"

She looked startled. "Oh, I'm not asking you for a service."

"You're not?"

"No, no. I intend to pay you."

I carefully controlled my reaction. "I see. Well, what is this negotiation about?"

"The sword, of course."

"Excuse me?"

"I want to offer her the sword we recovered from Fornia in exchange for Kieron's greatsword."

That threw me. I sat there for a minute, trying to figure out what it all meant, and then, to kill time as much as because I was curious, I said, "So far as I know, the sword we recovered from Fornia has nothing special about it. At least, insofar as any Morganti weapon has nothing special about it. Why do you think she'd be interested?"

"You know as well as I that there is more to the sword than that. If I don't know precisely what, that is because, well, that is because I have not yet taken the time to find out."

Because you aren't up to the job? I thought to myself. But that wasn't fair, of course. Several people, including Fornia, hadn't been up to the job. But it pleased me that, after snatching it, she hadn't been able to solve the problem either. I speculated that she'd been too proud to ask Sethra Lavode for help, but I had no way of knowing; maybe the Enchantress of Dzur Mountain had drawn a blank, too.

What I said was, "What would you do with Kieron's greatsword?"

I could see her trying to decide if I deserved an answer. At last she said, "Conquer the East. It would be a tremendous symbol for the leader of—"

"Spare me," I said.

She cleared her throat. "Yes, certainly. But you must see, you are the perfect choice. She trusts you, and even has some bizarre affection for you. And you could put it in terms that would make her see the mutual advantages. I don't know what the going rates are for such a service, but I have sufficient means to— where are you going?"

"To drink seawater. It'll leave a better taste in my mouth than this conversation. Excuse me."

And that was what Sethra the Younger wanted to see me about. It is, you see, all part of the same picture. It is not a picture I'd care to have on my wall.

Which doesn't keep me from continuing to paint it.

7

WHAT WAS THE QUESTION?

Loiosh said, *"No one's noticed you, yet."*

"Good."

I trotted to the top of the hill and took a good look around. The field on which my messmates were fighting was behind me, and farther behind me was the Wall; a long way off to my right was a match of cavalry against cavalry, and to my left was a company of bad guys marching at quicktime. They might be reinforcements coming to attack my own unit; I couldn't tell yet, and didn't want to wait around to find out. Ahead of me, about two hundred yards away, was a slightly higher hill, and on it was a body of soldiers, I guessed around twenty or thirty, standing alert and, I was fairly certain, protecting the sorcerers, in the center of whom would likely be what I was after.

"Okay, Loiosh. Forward at a march."

"You march, Boss. I'll just sort of hang around."

"Or you could fly overhead and let me know if you see Ori in that group."

"Whatever you say, Boss."

He left my shoulder. I headed toward the hill, wishing I had some sort of plan. But, after all, there were only twenty or thirty of them; what was there to worry about?

I'd covered about a hundred and fifty yards when Loiosh said, *"They've noticed you, Boss."*

"Great."

I kept moving, because stopping would have been worse, although I didn't enjoy it. I was, not to put too fine a point on it, terrified. My brain was working hard trying to come up with what to say, what to do that would not only leave me alive but let me finish what I set out to do, but each step took an effort, as if my feet had their own idea and wanted me to stop and re-consider the whole idea of forward motion.

I'd had the same reaction, now that I thought about it, to stepping through Morrolan's window; I hadn't wanted to go, but I did. And both times, in a way, I was driven by the same thing: the desire not to look craven in front of a Dragon. Why should I care? There's another mystery.

I knew, as I stepped through that window, that if I looked around there would be no window behind me, but I had to look anyway. No, there was no window; there was, instead, a breath-taking view of three mountain peaks, laid out as if they had been built just for how they looked from where I stood. Two of them were capped with snow, stretching out before me, too far away to pick out details. There was a purple sheen to them, and it took a moment to realize I was looking *down* on them. Then I noticed the sharpness of the air, and the fresh tang. I pulled my cloak closer around me.

"Let's go, Vlad."

"I'm admiring nature," I said, but I turned and followed him up the path.

I bent my head as we entered the cave—I suppose from some odd instinct, because it was large enough for Morrolan to enter unbowed, which he did.

The light failed quickly; after ten paces I could no longer see. Morrolan and I stopped and he made a light spell that caused a radiance to shine out from his hand, not too strong to look at but very bright wherever he pointed. We continued. The cave became narrower and the ceiling lower. "Watch your head," he suggested.

"Notice anything odd, Boss?"

"No, Loiosh, it seems just like every other time I used a necro-

*mantic window to step through onto the top of a mountain and walk
into a dark cave to meet someone of a half-legendary magical race.
What are you talking about?"*

"*What do you smell?*"

"Ah. Okay, point. I owe you a fish head."

What I smelled was brimstone. What it meant I couldn't say,
but I doubted it was a natural smell in that cave, at least as
strong as it was. I glanced at Morrolan, walking steadily and
emitting light from his hand. I could read nothing from his expression.

About fifty paces in from the mouth, the cave abruptly ended
in a natural-looking wall that could not have been natural. Morrolan stood there, frowning at it, and I said, "What now?"

"I am uncertain of the custom," he said. "Whether we should
wait or—"

There was a rattling sound, as of pebbles rolling on metal,
followed by a low rumble, and a portion of the wall before us
gave back, showing a narrow stone stairway heading downward.

"I think waiting is appropriate," I said.

He began going down the stairs.

There were only twenty steps, and those shallow, until they
reached another stone doorway, this one standing open, and we
continued, walking on flagstones that echoed sharply. The hall
was narrow and the ceiling low; I took a certain pleasure in seeing Morrolan walk with his head bowed. The smell of brimstone
grew even stronger.

"*I wonder what's for dinner?*" said Loiosh.

The hall ended without ceremony, leaving us in a nearly circular cavern about forty feet in diameter. The walls were rough
and cave-like, the floor polished smooth, and the ceiling just
high enough for Morrolan to stand straight. There was no furniture of any kind. A short person stood at the far end, looking
at us with what would have been an expression of curiosity in a
human or a Dragaeran. We approached until we were about six
feet away, and then stopped. The being was skinny and ugly,

wore what appeared to be blue and red silks in the form of lay-
ers of scarves, and as far as I could see, had no hair whatsoever.

He—I thought he looked like a he—gave no courtesy, but
spoke abruptly, in a pleasant, flutey voice. His accents fell in
odd, almost random places, and there was a certain clipped quality to his consonants, but there was no difficulty understanding
him. He addressed Morrolan with the words, "Greetings,
brother. Who are your friends?"

"Did you hear that, Boss? Friends?"

"Shut up, Loiosh."

"Good day to you," said Morrolan, adding a sound at the end
that was either the last cough from a man with Juiner's Lung or
the name of the Serioli we faced. "His name—your pardon—the
Easterner's name is Vlad Taltos, the Jhereg is called Loiosh."

"You don't mention the fourth, because we've met already;
but why do you leave out the fifth? Because she is not altogether
here?"

Morrolan frowned and looked at me. I gave him a helpless
shrug. I said, "I take it you two have met before?"

"Once," said Morrolan. "Far from here, but he told me where
to find him."

There was a story there, but Morrolan wasn't much given to
storytelling, and now wasn't the time to ask. I studied the Serioli, the only one I'd ever seen, and tried not to look as if I was
staring. He wasn't so polite; he was looking at me, and at Loiosh,
as if an odd specimen of vegetation had just occurred in his garden and he wasn't certain if it were flower or weed.

His complexion was very pale, almost albino, and his face was
more wrinkled than my grandfather's. His hair was thin, wispy,
and white, his eyes a pale, watery blue.

Morrolan said, "Who is the fifth?"

"Who indeed," said the Serioli, nodding sagaciously, as if
Morrolan had said something wise.

Morrolan glanced at me again as if wondering if I had any idea
what the Serioli was talking about. I shrugged with my eyebrows.

"You don't understand?" said our host. "How droll. But leave it for now."

"We've brought wine," said Morrolan, which was news to me. "Would you care for some? It is from the East."

"Grateful," said the Serioli. "Shall we sit?"

Morrolan sat himself down on the floor, leaning against the wall, legs stretched out, looking absurd. I sat next to him, but I don't know how I looked. Our companion walked around a wall that I hadn't seen was there—it blended into the back of the cave—and emerged with three handsome wooden goblets. Morrolan produced a bottle of wine and glass-cloth from somewhere, broke off the neck with a practiced hand, spread the cloth, and poured. Then he hauled out some sweet biscuits wrapped in cloth and spread those out on the floor. I ate one. It was all right. I wondered if it was the custom among the Serioli for guests to bring the refreshments; I made a mental note to ask Morrolan later, but I forgot.

I watched the Serioli eat and drink. I couldn't tell for sure if he had any teeth, but I almost became convinced he had no bones in his arms. I thought he looked graceful, Loiosh thought he looked silly. What good these observations did is, of course, a perfectly valid, if inherently rhetorical, question.

"You've brought good wine," said our host after eating and drinking for a few minutes. "And questions, too?"

"Yes," said Morrolan. "We've brought questions, but first there's the one we didn't bring, but found waiting for us when we arrived."

"Yes. You did not know of whom I was asking." Then he looked at me with his head tilted and his funny little eyes narrowed. "And you, too. Or are there secrets I am giving away?"

"None that I know of," I said. "Besides, I trust the Lord Morrolan completely as long as he has nothing to do with my business."

The Serioli made a wheezing sound accompanied by his whole face pinching up; I assumed he was laughing. He spoke in his own language, a clicking, snapping sound that seemed like one long word full of consonants and digestive trouble; it flowed naturally from his face, as if he ought to speak like that. Morrolan chuckled.

I looked at Morrolan and said, "All of which meant?"

"Three can keep a secret if two are dead."

I raised my glass to the Serioli, who said to Morrolan, "Let me then answer your question. You may be unaware of it, but by your side, descendent of Dragons, is—?" Here he croaked, coughed, and clicked something in his own language.

"Which means?" I said.

Morrolan answered, "Magical wand for creating death in the form of a black sword."

"Oh," I said. "Is that what it is?"

"Close," said the Serioli. "I should not, however, translate it as 'creating death.' " He paused, as if wanting to formulate the sentence before embarking on it. "It would be more precise to say 'removing life-substance.' " He paused again, "Or perhaps 'sending the life-substance to—' "

"Fine," said Morrolan.

"Our symbol for life, you see, is expressed in the phrase—"

"If you please," said Morrolan.

The Serioli looked at him. "Yes?"

"What—or who—is the fifth?"

"The fifth isn't entirely here. But your friend of the Old People should know."

"*You should know?*"

"*Old People?*"

"How should I know?" I said. "Old people?"

He made a growling noise in which words were hidden. Morrolan searched them out and said, "I'm not sure what that means. 'People from the invisible lights'?"

"Small invisible lights."

"Ah," I said. "Well, if you can't see them, I don't suppose it matters much how big they are." Then, "But were you speaking of Spellbreaker?"

"Is that what you call it?" He made his laughing sound again.

"What would you call it?"

"Spellbreaker," he said, "is as good a name as any, for now."

"You're saying I'm holding a Great Weapon?"

"No, you are not. Not yet."

"Not yet," I repeated. I let Spellbreaker, which I kept coiled around my left wrist, fall into my hand. I studied it. It seemed shorter than it had the last time I looked at it, and the links appeared to be smaller. "Not yet?"

"Someday, there will be a weapon—" He stopped and his lips worked. Then he resumed, "Someday, there will be a weapon called 'Remover of aspects of deity.' "

I repeated this name and shrugged.

"Godslayer," said Morrolan.

"If you wish," said the Serioli.

"What has this to do with my chain?"

"Everything," said the Serioli. "Or nothing."

"Do you know, I get tired of people speaking in riddles."

Our host made his laughing sound again. I wrapped Spellbreaker around my wrist. "Fine," I said. "How do I find this weapon?"

"*Uh . . . Boss? Why do you want to?*"

"*I'm not certain I do, but—*"

"To find it, you must first find—" He clicked some more.

I looked at Morrolan. "Artifact in sword form that searches for the true path." He looked at the Serioli to see if the translation was approved.

"Not far off. But I am uncertain if 'true path' would be precisely the way to say it. I might suggest 'an object of desire when the path is true.' The form of 'path' is made abstract by the final 'tsu.' "

"I see," said Morrolan. "Thank you."

I wondered if Morrolan had any idea what he was talking about. Probably, since he spoke the language. I said, "Would you like to tell me more?"

"The two artifacts were, or are to be, created together—"

"Excuse me, but is there a simple explanation for this 'were or are to be' thing?"

"No."

"I didn't think so. All right." I dropped it. Whenever anyone starts talking about the odd things time can do, I think about the Paths of the Dead, and I didn't care to think about that just then.

"Some of our people," he continued, "desired divinity and crafted artifacts to find and then destroy those who sit on the Thrones of Judgment. One of these became something other than what it had been designed to be; it became a device for the finding of—well, for the finding of whatever the wielder wished to find, based on the principle that all of life, including the desire of will, is part of—"

"If you please," said Morrolan. "The other?"

"The other was taken by the Gods, and an attempt was made to destroy it."

"I can imagine," I said under my breath.

"Both are now lost; when one is found, the other is likely to turn up."

"And what I have—"

"What you have," he said, staring at me with an expression I couldn't read, "is a gold chain that is useful for interrupting the flow of energies from—" He concluded the sentence with another word or phrase in his own language. I looked at Morrolan for a translation, but the Dragonlord was chewing his lip, frowning, and seemed to be busy with thoughts of his own. That was all right; I could make a pretty good guess.

I said, "Well, that's certainly something to think about. But I believe Morrolan brought us here to ask you something."

Morrolan blinked and looked at me. "Pardon?"

"I was suggesting that you ask our friend whatever it is you wanted to ask him about."

"Oh. I already have."

"You—all right."

"Loiosh, did you catch any psychic communication?"

"No, Boss. But I might have missed it. This character is weird."

"You think?"

Whatever information Morrolan had been after, he'd clearly gotten it. He made a few courtesies, which I did my best to mimic, then, bowing, he led the way back out of the cave. As we walked, I said, "I forgot to ask why the place smelled of brimstone."

He didn't answer.

Once we were back outside, I said, "So, how do you make the window reappear?"

He didn't answer that, either, but made a few nonchalant gestures in the air, and it occurred to me that there was no reason to make the window appear; he could simply teleport us to Castle Black. I'd have suggested that I preferred the other method of travel, but he didn't seem to be in a mood to listen.

My bowels twisted and the mountains vanished, and we were back in the room which we'd first left, and without so much as a pause Morrolan said, "Thank you, Vlad, I am glad to have had you along."

"Mind if I sit for a moment?" I managed. It wasn't just the aftereffects of the teleport, it was the realization that I'd have to teleport again when I left.

"Not at all."

He drew a curtain over the window we'd lately walked through. I looked around the room again, just to kill time. For the center of power for a powerful sorcerer, there wasn't a whole lot there: the table, two chests. And the windows. I counted nine of them. Then I counted eight of them. Then I counted nine again, then I counted ten. By then my stomach had settled down so I quit counting and stood up.

"Feeling better?"

I looked for traces of a sneer and didn't notice any. "Yes, thanks. Lead on."

He brought us back down the narrow metal stairway and through the labyrinth of Castle Black—a labyrinth I was beginning to learn, thanks to Fentor and the work I was doing on Morrolan's security (which I know I haven't mentioned much, but it doesn't really come into this story; there was a fair bit of work involved, and some interesting things happened, but I don't want to take the time to go into it right now).

"So," I said. "Would you care to tell me what you learned?"

"Of course not," he said. "Would you care for a drink?"

"No, thanks. I'm teleporting."

"Ah, yes, certainly." He reached into his cloak and removed a small purse.

"No, no," I said. "This one's gratis."

"Indeed?"

"Yes. I learned enough to pay for the experience."

"Oh? And . . ." He decided not to ask what I'd learned because he knew very well how I'd answer.

Loiosh said, *"Did I miss something? What did you learn?"*

"Nothing. I just wanted to give Morrolan something to think about."

"I hope it was worth whatever he was going to pay you."

Morrolan said, "Are you still determined upon the course of action to which you previously referred?"

"I beg your pardon?"

"I said—"

"No, never mind. I think I got part of that. Yeah, I'm still willing to do what I can to mess up this guy's program, if you think it'll help."

"Good. We will begin the muster tomorrow. The following day you may, if you are still willing, of course, report to your unit, Cropper Company, at noon. It will be assembling on the lea below Castle Black, north of the stone wall. Look for a green banner with a black horn upon it."

I opened and shut my mouth a few times, then said, "So soon?"

"If you can give me a good reason to delay, I'll consider the matter."

"I'll think about it and get back to you. But can't I just teleport to someplace where I'll do some good, instead of joining a company?"

"What makes you think the enemy will allow teleports anywhere in the area? Or, for that matter, that I will?"

"Will you?"

"No."

"I see. Well, what about your window?"

"I won't be here, I'll be with the army."

"Oh."

"Any other questions?"

"Uh . . . Why that company?"

"Is there another you'd prefer?"

"I haven't a clue, Morrolan. I just wondered what it is about them—"

"They'll be in the van during the first stage, which makes it most convenient for your activities, and Cropper, the Captain, is easier to work with than some. Anything else?"

"Yeah. How do I get home? I don't feel like doing my own teleport."

"Where are you going?"

"My office."

"I'll bring you."

"You mean you'll send me?"

"I was thinking of bringing you. I'd like to see where you work."

"Heh. That'll shake up the staff," I said. "Sure."

"Then open your mind and think of your office."

I had him bring us to the street outside, pointed out some sights to him while I recovered, and noticed that he was attracting a certain a mount of attention: Dragonlords aren't often seen in the company of Easterners. On the other hand, no one wanted to stare too blatantly; people mind their own business in my neighborhood.

I led him through the various fronts and up into the suite of rooms I worked out of. Melestav looked up when I came in, then saw who was behind me and nearly sprang to his feet.

"Melestav," I said, "the Lord Morrolan."

Melestav didn't find anything to say, which amused me. Morrolan looked around. "If I didn't know better," he said, "I should say that this was the office of an advocate."

"What were you expecting? Bottles of poison and shelves of garrotes?"

"I'm not certain," said Morrolan. "Perhaps that is why I wanted to see it."

"Here's where I work," I said, leading the way. Kragar, whom I hadn't noticed, stepped out of our way.

"Excuse me," I said. "Kragar, the Lord Morrolan."

"We've met," said Kragar.

"Forgive me if I don't bow," said Morrolan.

I showed him in, and had him sit in the chair opposite me. "So," I said, "you need more time to pay me back. Well, maybe we can work something out."

"There is a disparity," he said, "between what you do and the surroundings in which you do it. It is interesting." Which was when I suddenly realized that he wanted to be here because he wanted to learn about me—that is, he was learning about a potential ally or possible enemy, in much the same way he would investigate military positions, or I would study someone with whom I had business. It was reasonable, but it made me very uncomfortable.

"I had the same reaction, a few days ago."

He stared at me hard for a moment, then continued looking around my office.

"Ask him if he wants a job, Boss."

"Maybe later, Loiosh."

"Well, thank you, Vlad. I'll be going now."

"I'll show you out," I said, and I did, then returned to my desk, sat down, and said, "So, Kragar, it's like this, you see. . . ."

He waited for me to continue, his eyes narrowed, his head tilted, and his expression one of intense suspicion. At length, when I refused to finish the thought, he said, "What was he doing here?"

"Checking me out. But that isn't what I wanted to talk about."

"Oh?" he said. "It must be my latent Dragon instincts that tell me you've either done something stupid or you're going to ask me to do something unpleasant, or both."

"Both, I think."

He nodded, his expression unchanging.

"I'd like you to run things here while I'm gone. It'll be at least—"

"That's both, all right."

"—a couple of days, maybe a month or more."

He frowned and thought about it. At last he said, "I don't much like the idea. I'm an executive officer type, not a commander. That's how I like it, you know."

"I know."

He considered some more. "Offer me a lot of money."

"I'll give you a lot of money."

"All right."

"Good."

"What will you be doing?"

"Following up on your idea."

"Which one?"

"Sabotage and sundry nuisance for an army."

"I see."

"Morrolan has assigned me to a company."

"I imagine he has."

"Anything I should know about military life before I show up?"

He laughed. "I don't know where to start. For one thing, expect to hate it."

"Oh, I do."

"For another, if you start letting yourself get pushed around—I mean by your messmates, not your superior officers—it'll never stop, or else you'll have to kill someone, which won't be good for anyone."

"Got it."

"And for another, if your messmates even suspect you aren't going to be holding up your end in battle, they'll make your life miserable."

"One question."

"Go ahead."

"What's a messmate?"

"I can see," said Kragar slowly, "that you're going to need a great deal of preparation for this."

If you follow Dockside Road as it meanders generally east and a little south (following the docks, amazingly enough) you'll eventually reach a place where it opens up into a market area, from which Bacon Street springs off down a hill. Assume that the wind is from the north or west because if it is from the south or east you won't make it that far, and you'll soon see a row of short, squat, ugly brick buildings wedged right up against a very low section of the cliffs of Adrilankha. These are the slaughterhouses, and they're positioned so when the meat has been sliced, seasoned, smoked, salted, and packed it can be dumped over the cliff on shipping nets, from which it can then be stowed in the

holds of the merchant ships which will try to get it to its destination before too much of it has become too disgusting to be
eaten.

Go on past it, and hope the wind fortuitously changes direction right about there (nothing, but *nothing*, smells as bad as a
slaughterhouse on a hot day) and you'll start climbing up again,
and somewhere in there Bacon Street becomes Ramshead Lane,
and you'll notice that the stench diminishes and changes
(garbage doesn't smell quite as bad as a slaughterhouse) but
doesn't go away and that the dwellings are mostly wood, and
packed tightly together, and unpainted, and you're now in South
Adrilankha, and you are welcome to tell me why you bothered
to come in the first place. I was there because I had family in the
district.

I knew the streets here almost as well as I knew my own area,
so I paid little attention as we walked past bakeries and tanners
and ironmongers and witches and prostitutes, following the
turnings in the road and occasionally nodding at anyone who
dared to make eye contact with me, because I don't go out of my
way to be intimidating to other Easterners. It is a relief, in any
case, to see people who are sometimes bald and sometimes fat
and sometimes short and sometimes have whiskers, because
Dragaerans can't manage any of these things—what they see as
better I see as more limited.

We passed a street minstrel who was singing in one of the
more obscure Eastern languages, and I dropped a few orbs into
his instrument case.

"*Boss, was he singing what I thought he was singing?*"

"*A young man tells his beloved of his love for her.*"

" '*My little hairy testicle—*' "

"*It's a cultural thing, Loiosh. You wouldn't understand.*"

We came to a street called Strangers Road, and south of it was
a neighborhood called Six Corners where everything changed at
night; I know of nothing like it anywhere else in Adrilankha, or

in any part of the Empire. But here is a fish shop during the day; at night the unsold fish are thrown away and it becomes a place to buy homemade untaxed liquor, especially brandy. Next to it is a bootmaker's, until night, when the boots are locked away beneath the floor and it becomes an untaxed gambling hall. That baker goes home for the day, and another man comes at night, opens the back, unfolds rows of mattresses, and turns the place into one of the most wretched brothels in the City.

I rather preferred the district in the day, though at night it felt more like home.

And then, just after passing out of Six Corners, we eventually reached a small witchcraft supply shop at the corner of two unnamed and unmarked streets, and I walked in under the awning, setting the chimes ringing. I was greeted at once by Ambrus, the cat, who emerged from under the hanging rugs and was followed by my grandfather, who parted them carefully before stepping through. "Hello, Vladimir," he said. "It is good to see you. Sit down and have tea."

Ambrus crouched before me, preparing to spring. I made a basket of my arms, caught him, and carried him past the rugs and into the shop or the house—it was the same place and hard even for me to tell which items were for sale or use by customers and which were strictly personal. For example, you'd think the self-portrait was personal, wouldn't you? Just goes to show you. Loiosh and Ambrus, having established their relationship early on, determinedly ignored one another's existence.

I sat in a grey stuffed chair, set the cat on my lap, and took the small, delicate porcelain teacup from my grandfather. It was painted blue, and the tea was red. I squeezed lemon into it, added a trace of honey, and said, "How are you, Noish-pa?"

"I am as always, Vladimir."

In other words, he knew I had something on my mind and that I wasn't just coming over to visit. The thing is, I often come over just to visit, so how did he know? But never mind that. I took a tiny sip of tea, because I knew it would be very hot. It was;

it was also very good, and not in the least bitter. I could have gotten by without the honey. I should have sampled it first. I said, "I have joined the army, Noish-pa."

His eyes widened, and I was delighted to have actually managed to startle him. He said, "You have joined the army?"

"Well, after a fashion."

He leaned back a little in his chair, which was a great deal like the one I was sitting in. I suddenly realized that my own furniture tended to be like my grandfather's, as opposed to the hard wood and lightly padded stuff I had grown up with while my father was alive. "Tell me of it," he said.

"I was attacked not long ago. Beaten and threatened. It was by a man who had no reason to attack me, except to warn me to leave him alone. I'd have left him alone if he had left me alone. Now I'm going to hurt him."

"By enlisting in an army?"

"An army that is soon to attack him. I will be engaging in various special services—"

"Do you think this a good reason to enlist in an army?"

"Of course not, Noish-pa."

He cracked a quick, gap-toothed smile. "But you are doing it anyway."

"Yes."

"Very well."

He knew me, and knew when it was worthwhile to try to talk me into or out of something. He rarely tried to change my mind in any case, even when he might be able to. Loiosh flew over to him and accepted having his chin scratched. Noish-pa said, "What then do you ask me?"

"You were in the army once. What should I know?"

He frowned. "Vladimir, that was a different circumstance. I was a conscript soldier in an Eastern army; this is not the same as volunteering in an army of elfs."

"I know that."

"And we were soundly beaten in our first and only battle."

"I know that, too."

He stared off into the distance. "You will do a great deal of marching; protect your feet. Stay out of the way of officers—try not to be noticed. Do your share of latrine duty, but not more than your share, though you won't need to be told that. Sleep when you can, but you won't need to be told that, either. Trust your officers, even though they will not be trustworthy; you must trust them anyway because it is worse if you don't."

The implications of that last suggestion went home, and, in a certain sense, I became aware for the first time of just what I'd gotten myself into.

"*It's not too late, Boss.*"

"*Yes, it is.*"

I remembered to drink more of my tea before it got cold.

"Are you hungry, Vladimir?"

"A little."

"Come, then."

We went back into his little kitchen, and I sat on a stool at the tiny counter while he made the one thing I've never been able to get to come out right: It is an Eastern bread, only slightly raised, and pan-fried in a very light olive oil. I think the trick is getting the oil at exactly the right temperature, and judging when to turn the bread, which is just before it shows any obvious signs of needing to turn; the dough was pretty straightforward, unless Noish-pa was hiding something, which would be unlike him. In any case, I've never been able to get it right, which I regretted anew as soon as the first one hit the oil and released its aroma.

I watched my grandfather as he cooked. His concentration was total, just as when he was crafting a spell. The comparison between cooking and witchcraft has been so overdone that I can't make myself discuss it, but I'll mention I was reminded of it again.

I let the first "loaf" (it looked more like a large, raised square of light brown dough) cool just a bit. I took a clove of garlic, cut it in two with my teeth, and coated the top of the bread with it. When I could hold the bread without burning my fingers too much, I bit into the garlic, let it explode in my mouth, then followed it with a bite of bread. I closed my eyes to enjoy the experience, and when I opened them Noish-pa had put a glass of red wine next to my elbow. We ate in silence for a while, and I enjoyed it until I realized that this would be one of the last decent meals I ate for a while. I wondered if it would be possible to teleport out of camp late at night, get something to eat, and teleport back. No, they'd doubtless have teleport blocks in place to make sure the enemy didn't show up for reasons other than cuisine.

"You've really done it this time, haven't you, Boss?"

I didn't even tell him to shut up. I embraced Noish-pa and walked back through South Adrilankha. Not much time had passed, and the street musician was still there, this time singing something about a cockroach wearing leather pants. In a better mood I'd have laughed, but I still put some more money into his instrument case, just on the chance that it might bring me good luck.

I wanted to spend the next day preparing myself for what was coming; the trouble was, I had no idea how to do so. I wasn't even certain what to pack, except to make sure I had my most comfortable boots and, of course, a good assortment of weapons. I laid them all out with a heavy cloak, a spare shirt, some extra hose, and shaving gear, and stared at them, thinking they were inadequate and ought to tell me why, then I stuffed them all into a satchel and headed over to the office because I couldn't think of a good excuse not to.

Neither Kragar nor Melestav had much to say to me, from which I deduced that Kragar had, at least, hinted to Melestav about what I was up to. And, after all, what was there for them to say? Melestav kept shaking his head; Kragar smirked periodically. I didn't think it was all that funny.

I canceled a couple of unimportant meetings because I just didn't feel I could do them justice. I couldn't decide if I hoped there'd be nothing to do so I could go home and fret or if I wanted to be kept busy with my mind elsewhere. After an hour or so of hanging around being irritated I decided I didn't care and that I'd just take the rest of the day off. I'm the boss; I can do that.

I paced around my flat. I tried to read but kept getting distracted, so I went to a club that had music but only found it irritating, so I went to another club that had Fenarian brandy, and that helped. I wondered how many times, down through the ages, has Fenarian brandy or its spiritual equivalent, so to speak, come to the help of a man the day before he became a soldier.

Hell, that was stupid. I was *not* becoming a soldier. I was enlisting, as a formality, so I could march with an army and do nasty things to the enemy; I was certainly not going to be around for any battles. I drank some more brandy to that thought, then went home and went to bed, and some time later I fell asleep, and then I got up late the next morning and enlisted.

8

IN THE ARMY NOW

Fifty yards away there were about twenty Dragonlords, and among them, to the best of my knowledge and belief, were sorcerers skilled enough to be willing to take on the duties for an army. Now, don't get me wrong; I'm good at what I do. But marching forward across an open field, in plain sight, and just starting to cut away was not, it seemed to me, the best way to accomplish my goal.

"*Now what, Boss?*"

"*Funny, I was just asking myself that very question.*"

I walked forward about half the distance; I was certainly the object of their attention now. If I had arranged an attack from some other direction, and my approach had been merely a distraction, it would have worked perfectly.

Shame about that.

I unbuckled my sword belt, let it fall to the ground, raised my hands, and kept walking.

"*Got an idea, Boss?*"

"No," I explained.

"*Well, that makes me feel better.*"

Now it was just one foot in front of another, but with the destination in sight. There was horrid inevitability to it, as if I were just completing a journey that had started weeks before, with a teleport to where Morrolan's army was bivouacked; everything after that had been just continuing the journey. Maybe I never should have started it. I certainly felt that way when I appeared on the lea beneath Castle Black.

Skip the teleport; it's getting as boring to relate as it is to do, though perhaps not quite so sick-making. I arrived near a wooden bridge that was larger than it had seemed from a mile up (go figure). It was a strange bridge, too, with a high arch and sticks jutting out at odd angles and, as far as I could see, nothing at all keeping it together. On the other side were two sentries holding spears, and behind them rows and rows of tents, all of them beige, all facing the same way, all of them an equal distance apart. A few banners fluttered in the light breeze. It was a bit cool out.

I looked for the banner Morrolan had described. I wondered what I'd have done if there were no breeze; how much confusion would that have caused? No, of course a sorcerer would have gotten up a breeze. In fact, maybe that's what happened. I could probably find out by performing a—

"Well, Boss?"

"I'm procrastinating."

"I know."

I sighed and crossed the bridge. It seemed solid enough, and, yes, as soon as I crossed it I was stepping into an area protected from teleports. The sentries crossed their spears in front of me. One started to speak, but I said, "Vladimir Taltos, House of the Jhereg, to see Captain Cropper by orders of Lord Morrolan."

They stepped out of my way, and one of them gestured to my left. I nodded, turned that way, and began strolling, with the camps to my right. The stream on my left gurgled and laughed at me. It was all bloody damned pastoral in that direction. Looking the other way, there was actually not much activity; I saw a few people sitting on makeshift stools outside of tents, but not many, and those paid little attention to me. There were also a good number of wagons at the far end, and I could see a few people unloading boxes into large, pavilion-like tents. Occasionally

I'd hear laughter drifting over. A few small fires were going, and I could smell wood smoke and fresh bread.

"*There it is, Boss. Green banner, black horn.*"

"Where? Oh. I see it. *I'd been thinking of a Lyorn's horn or something, not the instrument.*"

I crossed the hundred yards or so to the flag and looked around. There were no uniforms as such, but everyone had a little cap on, and each cap was decorated with a green badge with a horn on it; they also wore sashes, with the same badge near the left shoulder. I drew a few curious looks from those assembled, all of whom seemed to be Dragons. One of them had a silver braid about his left shoulder. He was sitting on an empty wooden crate next to the banner. He looked up at me and said, "You want something?"

"I'm looking for Cropper. Uh, Captain Cropper."

"Who's looking?"

"I am."

He gave me an "I am not amused" stare and I reminded myself that I might be about to put myself in a position where this person would have control over my comfort, and maybe even my life expectancy. I mentally shrugged and said, "Baronet Vladimir Taltos, House of the Jhereg, sent by Lord Morrolan e'Drien, House of the Dragon."

He studied me a little, I guess trying to decide just how much of an attitude he ought to display at this point. Then he stood and said, "I'll tell him."

He went over to a rather larger tent, clapped, was admitted, entered, and reappeared. "Go on in," he said. I wasn't sure if I ought to salute, so I didn't.

Captain Cropper was old, probably getting close to three thousand, but had bright eyes, as well as bushy eyebrows and a pointed chin. He had a jacket with three silver braids around the right shoulder. He was seated on a rickety chair at a rickety wooden table and he was writing up reports or something. As I walked up he said, "I was informed that you were to be attached to my company. Welcome, I suppose. We will dispense with the swearing in because I'm not certain it would have any meaning, and I am unclear on your status with the company. I will find out in due time. For now, Crown will give you cap, sash, and bedding and show you to your quarters. And get rid of that thing."

"That thing" was, of course, Loiosh. It seemed we were going to have trouble right from the start. "That thing" said into my mind, *"Tell him if he gives me some of those silver things, I'll forget the offense."*

"Shut up, thing."

"He is required—"

"Sir!" He glared at me. I managed not to roll my eyes.

"Excuse me, sir. He is required for the operations I am to perform."

He worked his mouth like a horse and said, "Is it necessary that it go around on your shoulder?"

"I could stand on your head, Boss, but you might get tired of that."

"Yes, sir, it is," I said.

Cropper glared at me again. "Very well," he said. "That's all." And he turned back to his work.

He didn't seem to expect me to salute either. No one was expecting me to salute. I'd been looking forward to it, too—it's such a silly thing to do, when you stop and think about it.

I stepped out of the tent and found myself looking up at the man with one silver braid. I said, "You must be Crown, right?"

"Sergeant Crown," he snapped.

"Excuse me," I said, keeping all irony out of my voice. He had rather a square jaw for a Dragonlord, and very thick, bushy eyebrows. He wore a sort of jerkin that covered his arms to the elbows, showing off forearms that were thick and knotted with muscle and quite intimidating. I decided that if I ever had to go up against this man, I'd do so from a distance. I wondered if he was any good at throwing knives.

"Come along," he said.

"All right."

"Answer: 'Yes, Sergeant.' "

"Yes, Sergeant."

He grunted and turned away. I followed him. It occurred to me that achieving popularity was not the number one point on his program. He led me past the Captain's tent and then down a long row of smaller, identical tents, pitched in triangles with flaps all facing the same way. I was the subject of stares, all curious and sometimes unfriendly, from those sitting around outside of them.

He stopped at one and said, "These are your quarters. You'll find a cot, a blanket, canteen, and kit inside."

I said, "Yes, Sergeant."

"I see you have a sword. If you deem it, uh, insufficient, you may draw one of ours."

"Yes, Sergeant."

He turned away. There were two Dragonlords relaxing on wood-and-canvas backless stools outside the tent. They looked up at me.

I said, "And a very pleasant morning to you both."

It wasn't, really; there was a nasty wind that made it a bit cold, and it smelled like it was going to rain. I mention this because one of them, the woman, said, "It is, actually; at least compared to the last couple of days. I'm Virt e'Terics."

"Vlad Taltos."

"Jhereg?"

The question seemed curious rather than hostile, so I said, "Yes I am, or yes he is, depending on which you're asking about." I turned to the man and raised my eyebrows. He turned away.

"His name," said Virt, "is Napper. He's of the e'Drien line. Don't take him personally. Every squad needs someone like him to make bivouacs so unpleasant we look forward to battle."

Napper gave her a nasty look but didn't actually say anything.

"You may as well stow your gear," said Virt.

"Sure. Uh, what exactly does that mean?"

"Shove it under your cot."

"Oh. I can manage that."

Napper gave a snort which I couldn't interpret. Virt said, "For whatever it's worth, we may be moving out any day."

Napper spoke for the first time, saying, "What makes you think so?"

Virt pointed with her chin toward the supply tents. "The last couple of wagons have brought traveling rations. Besides, Sethra Lavode hates keeping her armies in bivouac. If she can't move them out, she likes to arrange billets."

"Don't matter," said Napper. Virt smiled and shrugged with her eyebrows.

At this point another woman walked up. She glanced at Loiosh, then at me. "You must be Taltos," she said. "I'm Rascha, corporal of your squad."

I bowed my head. "Uh . . . how do I address you?"

"By name is fine. And you don't have to salute."

"No one has made me salute yet."

She cracked a small smile. "I suspect no one knows quite how to deal with you." Of all the soldiers I'd run into so far, she seemed the most "military"—she stood straight and stiff, making her seem taller than she was, and she wore her hair short and brushed straight back from her forehead; her eyes were dark and narrow. She also carried a sword, which I noticed because she was the only one so far who did.

Virt said, "What's the story, Rascha?"

"Maneuvers this afternoon, and we'll probably be moving out tomorrow."

Virt nodded and didn't give Napper any "I told you so" sort of glance. Napper, on the other hand, gave a snort which may have been a response to either piece of news, or both.

"Move where?" I said.

Rascha gave me a quick glance, and said, "You'll know when we get there, Taltos," in a sharp tone of voice.

"Sorry," I said.

"Get your gear stowed."

"Right away," I said, and entered the tent, ducking low enough not to knock Loiosh off my shoulder. It was a bit cooler than it had been outside. There were four cots, and three of them had identical backpacks under them; I put my satchel under the fourth.

"You should have gotten a backpack, Boss."

"Good time to tell me."

I stepped back out. Rascha had moved on. I said to Virt, "The corporal seems easy enough to work with."

"Yeah. She's tough when it counts, though. She spent some time as a marine."

"A marine?"

"A shipboard soldier. They're the ones who go over the side and try to take a ship from the enemy. She saw some action in a skirmish with Easterners during the Interregnum."

"I didn't know there was a navy during the Interregnum."

"There wasn't, officially, but there was some fighting now and then around Northport and Adrilankha."

"Okay," I said. "Any idea where I might acquire a backpack?"

She shook her head. "Not around here, and we're not permitted to leave camp without permission. But I expect that when Aelburr gets back he'll be able to rig some straps for you. He's good at that sort of thing."

"Aelburr?"

"He's the other one who bunks with us."

"Oh. Where is he now?"

"He drew kitchen duty. He'll be back after lunch."

"Such as it is," put in Napper.

Virt added, "You can ask him about making you a stool as well; you'll come to appreciate whatever comfort you can find."

"I don't doubt that a bit," I said.

I sat down on the ground next to them. Yeah, a stool would be nice.

A little later there was the sound of drums, and my heart leapt to my throat, and I almost stood up and drew a weapon; I just barely saved myself from embarrassment by noticing that no one else seemed excited.

"That little tune," said Virt, "is called 'Graze the Horses.' It means lunchtime."

"It's our big excitement for the day," said Napper.

"True enough," said Virt. "Because of the danger. Grab your mess kit and come along."

Lunch was served up at a long table, which you walked along with your tin tray out so the cooks could put on it a hunk of tasteless cheese, as many biscuits as you could eat . . . in my case, that was about a third of one, and a piece of salted kethna that I wouldn't have served hidden in a stew full of lasher peppers. Then you filled up your collapsible tin cup with a horrid white wine and walked back to your tent to eat, and then down to the stream to clean your mess kit, and, then, perhaps, downstream to the latrines to divest yourself of what you'd just had the misfortune to consume. I fed Loiosh a bit of the kethna, and he liked it fine, which I think proves my point.

An hour after lunch were "maneuvers." We were called out and made to stand in a neat line, four abreast. On my left was Napper, next to him was a Dragonlord who turned out to be Aelburr. He was very tall—close to eight feet—and thin even for a Dragonlord. His black hair was brushed back like Virt's, and his arms were nearly as knotted as Crown's. In that formation, they marched us out to a field, where we had to do things like turn around all together, go from four abreast to eight abreast and back, spread out in different directions and come back, go from four abreast facing forward to thirty abreast and four deep, with proper distance between the lines, advance, retreat, quickstep, double-time, and all sorts of other things that everyone knew how to do except me.

We did this for about five hours, with a five-minute break each hour. During one of the breaks, I threw myself down next to the man who'd been behind me for most of the march.

"Not used to the work, Easterner?" he said.

I looked at him, and he didn't seem to be actively unfriendly, so I said, "Can't claim to enjoy it."

"Me neither," he said. He was a rather small man, almost mousy, and didn't give the impression of great strength, though he'd gone through the drills without being as winded as I was.

"But you're in it for the fighting, right?"

"Me? No. I've been in a few battles. I can't say I enjoyed them."

"Then why—?"

"Experience. I want to make a career of the Phoenix Guards. Or the Dragon Guards if the Cycle will be kind enough to turn for me. And you get along better if you start out with a few big fights under your belt."

"I see."

"What about you?"

"It's personal."

He laughed. "I would imagine so. The scuttlebutt is you know Sethra Lavode."

"We've met," I admitted.

"Is she really a vampire?"

"Well, she hasn't drunk my blood. At least that I remember." He laughed again. "I'm Tibbs," he said.

"Vlad."

"A pleasure."

"The same."

And the drum started up, and we were off on more senseless maneuvers. The next rest period found me next to Virt and Napper again. Napper had a look of disgust on his face that didn't encourage conversation. Virt seemed her easygoing self, so I said, "Mind if I ask you a question?"

"Sure," said Virt.

"Why is everyone so . . . hmmm. I'm not sure how to say this. I've dealt with Dragons before, and I'm used to, ah, I'm not used to being treated so civilly by them. No offense."

Virt smiled. "It's taken some effort," she said.

"Why the effort, then?"

"I can only speak for myself."

"Well?"

"We're going to war," she said after a moment. "We're going to be fighting. You'll be fighting next to me. I'd just as soon you didn't have any reason to let me be killed."

"Ah. I hadn't thought of that."

She smiled pleasantly. "It's probably in your best interest not to give me a reason to let you be killed, either. You may want to keep that in mind, Jhereg."

Napper looked up at me, then glanced away.

And again the drum, and again the marching and running, and then, a little later, we broke for practice in throwing javelins. I couldn't get anything like the distance most of the Dragonlords got, but I was awfully damn accurate. That gave me a certain amount of pleasure.

Then there was another drumbeat that announced time to sup. Supper was much the same as lunch except that a thin broth was substituted for the kethna. I sat next to Virt outside of our tent, and said, "Does the food get any better?"

"No."

"I see." Then, "Are most of these people volunteers?"

"All of us, of course. The units with conscripts have Teckla in them."

"Oh. Why did you volunteer?"

"I'm attending the Terics Academy, and one needs experience in battle before mastering theory."

"I guess that makes sense."

"Why you?"

"Why am I here? It's personal."

"Ah."

I decided after a moment that she deserved a better answer than that, so I said, "The guy we're going up against pissed me off."

"You're kidding."

"Nope."

"You joined the army because you're mad at the guy whose army we're fighting?"

"Yep."

She stared at me. "You know you probably won't get a chance to, uh, what do you Jhereg call it?"

"We usually call it killing," I lied. "And, yes, I know that. But I can be useful here."

"You're nuts."

"Thanks."

"But I mean that in the nicest possible way."

At that point we were joined by Aelburr, to whom I was then introduced. He seemed friendly enough, and agreed to modify my satchel and make me a collapsible stool. I said, "Is there anything I can do for you?"

"Yeah. Tell me how to win at S'yang Stones."

"Run the game, don't play it."

"I'm serious."

"So am I. It's a rigged game. In the long run, you can't win unless the guy running the game is an idiot. If you're really, really good at it, and you concede if you don't score well on your first couple of throws, and double-up every time you have an edge with your flat stones, and you get very good at tossing, you'll only lose a little, very slowly."

"Why is that?"

"Because in, say, a ten-fifty game you're paying twelve orbs for the stones, and you're risking fifty orbs if you lose, and if you win you only get back ten plus fifty, not including doubling, which works out even in the long run. So every time you play against someone as good as you, you lose two orbs. If you play against someone better, it's worse, and if you play against someone not as good, the luck factor is almost always greater than the two orbs you're losing. Usually about four coppers' worth."

"You've got it figured that precisely?"

"Yes."

He shook his head. "What about personal games, with no one running it?"

"That's different. Then if you're better, you should win."

"So how do you play?"

"Go for the big scores with your flat stones, and use the round ones at the end to knock off his big scores, and, if he gets a big advantage on the first round, surrender your ten and start over."

"I like to use my flat stones to knock out the other guy's early scores. Then I can get lucky with the round stones."

"Yeah, a lot of guys play that way."

"And I double when, well, you know, sometimes you can just feel that you're going to hit big?"

Sure you do. I said, "I don't know, I don't actually play a whole lot."

"Well, it seems like it works."

I thought, *I know exactly how you play, sucker,* but didn't say it. I said, "How do you do, overall?"

"I'm about even, or maybe a little up."

I almost said it with him. The consistent losers always say, "About even, or maybe a little up." But I just nodded and didn't say anything.

"Maybe I'll try it your way," he said.

"Let me know how it works."

"I will."

"So, why are you here?"

"Here? You mean, in the service?"

"Yeah."

He was quiet for a while, then said, in a low voice, "I've always dreamed of fighting under Sethra Lavode."

"Okay," I said. "I can respect that."

"It's better than the alternative, in any case."

"Oh?"

"My last posting was with a mercenary army. They've been hired to fight against her. I wouldn't care to do that."

"No," I said. "I wouldn't either."

A little later fires were lit, and we sat around them; apparently every three tents had one fire. Virt explained that, usually, the fires were where meals were cooked, but as this whole operation had been thrown together so quickly, they had gone to communal kitchens to save the extra work of dividing up the rations. I suppose that made some sort of military sense. Someone from one of the other tents said it only made sense if we weren't staying long. Virt said we'd be moving out any day, and explained her reasoning, which provided the subject for much lively debate and led to reminiscences about past campaigns that had involved a lot of waiting in bivouac.

"Well, Loiosh, what do you think of military life so far?"

"The food's good."

"Heh."

"And there's a lot of it."

"I didn't see a lot."

"That's because everyone hasn't been feeding you scraps."

"Everyone's been feeding you?"

"They sure have, Boss. I think they think I'm good luck."

"You're lucky they don't know you."

"Heh."

The conversation continued around me, and I occasionally put in questions, such as how they could tell the different drum calls apart, which were answered with the sort of patience I might display to a potential customer who wanted to understand the interest on the loan he was inquiring about. The drum, by the way, was called a juice-drum, and the peculiar sound it made was caused by steel balls rattling around inside the steel frame as it was struck.

Later they went on to talking about what they were going to do after the campaign. If they did what they said they were going to, I'd see a big increase in business at all of my brothels. Then they went on to telling humorous anecdotes, most of which I'd heard and none of which are worth repeating, although there were some particularly military ones that were interesting—most of these had to do with peculiar injuries, ways of bugging out of battle, or embarrassing things happening to officers (but never sergeants, for some reason). Loiosh thought some of the stories were funny, but then, he'd liked the food, too.

The drum started up again, and Virt explained that it was time to sleep. I wasn't used to sleeping on a set schedule, but I realized that I was sufficiently tired that it wouldn't be a problem, even with the unfamiliar bed and the nasty, prickly woolen blanket. And it wasn't; I rolled up my cloak for a pillow, lay down, and was gone.

The drum woke me up the next morning, beginning my first full day as a soldier. We were given ten minutes at the spring to make ourselves ready, which only barely gave me time to shave. I noticed various of my comrades looking at me out of the corners of their eyes as I did so, and I rather enjoyed it.

There were fires going by the cook-tent, so I went over there and discovered that not only was there no klava, but there was no cream or honey for the coffee, so I skipped it. I forced down a biscuit because I thought I might need it, then went back and heard that morning maneuvers had been canceled.

"I wonder why?" said Aelburr.

"Be grateful," said Napper.

"I have a guess," said Virt, staring over in the direction of the Captain's tent. It was very cold; I pulled my heavy cloak around me, thinking I'd trade half my territory in the City for a good cup of klava, and didn't say anything.

Rascha came by and wished us a pleasant morning. "What's the word?" said Virt.

"You'll know as soon as I do," she said, and continued on.

I studied the sky, hoping it wouldn't rain, but I couldn't tell anything. I knew Castle Black was somewhere above us, but I couldn't see it through the overcast, even though I knew that Morrolan would be able to look down and see us. It seemed wrong, somehow.

"Loiosh, what am I doing here?"

"If I knew, Boss, I'd be sure to tell you."

About forty yards away, over the Captain's tent, the banner of Cropper Company snapped and floated in the cold morning breeze.

The drums started up again, but we'd already eaten breakfast and it was too early for lunch. Virt stood up, smiling. "Do you know how to strike a tent?" she said.

I assumed she didn't refer to hitting it, so I said, "No."

"Time to learn, then," she said. "We're moving out."

9

SKULKING ABOUT

Loiosh kept asking what I was going to do when I got there, and I kept saying I didn't know. *"I'll think of something,"* I told him.

"Why am I not reassured?"

"Getting close enough is half—what's that?"

"More of the same battle, Boss. Just not our part in it."

"Look closer, Loiosh."

"Oh."

Off to my right, a bit over a hundred yards away, was a large body of Easterners—no doubt the mercenaries I'd been informed of. They were far enough away that I wouldn't have been able to tell they were human except that I could just barely make out a beard here and there, and that was sufficient.

They were going up against a cavalry troop, and I could just make out Morrolan's form, sitting on a dark horse and laying about him with—yes, it had to be Blackwand. With each cut of that blade, another died—and died forever, because there is no return, reincarnation, no afterlife of any sort to someone struck down with that weapon. The beliefs among humans regarding what happens after the death of the body are varied, peculiar, and often silly; but a hundred yards to my right Morrolan was making the question moot.

In spite of all I had seen, it was this that sickened me.

I discovered that I'd gotten all the way to the knot of sorcerers and their honor guard on top of the hill. Before any of them could speak to me, I said, "Can we stop all this nonsense, please?"

"*Good work, Boss,*" said Loiosh. *"You've gotten their attention."*

"That was my secret plan," I said.

They looked at me and I looked at them, and I realized with an almost profound sense of importance that I'd *stopped.* I'd reached the place. Whatever was going to happen would happen here, and then it would end, and a sudden, terrible delight filled me that, for better or worse, I was done marching. This meant, above all, that I was done marching in the rain.

It had started raining a little before noon the very first day I'd marched with Cropper Company, and sometimes it seems that it had rained ever since. We'd been marching for about four hours, and after the first I had decided I didn't care for it. The rain did nothing to change my mind. Marching through mud just isn't as much fun as they say, especially with a folded-up cot, a jury-rigged backpack, and a few pieces of tent on your back. I wore my heavy cloak because it was cold when we started, but at the first break I switched to the light one because marching turned out to be much harder work than I'd expected, and I became hot and sweaty inside the first mile. Then, of course, the rain started, so I was too hot while we marched, and too cold every time we had to stop because a wagon had gotten stuck in the mud and it was either in front of us and blocked the road or behind us and we weren't permitted to get too far ahead.

Virt kept looking around, as if trying to guess where we were going and what we were doing; occasionally she would make helpful observations about how the engineers would have been able to keep the roads passable if only there were wood in the region. Napper never said a word, but kept up a constant stream of invective through inarticulate grunts and hisses. Aelburr seemed cheerful, which was really annoying. Loiosh sometimes rested on my shoulder and sometimes flew over the company, enjoying his unexpected popularity and, fortunately, not making any wisecracks to me. I did my best to keep my thoughts to my-self, mostly as a matter of pride.

Somewhere in there we crossed into enemy-held territory. I didn't notice it at the time, but put it together some time later when I realized that our commissary was no longer paying for the supplies we took from the locals. Years later I found out that Sethra had cut the entire army off from its supply lines—a move she was fond of. I guess she was good at it, too, because the food never changed.

Pity.

The rainfall grew heavier. It's funny how little I notice weather in the City; but it just doesn't matter that much. A lit-tle bit of sorcery will keep the rain off, and then I'm at the office, or wherever I'm going. Here it was different; most of us had the sorcerous ability to keep the rain off our heads, but that did nothing for the road, and you can only keep up a spell like that for a certain amount of time before you start to get brain-fatigued, and then it can slip and you can lose control of the en-ergy. It would be humiliating to fry your brain because a Verra-be-damned *umbrella* spell got out of control.

Worse for a Dragonlord, though, because he'd be likely to show up in the Paths of the Dead and have to explain just how he Got It.

The Paths of the Dead.

I remembered them, then, as I was walking; I remembered thinking I'd never find my way out, and then saving myself, and Aliera, and Morrolan, with a homemade bit of witchcraft I hadn't known I could perform. And where were Morrolan and Aliera now? Probably snug and dry in Castle Black, waiting to teleport to wherever we ended up, while my boots went *flllp flllp* in the mud.

But it was my choice, and I knew I'd feel better when we made contact with Fornia's army and I did something nasty and dis-ruptive to it. Maybe only one or two things, then I could bug out.

Yeah. . . .

"Boss, you've got to let the spell go."

I wanted to argue with him, but there's no point in having a familiar if you don't let him do his job. *"Okay, thanks,"* I told him, and got wet. Looking at the line of march, I was pleased to see I'd held mine longer than many of them. I also knew that there would be some brain-fry casualties from this march; I wondered if that was one of the things calculated out by Sethra when she planned her campaigns: "Well, we're going to lose one percent every day to brain-fry if the weather's bad. . . ."

"You're right, Loiosh. My mind is getting numb."

"Soggy, too, Boss."

"You're not as funny as you think you are."

We stopped then—this one an official rest, as opposed to waiting for a mud-stuck wagon. I gratefully took off my gear, unfolded the stool Aelburr had made me, and sat down.

"We're bound for interesting country," said Virt.

I looked around; it was plain, and flat, with never a hill and hardly a tree to break up the terrain. "It is?"

"Well, this is good ground to fight on, but that isn't what I mean. I mean we're moving toward a hilly area, and it makes me wonder if Sethra plans to bring us directly into a fight or if we're reserves, because if we're reserves, I'd expect us to start heading north soon."

"Well, I know we're in the van."

"You do? How?"

"Morrolan told me. That's why I'm assigned to this company."

She looked at me as if waiting for me to go on.

"Boss!"

"Bloody death, Loiosh. I am brain-tired, aren't I?" "Never mind," I told Virt. "I've already said too much."

"All right."

"I'm not a spy, though."

"I didn't think you were," she said. "And I pretty much assumed that you weren't along just as a soldier."

"Yeah."

"But we're in the van, are we? Then, at a guess, we won't have more than a two-day march. Three, maybe, if the weather stays like this."

"And then battle?"

"I wouldn't be surprised. Will you be around for the fighting?"

I looked at her and knew what she was thinking—was I going to be sharing the danger, or was I just along for the ride and would bug out as soon as they went into battle. The answer, of course, was that I intended to bug out.

"I'll be there," I told her.

She nodded.

The bloody damn juice-drum again, and I stood up, refolded the stool, and eventually we moved out. The rain gave a last burst, then tapered off to a drizzle.

"Can't Morrolan's sorcerers do something about the rain?" I said.

"Chances are they just did."

I grunted. "Took them long enough."

"You're starting to sound like Napper."

Napper gave her a quick glare. I said, "I'm starting to understand him."

He gave no indication that he wanted to be understood.

I said, "I've been given to understand that bitching is the universal right of soldiers."

She laughed briefly, though I didn't think it was funny. "Not in an elite corps," she said.

"We're an elite corps?"

"Didn't you know?"

"How am I supposed to tell?"

"See any Teckla? See any conscripts?"

"Ah. Okay, I hadn't known to look for them."

"Well, there you have it. How do you feel, being part of an elite corps?"

"Bursting with pride," I said.

"That's the spirit."

Napper snorted. The breeze picked up and I shivered, but the rain stopped completely soon after that, and I was able to perform a quick drying spell, and then I felt better.

We put a few miles behind us, then stopped where we were on the road and ate salted kethna, cheese, and biscuits. I ate three biscuits. They tasted much better after not eating a decent meal for a day.

"If this goes on long enough, Loiosh, I'll have no more taste than you."

"I weep bitter tears."

"Reptiles don't weep."

"And we have other natural advantages, too."

I filled a pocket with some extra biscuits to eat on the way. They weren't all that bad, really, as long as you didn't compare them to anything good.

The grey clouds that had gathered beneath the orange-red overcast were gone, and in the distance there were now a few hills to be seen. That meant we were probably climbing, very gradually, which realization made my legs tired. Periodically, the Captain would ride by on a horse, presumably to make us feel even more tired. I hadn't seen much of horses before, and watching the Captain ride by while we kept trudging didn't give me any great affection for them.

As the light failed the drums rattled, and we stopped and I watched the other three put up the tent, making certain to show me how the pieces fit together. Then we lit fires, ate an evening meal that was suspiciously like the one yesterday, and sat around in front of the fire. Rascha approached and said, "Aelburr and Vlad, first shift on picket duty tonight."

"Okay," said Aelburr.

"Vlad?"

"Yes?"

"Did you hear?"

"Yes."

"Then acknowledge."

"Sorry."

Rascha moved on. I said, "How long does a shift last?"

"Two hours," said Virt, "unless they decide we're in imminent, in which case time doubles and personnel triples."

" 'In imminent'?"

"In imminent danger."

"Ah."

"Which I don't think we are."

I looked an inquiry at Virt, who shrugged and said, "I doubt it."

Aelburr stood up and buckled on his sword. I did the same. He led the way past the rows of tents to where we could just make out the banner in the fading light. Crown was there, and pairs would approach him to be sent off; to us he said, "North edge, forty yards out," and pointed. Aelburr saluted and turned away. I also saluted, which earned me a glance I couldn't read, then I went after Aelburr. But I was pleased; I'd finally gotten to salute.

"What do we do?" I said. "Stand in place like idiots or walk back and forth like morons?"

He gave a token chuckle. "Stand in place," he said. "More or less, anyway. As long as we keep watching, and we don't stray out of call, it shouldn't matter much."

We were out there for two hours, and nothing happened, but it was spooky. At first there was a hum of low conversation from the camp, but that died fairly soon, and then it was quiet, and I was one of those guards whom I'd spent so much time figuring out ways of circumventing, or sometimes knocking out, or occasionally killing. All of those occasions presented themselves to my memory with a snicker of revenge. I wasn't really worried, because Loiosh was there, but it was a position I didn't enjoy being in. I tried to start a conversation, but Aelburr let me know that we were supposed to use our ears, and that if we were caught conversing Bad Things would happen.

"What does the military consider a Bad Thing?"

"Latrine duty."

"Sold," I said, and shut up for the rest of our shift. We were relieved right on time by a couple of soldiers I didn't know and who didn't seem interested in either conversation or latrine duty. I followed Aelburr to the tent, which I couldn't have found on my own, and I climbed into my cot just an instant after I fell asleep.

Thirty hours later I got a practical demonstration of what "in imminent" meant. My feet were a day more sore, my legs a day more tired, and my spirits a day nastier. Virt seemed slightly amused at either my discomfort or my annoyance; Aelburr seemed lost in thought, and Napper, still scowling as before, appeared the only sane one of the lot of us. In any case, our entire tent was informed we'd be doing four hours of picket duty in the middle of the night, which made Virt nod sagaciously, Napper scowl menacingly, and Aelburr shrug philosophically. Then, an hour later, Rascha called me aside and informed me that I was excused and was not expected to do picket duty after all, and then she turned away before I could ask her why. I cursed under my breath.

"What is it, Boss? You enjoyed it so much last night that you want to do a double-shift tonight?"

"No, I just resent the implication that I'm not as reliable as anyone else."

"Getting a bit touchy, are we?"

"Bug off."

About then a mixed group of strangers—say a hundred of them—came rolling into camp on wagons pulled by horses. By mixed I mean I identified at least a couple of Vallista, and a few Teckla, and some Dragons. I looked an inquiry at Virt, who said, "Engineers."

"Ah. What will they be engineering?"

"Defenses. Earthworks. Bulwarks. We're apparently going to be required to hold this position."

"This position? Where in blazes are we?"

"You'll see the Eastern Mountains in the daylight."

"Oh. I guess we made good time today."

"We did at that." I recalled Sethra's plans, and then wished I hadn't known them, because I suddenly got the impression that our entire company was a marker on a gameboard that she was going to be maneuvering around with no concern for the individuals who comprised it. In an effort to distract myself, I strained my eyes eastward, but in the failing light couldn't see any mountain.

"We're pretty high up, Boss; I can tell you that much."

"How?"

"It's noticeably harder to fly."

"Why should it be harder to fly just because you're starting higher?"

"That's for you higher order animals to figure out; we avians just do our business on instinct."

"You're not an avian, you're a reptile."

"I still don't know why it works that way."

"If you had opposable thumbs you probably would."

"You want to drop that opposable thumbs bit, Boss?"

I suddenly had the impression that there was something I'd meant to do, something I should be thinking about, something . . . oh. Right.

"Who is it?"

"Morrolan."

"What do you want?"

"Aren't you even going to thank me, Vlad?"

"For what?"

"There's never been a soldier born who wasn't grateful to get out of midnight guard duty."

"I see. No, I don't think I'm going to thank you. I take it this is a good night to act?"

"The Captain is expecting you, and I'll be there."

"On my way," I said, relieved to know that I hadn't been let out of picket duty because they didn't trust me, and then annoyed with myself for caring.

I made my way through the camp toward where the Captain's tent should be.

"This way, Boss."

"Thanks."

It was very dark by this time, but I found it with Loiosh's directions and by hearing the flap of the banner. Then I wandered around it like an idiot until I found the entrance. The worst part of this nonsense was that I kept finding myself doing things I wasn't good at, and that meant looking stupid, in front of myself if no one else, and I've always hated that.

I clapped outside of the tent.

"Enter," said the Captain, and at the same time I heard Morrolan's voice: "Please come in."

"Well," I said, stepping in. "How pleasant that we should all run into each other here."

"Sit down, Vlad," said Morrolan.

I did so. I tried to read the expression on the Captain's face, but I couldn't quite make it out. But from the instant I'd stepped into the tent, things were different, and I think he sensed it: I was no longer one of his soldiers; now I was something else, though he wasn't certain what. I suspect I enjoyed the sensation more than he did.

"Their nearest outpost is three miles northeast of us," Morrolan began without preamble. "We can expect an attack tomorrow."

"Which means I have things to do tonight."

"Yes."

"What, exactly, do you want?"

Morrolan said, "Captain?"

The Captain's eyes widened, then he grunted, as if it all made sense to him now. "Let me think. We're still planning . . . uh . . ."

"You may speak in front of Vlad."

He grunted again. "We're still planning a withdrawal to the southeast?"

"Yes."

He considered some more, then said, "How much of his army are we facing?"

"About a third. We know another third is marching to reinforce, and he probably has a division that's trying to move around our flank."

"What if he decides not to attack? Maybe he'll wait for the other divisions to arrive. Functionally, they're an outpost; they're losing a big part of their advantage right from the start if they launch an attack."

"They may not; if they don't, we'll attack."

The Captain shook his head. "We're an advance guard. I don't like the idea of attacking."

"We won't commit a great deal of force, just enough to encourage a counterattack."

"Right. I know. But if they don't counterattack?"

"We have sufficient force to overrun this outpost. If they won't counterattack, we'll take it and let them try to take it back from us. As far as Sethra is concerned, that's just as good."

"She's the general."

"Yes, she is. But, in any case, Fornia is very aggressive. Sethra thinks he'll test us tomorrow."

"All right. In that case, assuming he *is* planning a morning assault, anything that will delay it for even an hour or two would be useful. I'd like to give the engineers a little more time."

Morrolan nodded and said, "Vlad?"

I shrugged. "I don't know this work. How would I go about it?"

"There are a number of possibilities," said Morrolan.

The Captain said, "Do you care if they identify it as sabotage right away?"

"All things being equal, it would be better if they didn't, but that's not a high priority."

"Okay, then. What if you just went in and put holes in their water barrels? They're going to need coffee, or at least water, before they go into action. That should set them back a bit."

"Not very elegant," I said. "But I should be able to do it."

"I have a better idea," said Morrolan, with a sudden glint of
humor in his eyes. "I believe you are going to like this, Vlad."

"I'll just bet," I told him.

Thirty-four hours earlier I had been on picket duty, assigned to
make sure no one could get in the camp unseen; now I was on
the other side, trying to do exactly that. This side felt more natural to me, and my new sympathy with the opposition didn't
get in my way.

Loiosh flew overhead, keeping an eye out for exactly where
they were stationed, as I moved slowly toward where I had been
told the enemy was camped. My feet made no sounds, my grey
cloak blended into the night, and in my left hand was a small rod
that would alert me well before I crossed the line of any sort of
detection spell.

"*Anything, Loiosh?*" I asked, just because the silence was hard
on my nerves.

"*Not yet, Boss.*"

"*Maybe they've packed up and left.*"

"*I'll believe it if you will.*"

Then, "*Found 'em, Boss. Three of them, straight ahead of you.*"

"*I'll bear to the left, then.*"

"*It's clear that way.*"

I kept moving, not too fast, avoiding any abrupt motions.
Now I could see the embers of campfires, which not only gave
me a target but made it harder for me to be spotted from within
the camp. I remembered from last night that I'd only rarely
looked back toward the camp; my attention had been focused
outward. Still, I made certain not to stand between any of the
fires and the picket spot Loiosh had identified.

There should have been an interior line of pickets as well, and
there probably was, but I didn't see them and they didn't see me.
Once I was in the camp it was easier; the fires had mostly burned
down, and nearly everyone was asleep. I walked with confidence,

as if I belonged there, and the few guards who were wandering around pretty much stared through me.

"Do you see their banner?"

"Forty yards, this way."

I went that way. Light glowed from the overlarge tent to which Loiosh directed me, the flickering light of lamps. As I got closer I heard low voices—officers, no doubt, discussing plans for the morrow, when our "advance guard" would be "tested" by their "outpost."

There was a guard posted right in front of the tent, a very inconvenient place. But that was all right.

"Okay, Loiosh. Take it away."

"I'm there, Boss."

He launched himself from my shoulder and swooped on the guard, missing his head by about three feet. The guard swore and took a step back. Loiosh swooped again. The guard drew his sword and took an aimless swipe into the air. I drew a knife from my belt and found the flagpole.

It took about a second to cut the rope, and the banner slid down silently. Another second, and I was holding the banner in my hands. I slipped into the darkness behind a nearby tent and said, *"Okay, Loiosh. I've got it. One down."*

"I'll be there in a while, Boss."

"Loiosh . . ."

"Oh, come on, Boss. I'm having fun."

"Loiosh."

"All right, I'm coming."

Someone from inside the tent called, "What's that ruckus?" but I didn't hang around to hear the answer.

The others were easier; they were next to dark tents that had no sentries posted outside of them. It was just a matter of being careful and, as always, not getting caught. All in all it took about an hour, and then another twenty minutes to work my way back to our own lines.

Just for practice, I snuck past our own sentries and made my way to the Captain's tent. There was a sentry there, too, but to him I announced myself. He glanced at the bundle in my arms but didn't seem to recognize what it was. He announced me, then pulled aside the flap. The Captain and Morrolan were sitting around the Captain's table, drinking wine. I tossed my bundle onto the floor and said, "I'll have some of that, if you've any left."

"I think we can spare some," said Morrolan.

The Captain looked at the banners and laughed. "Well done," he said. "How many did you get?"

"Eleven."

"Well, well. We've captured eleven colors and haven't drawn sword. I wonder if history records its equal?"

"I very much doubt it," said Morrolan.

I drank some wine. Wine tastes especially good after you've pulled off something scary and you're easing up on muscles you hadn't known were tense.

"Any trouble?" said Morrolan.

"Nothing Loiosh couldn't handle."

"Heard and witnessed, Boss."

"Shut up, Loiosh."

The Captain said, "We ought, then, to have gotten a couple of hours' reprieve while they rig up some new colors, but we can't count on it. That means I still need to check on the earth-works."

"And you, Vlad," put in Morrolan, "should catch some rest. Tomorrow you stand to battle."

"Heh," I said. "What makes you think I'll be there?"

He shrugged and didn't answer, which left nothing to say, so I finished my wine and went off to get some sleep.

I think Morrolan's little scheme worked. At any rate, it wasn't until the ninth hour of the morning that they commenced their assault on our position.

10

I scanned the faces before me; mostly I was looking at warriors, all of them large and, well, scary-looking. Most of them were Dragonlords, but I saw at least two Dzurlords among them. They were all noticeably lacking in sympathy. Behind them were the sorcerers, and, though I couldn't see him, I knew Fornia was behind them somewhere, watching the progress of the battle— the slaughter—and making decisions that would let his forces do more of the slaughtering. That, after all, was what war was about.

Someone came forward, a Dragonlord I'd never seen before. He said, "I am Jurg'n e'Tennith. You are here to ask for terms?" He seemed doubtful. He probably didn't think Morrolan would send an Easterner.

I said, "Not exactly."

"To negotiate, then?"

I was considering how to answer this when someone else pushed his way through the warriors, and I recognized Ori. He said, "He's no negotiator; he's an assassin. Kill him."

Well, I reflected, that certainly put the negotiations on a different footing. Now would be a really good time to hear the juice-drum signaling "charge," and have the company come suddenly to my rescue. Unfortunately, I'd left them rather far behind, and any drum I was likely to hear would be support for those in front of me; not that they needed it.

All of which reminds me that I never much cared for the

sound of the juice-drum, and provides another splendid opportunity to leave you hanging for a while. Don't worry, I'll come back to the fight in a little bit.

Where was I? Oh, yes: the juice-drum.

I'd pretty much hated it since the first time its call had woken me up earlier than I'd had to get up since I quit running a restaurant. It had woken me up even earlier than usual the morning of the attack. That day there wasn't a nearby creek, so those in charge had set up casks of water. I forced myself to shave. Shaving in cold water, by the way, isn't as much fun as they say. I decided it was a good omen, however, that I didn't cut myself. Virt, who was next to me at the water casks, explained that one difference between an elite corps and the usual sort of conscript army was that we were trusted to get ourselves up in the morning; in a conscript army the corporals came through the tents throwing everyone out and striking them with sticks if they weren't fast enough.

"And they aren't killed?"

"Corporals are hardly ever killed by conscripts. Officers, now, have to be a little careful."

I wanted her to explain that, but the juice-drum cut in again, and I realized with a kind of horror that I recognized the particular rattle and bang as the call to breakfast. Of course, there was a kind of horror associated with breakfast, too.

I tried forcing plain coffee down my throat, but only managed a swallow before I had to give up. Around me, everyone was swilling the stuff like it was peach brandy. I shrugged and ate a few biscuits, washing them down with water. Then I wandered back toward our tent, and only then noticed that, during the night, dirt had been piled up between us and the enemy camp, forming a kind of wall. Okay, now I knew what earthworks were.

Someone I didn't recognize came by and dumped a pile of javelins in front of the tent. Aelburr, who was standing there, picked up three of them, Virt did the same. That left six. I looked at them, then at Virt, then I picked up three of them.

Aelburr said, "You know how to use one of these?"

I thought he was asking about the javelin until I noticed he was handing me a whetstone. Wisecracks passed through my mind, but I only said, "Yes," and took it. He passed me a small flask of oil. There was already, all around, the scraping sound of weapons being sharpened. I added my voice to the chorus, but I only sharpened the javelins and my sword; I was feeling a bit bashful about my collection of nasties.

The bloody damn drum called out again. I hadn't heard that drum call before, and I hated it that I could tell it was unfamiliar. I asked Aelburr what it was. "It's called," he said, " 'Corporal's Tears.' It means squad leaders report to the Captain. They're getting final instructions for the battle." My heart skipped a beat, but I kept my face expressionless.

"Loiosh, keep your eyes opened for a good time to make myself scarce. Preferably before the fighting starts."

"Noted, Boss."

I continued sharpening javelins. Virt said, "How far did you throw that thing?"

"About sixty-five or seventy yards."

"All right, ignore the first command to launch; if you wait for the second they should be in about the right place. The first throw is just for annoyance anyway; the last two we send at them quickly, and you can aim."

"From that far away we should have time for more than two casts."

"You'd think so, wouldn't you? But over this kind of terrain, you'd be amazed at how fast they can cover ground at a charge. Depending on what sort of troops we're up against, of course."

"Do the javelins do any good?"

"A little. We dent some shields, anyway."

"Shields? They have shields? Why don't we get to have shields?"

"Do you know how to use a shield?"

"Uh . . . no. But still they'll have them."

"Probably. As I said, depends who we're up against. If it's cavalry, they won't have shields, but then we'll have other problems."

"Cavalry?"

"Or it might be a spear phalanx, in which case the javelins will be pretty much a waste of time, and we'll have to countercharge and try to flank them. It's up to the enemy what they throw at us. That's the advantage of attack."

"So, what do we have instead of shields?"

"We're light infantry. We have javelins and the capability to maneuver quickly."

"Oh, good."

"*Boss, why do you care? You won't be there.*"

"*I know. But I can't help thinking about what it would be like. This is no place for a self-respecting assassin.*"

"*You knew that all along.*"

"*Not viscerally.*"

The engineers came by, with more dirt to unload, build up, tramp down. I realized for the first time that as they went they were also digging a ditch in front of the thing. Virt and I watched them.

I said, "What do they do when it rains?"

"Hope there's a lot of wood around."

"For what?"

"For—"

And the juice-drum started up again.

"I've heard that one before," I said.

"Strike camp."

"Ah."

I was able to be a bit more help this time, and soon we had our backpacks in place, and, with our stools packed, we sat or knelt on the ground. There was no sign of the camp except for the pits where the fires had been. Then there came another call, this one I didn't recognize. "Let's go," said Virt. "Leave your pack by this mark and take the line."

"All right."

She walked toward the earthwork. Rascha motioned us toward a position, and I found myself between Virt and Napper. Napper wasn't scowling now; his eyes gleamed and as I watched he licked his lips, then bit them, first the top, then the bottom, then licked them again, and repeated.

"You okay?" I said.

"This," he said. "This is what it's all about."

"Oh," I said.

"Here they come," he said, his lips pulling back into a grin.

Oh, good. I was about to take a step back and get myself lost behind the lines when I noticed Virt looking at me. I stuck my javelins in the earthwork in front of me, drew my sword, and transferred it to my left hand. Maybe they'd throw something back at us and I could pretend to be hit, roll backward, and get out that way. No, that didn't sound practical. Maybe—

Virt clapped me on the shoulder. "You'll do fine, Easterner. Everyone—at least, everyone who isn't an idiot—is a little nervous before his first battle. You're worried you won't stand up to the test. It's normal. But once things get hot, you'll do fine. Trust me."

I'd never heard that line before, but it still sounded trite. For how many soldiers had words like that been the last thing they ever had spoken to them? Damned reassuring.

They appeared in a line in front of us, all at once. A whole lot of them. More than there were of us, I thought. They seemed to be walking at a steady pace, and I guessed the distance at about two hundred yards. A long way.

"Heavy infantry," said someone.

"Aim low," said someone else.

Virt tapped me on the shoulder. I jumped, but she was polite enough to ignore it. She said, "Their shields won't be long enough to protect their legs, and they'll naturally raise them once we release our javelins, so—"

"Got it," I said.

I guessed there were at least four or five thousand of them, which was more than ten times the number of our Company. Of course, it was more than just our Company on the line. I wondered how many of us there were all together. Not as many as there were of them. Soon they were close enough so that I could see they carried spears.

"Conscripts," someone said. "They'll break if we make it hot enough for them."

Napper was gnashing his teeth next to me, as if it were all he could do not to charge out at them. Aelburr, just beyond him, was tapping a javelin against the ground and whistling.

"Boss, what are you waiting for?"

"I can't run while she's watching me."

"Why not?"

"Because . . . I don't know. I just can't."

"Boss . . ."

"Loose javelins!" came the call from somewhere, and everyone except me did so. The enemy had gotten much closer, say a hundred yards away, and as our javelins flew they broke into a run. The flight of the javelins looked like we'd picked up a piece of black metal and thrown it as a body, dropping in on an enemy—

"Loose javelins!"

—who might not even have noticed for all the good they did, as I threw mine and instantly lost sight of it, and then I remembered that I was supposed to aim low, but the idea of aiming was beyond me as I picked up my second, readied it, and—

"Loose javelins!"

—threw it, and who knows where it went, because they were *awful* close now, as I picked up my third—

"Prepare to engage!"

—and transferred it to my left hand while switching my sword to my right as they made it to the ditch, and over it, clawing at the earthworks, and everyone was yelling, including me, and there was this annoying wooden shield in my face, so I stuck my javelin into it and used it as a lever to force the thing away and then cut someone's face open, and I kept trying to move ahead, but there was this damned mound of dirt in front of me and I cut once more, hit someone's shield, then dropped to my knees and cut at the side of someone's legs, and then Virt was pulling me backward and saying, "Vlad! Vlad! It's over! Didn't you hear the drum?"

I stood there, panting for a moment, then, moved by exhaustion or disgust, I'm wasn't sure which, I pitched forward onto my face, rolled over onto my back, and lay there staring up at the sky and breathing. Oddly, it was only then that I became aware of screaming and invocations to various Gods from all around me. There was also some quieter moaning from nearby, but I didn't turn my head to look at it. I had an idea of what I'd see if I looked: bodies strewn here and there, many of them alive, some of them missing portions of themselves. The sound told enough of a story.

"You injured?"

"No," I heard myself say, and I wanted to laugh because the question was funny. Of all the things I could have said I was—hurt, damaged, destroyed, demolished, ruined—she'd asked the one question to which I had to answer "No."

Napper's face suddenly appeared above me. I couldn't read his expression because his face was upside down. There was blood spattered all over him, clothing and face. It seemed natural. He said, "You'll do, Easterner."

If I'd been able to move, I think I would have killed him.

I spent about five or ten minutes lying there before someone I didn't recognize knelt down next to me.

"We'll have to get that jerkin off," he said.

"I beg your pardon?"

"The jerkin has to come off."

"Shouldn't we be introduced first?"

His smile came and went, like he'd heard that sort of thing be-fore, and someone behind me grabbed my shoulders and pushed me up, and he started to pull my jerkin off.

"Wait a minute," I said.

"You'd rather bleed to death?"

"I—" I looked down and saw a gash in the jerkin, and there was a great deal of blood coming from it. Be damned. I *was* in-jured. Well, that gave me some justification for lying flat on my back staring up at the sky.

The funny thing was I still didn't feel anything. But, yeah, I'd managed to get myself cut. I didn't look closely, but it was within a couple of inches of the same place I'd been cut a few days be-fore. My grandfather would have told me my fourth position guard was drifting up. My grandfather, no doubt, would have been right. I'd have to—

"The jerkin?" said the physicker.

"Go ahead," I told him.

He pulled the jerkin off, dropping four knives, a couple of shuriken, and three darts onto the ground. He gave me a look. "What?" I said.

He shook his head. "Lie down."

"I can do that."

He poured something onto my side; it felt cold, but there was still no pain. However, I did feel a few drops of rain on my face, then a few more. The first couple felt nice. After that I hated it, and I only wanted to get out of the mud.

Mud.

Gods, but I hate mud. I'd never noticed it before, but now I think I'll hate it until they bury me in it. I had always thought my boots fit well, until the mud kept trying to pull them off my feet with each step. Sometimes it would succeed well enough that I had to step out of line, adjust, then run to catch up, and even without that I felt like I was constantly out of breath just from the extra effort. The water that leaked into my boots wasn't that much fun either. And now I was lying in it.

I began to shiver, which, more than the knowledge of the wound, made me feel weak and vulnerable. The physicker did a few things I'm not sure of, probably sorcerous but maybe not, then he slapped a bandage onto my side and put some sort of cloth against my skin that held the bandage in place. They were both instantly soaked with water; maybe they'd have carried me to someplace dry if I were more seriously injured or if there were any such place.

The rain increased to a driving torrent, and I hated it.

"Why didn't you tell me I was wounded?"

"I was afraid if I did it would start to hurt."

"Oh. You're pretty smart for a guy with no opposable thumbs."

"Thank you so much."

"That should do," I was told. "Take it easy with that side for a few days."

Physickers always say things like that. What exactly did he mean? Was I supposed to avoid having any more holes put in it? Good plan. I'd go with it.

"Okay," I told him. "Thank you."

He grunted and moved on. There were no more screams, but there were still a few moans that I could hear over the sound of rain striking wooden shields, metal swords, and whatever else was there to make sound against. Whoever had helped with my jerkin now helped me stand up, which made my side hurt, but not badly, which was just as well since I don't much care for pain. It turned out to be Aelburr. I said, "Anyone else hurt?" which of course was a stupid question, but he knew what I meant.

"Napper lost some skin on his left hand, but nothing else."

"Can't one of our sorcerers stop this Verra-be-damned rain?"

"I suspect our sorcerers are more exhausted than anyone else on the field."

"Oh. I suppose. Any idea what happens now?"

"We've picked up our wounded and our javelins, that's always the first thing. Now, I imagine, we'll re-form and—" The juice-drum cut in again. I was getting very tired of the thing. Aelburr paused, then said, "Or maybe we retreat to a prepared position."

"What does that mean?"

"With luck, it means the higher-ups had this in mind all along. Without luck, it means we're running and they don't want us to fall apart."

"Oh. Yeah. I didn't have to ask: They had it planned."

"How do you know that?"

"Uh . . . I'm an Easterner. We know things."

He didn't look convinced, but he did help me find my pack, get my heavy cloak out and on, and then put the converted satchel onto my back. That hurt, too, but I could carry it.

"Carry it on the wounded side," said Aelburr.

"Excuse me?"

"If you carry it on the healthy side the wound will open up."

That made too much sense for me to ignore it, so I did as I was told, then made my way up to the mudworks, which were vanishing into the field, and stared out; I could just make the enemy out through the drizzle, formed in a solid, even line, not moving, about a hundred and fifty yards away.

The command came a little later, and this time it was in plain words: "Fall back!" Seemed like a fine idea. Rascha came along and formed us into something like a line, and then Crown yelled something and everyone else turned around so I did, too; we began to move, in one long line, the Captain to the extreme right, our backs to the enemy. We started out at a quick trot, which I can safely say that everyone in the company was better at than I was, but I kept up. Eventually, on command, we dropped it back to a fast march, which we kept up much too long, and then we halted and turned and waited.

The rain stopped at last, and it was followed by a bitter wind that was only partially blocked by my rain-drenched cloak. Happiness, I decided, would be a nice campfire, proving once again that happiness is minor misery where before was extreme misery, if that ever needed proving. But there was no fire, and we waited.

At the time I had no idea what was going on, or how our part fit into Sethra's grand design, nor, to be honest, did I give it even a passing thought; but it is rare that a foot soldier has the chance to ask questions of his commanding general over a glass of red wine, and I had that advantage, so I ought to give you the benefit of what I was able to learn, later, when I had the leisure for curiosity.

Most of the division led by Morrolan had been about half a day's march away from us the entire time, and while we pulled back after their first attack, they were advancing. The engineers had been killing themselves preparing a defensive position for just this circumstance, and it was Sethra's hope (though not, she says, her expectation) that their entire corps could be lured into battle against our company and the other companies in the van, which would hold them just long enough for Morrolan's division to arrive and scatter, trap, or crush them. Of course, it didn't work that way, and what happened instead is that we fell back to the "fortified" position and stayed there for an entire day convinced we were to be attacked any minute, and then we abruptly broke camp and marched away in another direction entirely, which turned out to be due east, rather than the southeast that Sethra had originally planned on. I don't know what led to the change; none of my business, I suppose.

I found it annoying, but everyone else seemed to take it as just part of the routine. The rains plagued us for the next day, and most of the conversation was about incompetent sorcerers who couldn't manage the simplest weather control, and speculations about whether the whole thing was the work of Fornia's sorcerers. We could all see that the weather system above us was too large and complex to be considered "simple" but that didn't stop the remarks. I'd have hated to be a sorcerer; I'd have had to kill someone.

At the end of that day's march, with the rain still coming down, all of us soaked to the skin, and the ambulances having already carried our wounded back toward the rear, we held services for the nine soldiers in our company who'd been killed. The Captain gathered us together in formation facing the presumed enemy (I don't know if they were five hundred yards from us or twenty miles at that point) and stood there flanked by tall torches, so we could see him. The bodies lay naked in front of us, wounds hidden, torsos glistening with rain and the embalming oils that would preserve them between here and Deathgate. I knew they were dead because they were the only ones present who weren't shivering.

The Captain spoke of the pride of the House of the Dragon and promised the souls of each of the fallen that they would be sent to the Paths of the Dead, where he was confident they would be received with honor. He named them, and their rank (none higher than corporal), and asked the Lords of Judgment to look kindly upon them, and then said a few words in the ancient tongue of the House of the Dragon.

I felt as out of place as I'd ever felt anywhere, and I kept waiting for my natural cynicism to rescue me, but it was off catching up on the sleep that the rest of me wanted. Loiosh, too, was silent, and there was little talk as we broke up into squads and returned to our tents. I did ask Virt, in a quiet voice, how these things were handled, and was told that the bodies were to be placed on wagons and an honor guard sent to convey them to Deathgate Falls.

"Beyond that," she said, "who knows?"

Well, I did. At least, I had a pretty good idea, but it didn't seem right to say so. I was the only one in the company who had personal experience of what lay beyond Deathgate; I was also the only one in the company who had no right to the knowledge and the only one who, if killed in action, would not be sent there.

My natural cynicism finally appeared, but by then it was time to sack out for the night, so I could arise, rested and alert, and spend another day marching through rain and mud and eating bad food.

After a couple of days, the rains realized that we weren't going to quit so they stopped, and even the overcast became higher and thinner. There were mountains before us now: the Eastern Mountains in general, and Mount Drift in particular; I remembered it from the map. There was no more rain at all, as we had reached the dry lands west of the mountains; by whim of the Gods or freak of nature, the eastern slopes of the mountains were lush and forested while the western would have been desert were it not for the mountain streams, washes, and rivers that made their way across.

Now that the rain was gone, however, it was too hot, much too hot for marching, anyway. Both of my cloaks were stowed, my pack weighed a million pounds, give or take a couple, and even the little uniform cap was an irritation; the first thing everyone did when we stopped was take it off. On the other hand, I learned then what it was for: It kept the dust out of our eyes as we marched. Apparently cooling spells, or even wind spells, were too much work for the sorcerers of the company, and so those of us who knew a little sorcery, which was fortunately most of us, took turns attempting to summon up a breeze. This broke down by the second day of marching, after which we just put up with it.

I was now consuming six or seven biscuits at a meal, to show to what depths the human animal can be reduced. And we still had no idea to where we were marching, nor for what purpose. Well, I had a vague idea, thanks to having been at the one planning session, but it is one thing to hear elaborate strategic plans; it is quite another to spend a week marching with no knowledge of what was ahead except, in the most general terms, that we'd probably fight at some point. Stopping was a relief, but now, ironically, there was little reason to stop. We were on a good road cut by someone sometime for some reason through the harsh, rocky ground, but even the ground would have been passable, so we just trudged on and tried to make it to the next water break without screaming or choking on the dust kicked up by those in the front. My side did feel better.

Eventually, late one evening, we reached the Eastern River. I had assumed we would stop there, but whoever was in charge—that is to say, Sethra Lavode—wouldn't hear of it. We were to cross at once, we heard. I studied the river in the fading light and would have scowled but I didn't want to look like Napper.

There were grey, water-smoothed stones on the far side of the river, and smooth sandy banks near us; I'm willing to listen to explanations for that if you have any. Beyond it Mount Drift was getting close, and its companions were appearing tall and impassible. Impassible didn't bother me, because I didn't think we were going to pass them; as opposed to the river, where the engineers were already at work with wooden planks, floats made of sheep bladders, and prefabricated fittings. The river was wide here, and fast, but, we were informed, not more than four feet deep. "Not more than four feet deep" had a sound I didn't like. The evening, ironically, had turned quite cool, so walking through water, for which I'd have traded my best dagger the day before, had, now, nothing to recommend it.

"Are they going to ask us to ford it?" I asked Virt, gesturing significantly at the engineers busily putting together their makeshift bridge.

"That's what I'd do," she said irritatingly. "We should have a force on the other side before we start to bring the wagons across, and the sooner the better."

"Why?" I said, just because I was annoyed.

"Well, we have to figure the enemy is nearby; we've been skirting his territory for days, and he can't let us just wander anywhere."

I mentally pulled out the map of the area. Oh, *that's* where we were. Okay, that made sense; once we crossed the river, we could follow it downstream right into the heart of Fornia's territory; if Sethra wanted to force him to attack us, that would be the way to do it.

The drum ripped out, and by now I had no trouble recognizing the call to form up and prepare to move. We did, grumbling. Virt and Aelburr seemed like the only two in the company who didn't mind; just my luck to be in the only squad in the company with two irritatingly cheerful footsloggers. I made a remark to that effect to Napper, who nodded glumly.

Rascha approached before we started across and said, "Taltos, you're a bit shorter than the rest; if you want to wait for a wagon you can."

"I'm fine," I said.

"*Boss, I'm never going to figure you out.*"

"*Shut up.*"

The Captain led the way, dismounting and leading his horse across, then we moved out, and got wet and cold and fought the current, and climbed up over the rocks on the other side and moved back about a hundred yards from the bank. Eventually fires were lit, and we put up our tent by their light, and they served the food, and we sat around the fires getting warm and dry, which translated to happy, which in turn translated to not too discontented.

At the next fire over, they were playing S'yang Stones, and I knew that Aelburr would be there, maybe following my advice and winning, but more likely playing his own game and losing. I thought about playing myself, but sitting by the fire was too pleasant. Napper was off somewhere; the rumor was he'd formed a liaison with a woman in another company. I ended up sitting next to Tibbs, who kept trying to find humorous anecdotes that I thought were funny, and failing. When he got to the one about the headless private carrying the legless corporal back to the physicker, Loiosh said, "*Aw, c'mon, Boss. That was funny.*"

"*If you say so,*" I said.

"*If you stay in the army long, Boss, your sense of humor is going to vanish entirely.*"

We were joined by a young-looking Dragonlord; in the flickering of the campfire he seemed little more than a boy. Tibbs said, "Hey, Dunn. Where have you been?"

"Fishing."

"Catch anything?"

"No."

"Told you."

"I had to try."

"Yeah, you did, didn't you? This is Vlad. Vlad, Dunn."

"I've seen you."

"*A nice guy, Boss; he's fed me.*"

"*All right, Loiosh. I won't kill him, then.*"

Dunn and I exchanged greetings. Tibbs said, "What are you looking so glum about?"

Dunn said, "Crown says I still can't carry the colors next time we go into action."

"Congratulations," said Tibbs. "Why are you so all-fired anxious to be killed?"

Dunn didn't answer. Tibbs shook his head and remarked, "You should have been a Dzur."

"I'd challenge you to a duel for that," said Dunn, "but there aren't enough of you."

Tibbs gave a short, barking laugh.

Rascha came by about then, wished us all a good evening, and said, "You may want to sharpen your weapons tonight."

Tibbs said, "You think we'll see action tomorrow?"

"Nothing's for certain, but it looks likely."

We nodded and thanked her for the information. I went back to the tent and borrowed Aelburr's whetstone, then returned to the fire and put it to use.

Loiosh said, "*What about the whole plan to bug out when the fighting starts, Boss?*"

"*Shut up, Loiosh.*"

I spent last night with Cawti, an Eastern girl who has agreed to marry me. She has a wonderful smile and a good hand with a dagger, and she knows how to listen. We lay in my bed, pleasantly exhausted, her hair all over my chest and my arm around her shoulder, and I spoke with her about the proposal from Sethra the Younger. She listened without a word until I ran down, then she said, "And?"

"And what?" I said.

"And why did you expect anything different?"

"Well, I don't suppose I did."

"Are you still angry?"

"Not so much. Like you said, I should have expected it."

"And what about her proposal?"

"What about it? Can you imagine me accepting it?"

"Certainly."

"You can?"

"I have a great imagination."

"Among other things, yes. But—"

"But, if she hadn't been so annoying, what would you have thought about it?"

"Why should I care?"

"Aliera."

"What about her?"

"She's why you should care."

I sat up just a little, found a glass of a very dry white wine that we'd kept cold by setting it in a bucket of ice. I drank some, then held the glass for Cawti. She squeezed my shoulder by way of thanks, and I said, "You think I owe her something?"

"Don't you?"

"Hmmmm. Yeah. What with one thing and another, I suppose so."

"Then you should probably tell her about the offer, so she can decide for herself."

"I hate the idea of doing a service for Sethra the Younger."

"Yes, I know. I hardly blame you, but . . ."

"Yes, but."

The wine went down nicely. A welcome breeze came through the window.

"I think it's going to rain," said Cawti.

"I'll speak to Aliera tomorrow," I said.

"Would you like me to come along?"

"Very much," I said.

"All right. I think I'm sleepy now."

"Sleeping comes highly recommended as a cure for that."

"You think? Next you'll tell me that eating is a good cure for hunger."

"Temporary, but it'll take care of the symptoms. Are you hungry?"

"Yes, but I'm more sleepy."

"Then we'll have breakfast tomorrow. One problem at a time."

"Good idea," she said sleepily, and nestled into my shoulder.

"I wonder what Aliera will say. She doesn't think much more of Sethra the Younger than I do."

Cawti didn't answer. If she wasn't already asleep she was close to it. I set the wineglass down next to the table, then pulled the covers up. Outside, it began to rain. I thought about shuttering the windows, but it was too much work, and the rain smelled nice.

That was yesterday. This morning Cawti and I found Aliera

in the library of Castle Black. Going there today, after spending so much time thinking about, remembering, those first few times I'd been within the walls of that peculiar place, caught me up. I looked at it as if seeing it anew—as I'd first seen it years ago before war and love and war. To me Castle Black has always seemed palatial, with the grand, sweeping stairway and the three great chandeliers lighting the enormous hallway, all of them decorated by artwork one might expect to find in the Imperial Palace itself, artwork that is violent and beautiful at once, as, I suppose, are the Dragons at their best.

At their worst they are brutal and ugly.

Aliera said, "Greetings, Vlad, Cawti."

We both bowed. Cawti said, "How is Norathar?"

"Adjusting. Becoming reconciled. She'll make a good Empress."

I glanced at my betrothed, but if the subject was still painful for her, which I was certain it was, she gave no sign of it. Every once in a while I wondered how the House of the Dragon felt about its next Empress having once been a Jhereg assassin, but chances were good I'd be long dead by the time the Cycle turned, so I didn't give it that much thought, and it was one of the things Cawti and I still had trouble talking about so I don't know how she felt about it.

I said, "I have a proposal for you."

Aliera put down her book—I didn't catch the title—and tilted her head. "Yes?" she said, in a tone that indicated, "This is bound to be good."

"It comes from Sethra the Younger."

Her green eyes narrowed and appeared slightly grey. "Sethra the Younger," she repeated.

"Yes."

"What does she want?"

"Kieron's greatsword."

"Indeed? The sword of Kieron the Conqueror. She wants me to give it to her. Well, isn't that sweet."

"I'm just passing on a message."

"Uh-huh. And what is she offering for it?"

"I think you can guess, Aliera."

Aliera studied me, then slowly nodded. "Yes, I suppose I can, at that. Why don't you both sit down."

She looked at us, her grey eyes squinting. She held her wineglass, a fine piece of cut crystal, so that the chandelier made a rainbow through it that decorated the dark wood table next to her.

"What do you two think?" she said at last.

"We're delighted, of course," I said. "We'd like nothing better than to have Sethra the Younger butcher a few thousand Easterners."

She nodded. "There's more to this than that, however."

"Yes," I said. "There is."

"I'm surprised you're even bringing me the proposition."

"I wasn't going to," I said. "But Cawti talked me into it."

Aliera turned an inquiring gaze at Cawti, who said, "It's something you should know about."

She nodded. "Morrolan claims to have an idea what it is, but Sethra the Younger claimed it, and he didn't have the—well, he chose not to dispute it."

"If you get it," I said, "he still won't. Unless you give it to him."

"It may be," she said, "that, whatever it really is, a Great Weapon, as we suspect, or something else entirely, it has been trying to come to me all along."

I thought back on the Serioli, and on the Wall, and on everything that had happened, and I said, "That is a disgusting thought."

She turned her glance to me, frowning as if I'd spoken in a foreign language, but continued her thought without answering me. "If so, to fail to take it would be to ask for more trouble, and greater."

"On the other hand," I said, "I seem to remember Kieron the

Conqueror promising to come after you if you gave his sword away."

"Yes," said Aliera. "And that is, of course, another advantage."

11

BREAKFAST WITH CHEF VLADIMIR

There was a certain amount of doubt in the eyes of the soldiers in front of me, either because they weren't all that happy about cutting down a single unarmed Easterner or, more likely, because Ori was not authorized to give them orders. But for whatever reason, they hesitated; Ori, on the other hand, did not. He took a step forward, and as his arm came up, I let Spellbreaker fall into my hand, and then there was something black and ugly crackling and coming toward me.

And here my memory plays tricks on me again, because I know how fast such things move, and so I know I didn't really have time to make the cold, disinterested observation that I remember making, and I certainly wouldn't have had time to deliberately fall over backward while swinging Spellbreaker before me, and to listen to the crackling in the air, and notice that particular odor that accompanies thunderstorms, and be simultaneously planning what I was going to say if I were still able to say it, but that's how I remember it happening, and if my memory is to defy reason, well, I still have to go with my memory, and so there is the smell, the crackle, the roll, and even now the muscle memory of Spellbreaker's weight in my hand, and the feel of the ground beneath me, and even a small rock that bruised my shoulder as I hit, rolled, and came up, aware that my left arm was numb, and my brain was going *tick tick tick* as I made deductions and decisions and was able to keep my voice cool and rational as I said, "That was uncalled for, Ori. Do it again and I'll destroy you. I'm here to talk, not to kill, but if I change my mind I'll burn you where you stand even if your bodyguards slice me to ribbons in the next instant. Now stop it, and we'll talk."

I caught his eye and held it, and for a moment I didn't even notice the twenty-odd Dragonlords who might or might not be about to cut me down. I waited. Before me stretched gentle, green hills; behind rose the cliff called the Wall, with the plain flat monument to Baritt, his "tomb" standing up before it; and around me were the Eastern Mountains; they all seemed to hold their breath with me. I wondered if I were to die here. It would have been appropriate if I'd had some sort of premonition, but I don't get premonitions, at least, not reliable ones. In any case, I'd had no premonition when I had first reached the Eastern Mountains.

At their feet, I had learned when we first reached them, long miles from where I now stood, the day arrives suddenly. For once I was almost glad to be made to wake up early, because otherwise I should never have seen the red and gold tickling the peak of Mount Drift in the false dawn, with the overcast, very high and thin, looking like a product of the mountain, and the splintered light turning the camp into a giant field of mushrooms and the river into a ribbon of purple.

Forgive me; you know we hardened soldiers are all philosophers, and philosophers are all poets. Well, actually, we hardened soldiers are usually drunks and whoremongers, but philosophy's a good way to pass the time in between.

I was poetically given latrine duty that day. Rascha explained, apologetically, that there hadn't been enough "defaulters" to do the job, so lots had been drawn, and my name had come up. But I could breakfast first. I took it philosophically.

I won't spend a lot of time describing latrine duty, but I can say it wasn't as bad as I thought it would be—a lot of digging, mostly, and, in any case, everyone else was involved in digging more earthworks under the guidance of the engineers, so it wasn't much more work than what everyone else was doing, just slightly more unpleasant. I did get a laugh out of a few of my comrades by taking a piece of salted kethna, throwing it into the pit I'd just dug, and covering it over. "Just thought I'd cut out the middle part," I explained.

But I learned one thing of real value that impressed itself upon my consciousness even more than it had during the march, which is when I first began to suspect it: A Dragonlord squatting over a field toilet looks no more dignified than anyone else in that position. That is knowledge I am happy to carry with me.

We held the position on the riverbank for three days, three relatively pleasant days, in fact. It was hot, but we didn't have anything to do except relax or bathe in the river, and, best of all, no one tried to kill us. I had thought we were waiting there with the expectation of being attacked, but I learned later that, in fact, what we were doing was letting the other divisions move into position for a three-pronged attack on the heart of Fornia's realm. Fornia, of course, was busy with marches and counter-marches to defend against exactly this. We heard rumors of skirmishes on our flanks, and they turned out to be true, but they were only minor, unimportant little probes of our defenses— unimportant, that is, except to whoever was killed or maimed in the actions. Since the fatalities were all in other companies, we didn't have funeral services for them.

Most of our time was spent sitting around gabbing—or, in the case of Napper and me, complaining. Most of the conversation was pretty low on the scale: sex and liquor, with drugs and food coming second. The rest of the conversation was at a considerably higher level—there was very little middle ground. Philosophizing, as I mentioned before, is a highly respected activity. At one point I said to Virt, "The trouble with you Dragonlords is that to you killing is so impersonal."

She raised an eyebrow. "That's not what I'd expect to hear from a Jhereg."

"How so?"

"I'd thought some of your associates were in the habit of having people killed for business reasons."

"Sure," I said. "But one at a time."

"I imagine that's an important distinction to whoever gets it."

"Well, no; but it matters a great deal to everyone else in the neighborhood."

"Maybe to the House of the Dragon," she said, "the means must be broader because the ends are more sweeping."

"Excuse me?"

"We're not fighting for control of this-or-that brothel, but for this-or-that barony. While that may not be better, it is certainly bigger, so there would naturally be bigger forces involved."

"You think that accounts for it?"

"It is, at least, the most widely accepted theory, and I believe it."

"Uh . . . 'the most widely accepted . . .' There are theories about this?"

"Oh, certainly. There are theories about every aspect of war."

"I see. And are they useful?"

"Some more so than others. But the ones that aren't useful are usually entertaining."

"I see. I hadn't thought of 'entertaining' as having much to do with war."

"No, you wouldn't have. And the idea that it might be probably disgusts you." I didn't say anything. After a moment she said, "Haven't you ever been in mortal danger and discovered after it was over that you'd been having the time of your life? Haven't you ever taken pleasure in making detailed plans, pleasure that had nothing to do with how good, or bad, or important, the end result was? Can't you imagine the pleasure in setting up a complex problem and watching the pieces line themselves up, and all the forces come together, and having things work out the way you wanted them to?"

This, of course, set me thinking of Assassinations I Have Known. I said, "Yes."

"Well?"

"Yes, but."

She nodded. "Go on." It occurred to me suddenly that she was enjoying the conversation. Then I realized that I was, too. Was this significant of something?

I let my mind run and my eyes wander; she waited patiently. I said, "Well, maybe it's just numbers. But it seems that the more lives are being lost, the more important the cause ought to be. Don't you think?"

" 'Ought' is a tricky word. So is 'important.' "

"I can't deny what you say about danger. Yes, certainly, even though I try to avoid putting myself in danger, I know what you mean about the feeling of, well . . ."

"Of being fully alive?" she said.

"Yes, that's it. But that's me, and maybe even the guy I'm facing, if he's another volunteer. But what about those conscripts you've mentioned?"

"They're Teckla," she said.

"True," I admitted. "Okay, back to 'ought' and 'important,' then—"

She laughed suddenly. "You'd make a good tactician. I don't know about strategist, but certainly a tactician."

"I don't think I want to know why," I said.

"All right, then. Back to 'ought' and 'important.' They're moral judgments, aren't they?"

"Is that illegal in this dominion?"

"Not at all. But, traditionally, they're considered too important to be trusted to foot soldiers."

"Ah, tradition," I said. "Well, do you believe that?"

"Of course not," she said. "At least, no one can help thinking about the why's of what we're fighting for. And it does no harm, as long as you don't think about it just when someone is trying to skewer you."

"Well then," I said. "Let's get down to specifics. Fornia is as power-hungry as—well, he's power-hungry." I'd been about to say "as Dragons always are," but caught myself. "So is Morrolan. Their lands are next to each other, and Morrolan wants to make sure Fornia isn't able to threaten him, and, of course, Fornia doesn't want his lands invaded, so they make up a pretext of insult, and a few tens of thousand of us start hacking at each other. How do we fit that into 'ought' and 'important'?"

"You're here for much the same reason, aren't you? Fornia offended you, so you're going to kill a few perfect strangers?"

"I'm one man. I'm not commanding an army to do my killing for me."

"You think Morrolan should challenge him to a duel?"

"No, I think Morrolan should kill him."

"How? Assassination?"

"Why not? Anyone can be assassinated."

"So I've heard," she said dryly. I expected her to start in on the cant about how horrid it was to assassinate an enemy compared to honorable battle, and I was all set with a tirade about the death of one versus the death of hundreds or thousands, but she didn't go there. She said, "And, if he succeeded, what would then happen? Do you imagine Fornia has no friends, no family, none who would take offense?"

"If no one knew—"

"Is that how it usually works, my dear Jhereg? When someone is killed in your House, is it not usually known who benefits from his death?"

I didn't have a good answer; she was right. In the Jhereg, you usually wanted it known who had the guy shined; that way it served as a warning to the next guy who might think about committing whatever offense had put a polish on the victim.

"All right," I said. "I concede the point. Assassination would be impractical in cases like this."

"Well, then?"

I grinned. "There's always negotiation."

"Certainly," she said. "As long as you can threaten war, you'll always be able to negotiate."

"I was kidding."

"I know. I was being serious."

"You'd make a good enforcer. I might not want to give you your own territory, but I'd certainly hire you to collect debts."

For an instant she looked annoyed, then she gave me a smile and said, "All right. Well taken."

"Who is that?" I said, gesturing with my eyes.

"Who? Oh. His name is Dortmond. I'm not sure what line he is of. He's been in the company for most of two hundred years. He certainly knows how to campaign, doesn't he?"

"Except that he has to carry it all."

"He's big enough. It all collapses, and I believe he's been known to bribe the wagoners to bring some of his excess along."

The man in question was a couple of tents down from us. He was, indeed, a very large man, of middle years, with long hair and good features for a Dragon. He had his cap pulled down over his eyes and was sitting in front of his tent on what seemed to be a canvas-and-wood chair, complete with back. His feet were on a small footstool of similar construction, and by his elbow was a table, on which sat a wine bottle; a goblet was in his hand, and he was smoking a large black pipe. I watched him for a moment. The complete soldier, all his spare energy devoted to wresting luxury from the tedium of camp life.

"You should see the inside of his tent," said Virt.

"Oh?"

"Double-sized cot with extra padding, pillows, and bug netting. He's painted the bug netting, too; it shows a mountain scene with a wolf howling."

"That *is* a lot to carry."

"The cot is awfully comfortable, though."

"How—never mind."

Virt didn't answer the question I'd almost asked, but silently watched him along with me. He probably expected to serve as a foot soldier all his life, perhaps someday reaching the rank of corporal. He gave the impression of perfect contentment with his lot. Virt seemed to share my thoughts; eventually she said, "There are worse lives than that of the soldier, you know."

"Evidently," I said. "But you'll never be content with it."

"Me? Oh, no. If I'm killed in battle, it'll be on the way up the ranks."

"And what about Napper?"

"Him? You know, I think he's every bit as contented with his life as Dortmond."

"What about her?" I asked, gesturing toward a slim lady who had just walked up to Dortmond. "She looks, oh, I don't know. Peaceful. Nice. Friendly. Something like that."

"Neera e'Lanya. She is. As sweet a girl as you'd ever meet. She's the peacemaker whenever two people in the squad start getting on each other's nerves."

"And now you're going to say that, in battle, she turns into a berserker, right? Dragon rage, spitting, killing with her bare hands?"

"You got it."

"She's really like that?"

"She really is."

"Dragons are weird," I said.

After the evening meal, such as it was, I was called to the Captain's tent once more, and once more the Captain seemed a bit nervous, and once more Morrolan was there.

"Well, Vlad," he said. "Are you prepared to strike another blow for freedom?"

"Is that what we're doing?"

"No, but it sounds better than helping a wealthy and powerful aristocrat maintain his wealth and power."

"Have you been listening in on my conversations?"

"No, why?"

"Never mind. What do you want me to do?"

"Fornia," said Morrolan, "likes to send troops into battle with a full belly. It—"

"The dastard," I said.

"—would be to our advantage, then, if that proved to be impossible."

"I imagine. You're expecting them to attack?"

"It seems likely. They've brought up a number of units, and ours are still arriving. The longer they wait, the stronger we are. Mill's brigade should be arriving sometime tomorrow morning between the eighth hour and the ninth; if they're here before the action begins, we should be able to mount a nice counterattack."

I nodded and didn't express my thought about how "nice" a counterattack was likely to be. I said, "All right. Yeah, I'll interfere with their breakfast. You have something specific in mind?"

He did. I laughed, though it wouldn't be all that funny to the soldiers on the other side. I said, "Won't that just put them in a bad mood?"

"Yes. No doubt their officers will blame it on us and give them good rousing speeches. But it'll also disorganize them and delay their attack. And, of course, it won't help their morale to realize that we can get in and out of their camp any time we like."

"Well, that's what I signed on for," I said. "Where are they?"

"Downriver about half a mile."

"Right along the river?"

"Yes. For the same reason we are."

"We could make use of that, you know. We could mess with their drinking water or—"

"There are traditions involved, Vlad; we don't do that. Officially."

"Officially?"

"I mean nothing organized. But I've never heard of a unit that was upriver of the enemy who could resist a few pranks, at least."

"You must tell me about them."

"Another time."

"All right. In any case, it should be easy enough, with them right next to the river. How many of them are there?"

"More than there are of us," he said. "But then, we're dug in pretty good. Why do you need to know?"

"I have to know how much I'm after, don't I?"

"Oh. Yes." He did some calculation. "More than one wagon, probably more than two, fewer than six."

"Ah. An exact science, I see."

"Plus, of course, whatever they've already taken off the wagons."

"Right. Plus that."

"They won't have unloaded much; they won't know exactly when they'll be moving out. Of course, your target will be toward the rear."

"Okay," I said. I did some calculating, trying to figure out the best way to go about it; difficult, without complete information. "It'll be easier if I have some help. A lot easier."

The Captain spoke for the first time: "How much help?"

"Two should do it. Just extra hands to speed matters up."

"I don't want to lose valuable troops."

"Glad to hear it. I doubt they want to be lost. I know I don't."

He started to respond, glanced at Morrolan, cleared his throat, and said, "Perhaps some of your tent-mates, to keep the gossip down."

"They'd do."

"Who's your corporal?"

"Rascha."

"Very well, I'll speak with her."

"Good enough," I said. "I'll set off around midnight."

He nodded. Loiosh said, *"This should be fun, Boss."*

"Sure, Loiosh. Maybe you'll get a promotion out of it."

I went back to my tent and pulled my cloak out of my satchel. Virt and Napper were sitting in front of the fire, sharpening their weapons. Aelburr was inside, catching a nap. He opened one eye and said, "Not going to sleep like a sane person?"

"A sane person wouldn't be here."

A corner of his mouth twitched and he went back to sleep. I stepped out of the tent and sat down next to the others.

"Nice night," said Virt.

It was, actually. I hadn't noticed. I realized that I didn't notice the weather unless it was bad. Napper, however, said, "She means she doesn't have picket duty tonight."

"How 'bout you?" I said.

"No. Probably tomorrow, though."

"Tomorrow," said Virt, "we'll be somewhere else. Either upriver or downriver."

"There will still be picket duty, though. And, most likely, worse weather."

"True enough," I said, because I agreed with him. I checked the various goodies in my cloak, then checked the time and found that I had a few hours to wait, so I set about sharpening my blade.

A little later Rascha came by. She gave me a funny look, worked her mouth a couple of times like she was having trouble talking, then she said, "Aelburr! Virt!"

Virt said, "I'm right here, you know."

Aelburr poked his head out and said, "Yeah?"

"You're both assigned to Taltos here for tonight."

I felt them looking at me while I studied the top of the tent in front of me, just to see if it was straight.

"What is it?" said Virt.

"He'll explain," said Rascha with distaste, and moved along quickly.

They both gave me inquiring looks. So did Napper. The top of the tent was reasonably straight. I said, "It's nothing much. I've been asked to cook tomorrow."

Napper made a grimace. Virt said, "There's something you're not telling us."

"Yeah, well. I'll explain later."

"How much later?" said Aelburr. "Is this going to interfere with my sleep schedule?"

"Think of it as picket duty. Sort of."

The three of them exchanged glances. "All right," said Virt. "When *are* you going to explain?"

"Around midnight, we're going to take a walk. We'll go past our own pickets. Then I'll explain."

"Ah," said Aelburr. "An adventure." He didn't look pleased.

Virt said, "I don't know how good I'd be at sneaking around."

"You don't have to be either silent or invisible; you just have to not be heard sneaking or seen skulking."

"Excuse me?"

"Once we get to, uh, where we're going—"

"I like the sound of that."

"—you hide behind any handy objects, but in getting to them you just walk. Don't crawl, and don't try to walk silently. If there's any of that to be done, I'll do it. And you'll be going without your swords."

"How did we get so lucky?" said Virt.

I shrugged. "You have the good fortune to bunk with me. Not only do you get to listen to me snore, you also get to go and get killed with me."

Napper cleared his throat and looked at me with narrowed eyes.

"Sure," I said. "You can come, too."

He nodded.

Soon after midnight we set out, creeping along the river. At roughly the halfway point between the pickets, I stopped and sketched out the plan in a whisper; then I motioned them to follow me before they could ask questions I didn't want to answer or, more important, think about what we were doing. Having them thinking would do no one any good.

Loiosh spotted the enemy pickets and guided us past them. I don't think any of my little band figured out what Loiosh was up to; they just followed me. That was best. Once past the pickets, we had to remain hidden until Loiosh and I could identify the cook-tent. We entered the enemy camp and I had them wait while Loiosh and I searched. The supply wagons were near the mess-tent, which was both good and bad for my purposes. The cook-tent was less than thirty yards from the river, which was good.

"Well? Are they guarded?"

"Four guards, Boss. Moving rightwise around the wagons and the tent. You want to try the same trick we used last time? That was fun."

"No. Too much danger they figured it out. And I won't discuss your idea of 'fun.' "

"What then?"

"We wait."

"Clever, Boss. Do you think if I had opposable thumbs I could come up with plans like that?"

"Shut up, Loiosh."

I returned to where my compatriots were hidden, and, in the flickering half-light of the enemy campfires I indicated that we would just be sitting there for a while. I couldn't see their expressions. I was just as glad.

It was neither warm nor pleasant, but they were used to waiting for action, and, for that matter, so was I. We waited a little more than two hours for the guard to change, assuring us of several hours before they were relieved again. I had their movements figured out. And there had been no one checking on them. Loiosh said, "If this had been your operation, Boss, you'd have gotten all the details before you went to work."

"If this had been my operation, Loiosh, I would have hired someone else to do it."

I signaled to my temporary squadron that they should stay there, and I moved a little closer to the guards. I drew a dart from my cloak, waited for the guard to pass by me, then threw the dart into his back. He cursed.

"What is it?" said someone.

"Something bit me."

"Bees sleep at night."

"Well, that makes me feel better."

"I'm just saying—"

"I better see the surgeon; I'm starting to feel queasy."

"You have any allergies?"

"Not that I know of. What is there that bites around here?"

He didn't get an answer, because the woman he'd been talking to was out cold by this time. At least out cold, maybe dead, because a blow to the top of the head with the hard pommel of a dagger can kill, even if you don't intend it to. Fortunes of war and all that. And then, as the man succumbed and collapsed, I stuck a dart into the woman to be certain—the poison on the dart probably wouldn't kill her, but it wouldn't make her feel any better, and, in any case, neither of them would wake up any time soon. I hoped I hadn't killed either of them; I hate killing people I haven't been paid for. Were this a Jhereg operation, it wouldn't have come up. Jhereg operations are cleaner.

So, okay, you don't need the details; I took care of the other two guards as well, and I didn't kill either of them for sure, though I may have hit one a bit too hard. . . .

Oh, skip it. I went back to the others and motioned for them to follow me.

The rest of the job involved one decision: Was it safer and easier going to the water or from the water? One was quicker, the other safer; I opted for quicker. I was fairly certain I could vanish into the night if by chance I was seen, but I doubted my companions could. I called them close and whispered, "If there's an alarm, we go straight into the river, drop everything, and swim downstream as far and as fast as we can, okay? Remember to get rid of your boots."

They nodded. I didn't think they were very pleased with the prospect. We entered the mess-tent and took care of business there, which took only a few minutes. While we did so, I had Loiosh smell the wagons so he could tell me which ones we were interested in.

"*Three of them, Boss.*"

"*Good show.*"

I left the tent first and looked around in spite of Loiosh's assurance that all was clear, then I led my little band over to the wagons and pointed out the ones we wanted. There was a little more light here, and I could see them wondering how I knew. I resolved not to tell them.

We dumped kerosene over them. Now was when we had to be fast, because no one is going to pay much attention to someone half glimpsed who is moving about the camp as if he belongs there, but the smell of kerosene is strong and sets off alarms in anyone.

It only took a minute or so to drench the wagons, then I signaled that we should retreat back toward our own camp. Virt looked a question at me, presumably, How are we going to set them on fire? I smiled back at her and led the way.

We made it past the pickets without incident, at which point Virt said, "How are you going to start the fire from here?"

"Oh, I don't know." I picked a stick, drew on my link to the Orb, and started it burning. "I'll think of something," I said, and handed it to Loiosh, who flew off into the night.

They stared in wonderment for a moment; none of them, I think, had any previous clue of Loiosh's intelligence. Just for fun, I led them past our own pickets.

Once back in camp, all three of them reacted as I should have expected: laughter bordering on the hysterical, which was a little terrifying in Napper's case; and, along with the near hysteria, an unreasonable desire to continue being silent, as if the habit had been ingrained for life in the few intense hours.

Eventually they quieted down, and then Aelburr whispered, "Hope they like toast," and they all burst into giggles again, with hands clapped over mouths to keep it quiet, which, of course, made it even funnier. I found myself laughing with them, until we were informed that if we didn't quiet down at once we'd be put on report. Napper, tears streaming from his eyes, tried to whisper something that struck him as funny about that, but couldn't get it out, and the effort made him laugh even harder.

Virt, however, hysterics or not, was not anxious to be put on report, so she gestured that we should follow her. She started jogging toward the river, then veered away to stay within the boundaries of the camp. I wondered what she was up to when my question answered itself; it is hard to stay hysterical when you're out of breath from running, and hard to run when you're out of breath from laughing. In a few minutes, we weren't laughing anymore, and Virt led us back to our tent.

It actually worked; I, at least fell asleep quickly, and I think the others did as well, and there was really nothing more to the incident until breakfast the next morning, when we each took our biscuit and looked at it.

"Yes," said Napper. "They taste rather better today than they did yesterday, don't you think?"

Whatever happened in the next few hours, I decided, getting a pleasantry out of Napper counted as a moral victory.

12

A FEW BUMPS AND BRUISES

Sounds broke in to interrupt my stare-down with Ori: the sounds of Easterners being slaughtered. Mostly screams—and screams that were different from the cries of the wounded, because these had the edge of terror. I realized then that even from here I could feel the presence of Blackwand. On the field below me, to my right, Easterners were dying and my side was winning; the souls of my kind were gone, swallowed up, vanished forever, destroyed; and my side was winning the engagement. You could say I had mixed feelings about this.

On the other hand, if I wanted to present myself as a negotiator, it did put me in a stronger position. As I considered this, another interruption came, this one in the form of someone pushing through past the honor guard and coming up next to Ori.

It was about here that everything speeded up and slowed down; that is, things began to happen faster, but it seemed as if I had more time to observe and think it all over, to weigh the options, note the dangers, and be afraid.

"Well," I said. "My Lord Fornia. I hadn't expected to find you here."

He didn't appear any better disposed toward me than he had been when last we met, which, now that I thought about it, was only about a quarter of a mile from this very spot. Coincidence, if you like. I don't, terribly. I did think, for a moment, about taking a shot at him; the reasons against were legion, including not having much chance of killing him, having less chance of es-

caping alive, and being certain that Morrolan wouldn't thank
me even if I managed. But I did think about it.

Ori said again, "He's an assassin. Kill him."

I said, "Oh, let's not."

Fornia said, "No, he's not here to assassinate me. Whatever
his threats, Morrolan would never countenance such an act."

"In war, my lord? In battle?"

"On the other hand," said Fornia, "I do not believe you are
here as a negotiator. Morrolan would no more send an Easterner to negotiate with me than he would send a Jhereg to assassinate me. So what *are* you doing here, exactly?"

The warriors stared at me; behind them, no doubt, were more
of Fornia's sorcerers. I turned my head and gestured to the battle to my right. It was worse than it had been; I could make out
Morrolan, and around him, even from this distance, I saw
corpses lying in heaps. Or, at any rate, bodies; I didn't have to
be there to know they were dead.

I turned back to Fornia. "They're getting closer," I said. "Morrolan and his brigade. With Blackwand," I added.

He didn't seem unduly worried. I went on, "Morrolan didn't
send me to kill you or to negotiate with you. He didn't send me
at all. I'm here on my own."

"Indeed," said Fornia. "Do you, then, imagine you can kill
me, here, now?"

Why wasn't he worried? If Blackwand was coming for me, I'd
be worried. I'd be more than worried, I'd be bloody terrified.
"No," I said. "Or, perhaps yes, I could, but it is not my intention
to try."

His eyes strayed to the carnage below, now noticeably closer
than when I'd reached them. He seemed unconcerned. "What
then?" he said.

"I want to stop the slaughter."

He gave a short laugh. "You *have* become a soldier. Soldiers
have wanted to stop the slaughter as long as the profession has
existed."

That I believed. That, at any rate, had been my desire since
the first time I was in battle. No, I suppose, since the second
time; the first time was too confused, the second time, the
morning after we had burned up the enemy's biscuits, is the battle I have the clearest memory of, and the greatest feeling of disgust, at least up until this point. It all seemed to happen slowly,
with a neat succession of images burning themselves into my
memory.

That time, the engineers, instead of digging the ditches and
building up the earthworks, passed out shovels and guided us in
doing so. The ground, I remember, was soft and easy to work
with, a fact the engineers never let us forget. The air was dry—
almost throat-parching dry—but cold. The sort of cold where
any little bump or bruise has an additional sting to it. I hoped we
wouldn't be doing any fighting, but I expected we would, and I
was right.

So we dug a deep ditch and piled up dirt until it reached the
height of our chests, and whether our clandestine activities in
the night had anything to do with the fact that we were able to
finish before they attacked, I don't know, but I'd like to think so.
It makes me feel useful.

The juice-drum gave the call, "Rubbing Elbows," which
meant to form the line, and we did, under Rascha's guidance.
We were each given three javelins, which we stuck into the
ground near us. Rascha had a spyglass, and her first word as she
studied the enemy that was just too far away to see with the un-
aided eye was "Cavalry." Then she said, "Pass the word for
pikes." Then, almost at once, "No, never mind. They're re-
forming."

This time Loiosh did not suggest I bug out; he probably didn't
know why I'd stayed in the line last time, any more than I did,
but figured there was no help for it and I was just bound and determined to remain for the fight.

Rascha continued studying their lines, occasionally making
aimless gestures with her left hand; I assumed some sort of spell

to help her see or to counter any clouding spells the enemy might be using.

"No cavalry," said Virt. "You won't have to fight your own kind yet."

"Good," I said, meaning it.

She said, "Smart, too. I wouldn't send horses against ditches and earthworks."

"What would you send against us?"

"Well, certainly not a spear phalanx—they don't like ditches and they hate earthworks. I'd say either mounted infantry or heavy infantry, like last time."

"Mounted infantry?"

"Ride like bastards up to the ditch, dismount, and come right over. They could get here awful fast, and the horses will shield them from javelins once they've dismounted. Why do you ask? We'll know for certain in a few minutes."

"Just killing time."

"Best to be killing something," put in Napper. His eyes were shining and he kept baring his teeth.

I shook my head. "You really like this, don't you?"

"Yes," he said. "And so do you, you just don't want to admit it."

"Mounted infantry," said Rascha.

"Good call," I said. "So, what do we do? Think the Captain will pull something clever?"

"Nothing clever to be done, really. We just have to hold this spot. Maybe Sethra will send someone in on their flanks, maybe not. Depends on how much of their forces they've committed and, well, on a lot of things we don't have any way of knowing."

I grunted.

Crown, from far down the line, called, "Make ready."

I drew my sword, transferred it to my left hand, and picked up a javelin.

"You really ought to borrow a heavier blade," Aelburr told me. I grunted again.

Virt said, "We'll be lucky to have time for two throws before they're on us."

"Yes," said Aelburr.

That meant one for me.

Rascha said, "Aim for the horses." That was funny; how was I supposed to aim for anything else? We could now see the line clearly—it stretched out to more than cover us; we were flanked on both sides, then. But that, of course, was not my concern. Whoever was guiding the battle was supposed to make sure our line didn't get rolled up, and if whoever that was blew his job, it wasn't my concern.

It was, of course, my life. I remembered what my grandfather had said about trusting your officers even though you know they aren't worthy of trust. My hand was cramping from gripping the javelin tightly and I made an effort to relax it.

I wasn't used to this. Analogous situations in the Jhereg just weren't analogous.

"You know, Loiosh, I don't think I'd care to make this a career."

Whatever answer he was going to give was masked by an intrusion into my head. It took a minute for me to figure out what it was, then I realized that it was Kragar, choosing just then to get in touch with me.

"What is it, Kragar?"

"Nothing important, Vlad, but—"

"Then forget it, for the love of Verra. I'm just a little busy right now."

"Okay. Later."

I looked up again, and there were many horses riding down on us, and Rascha said, "Javelins ready!" We all prepared to throw; I prepared to ignore the order to throw until I had at least some chance of hitting something. I wondered abstractedly if this time I'd be able to follow the flight of the javelin as it left my hand. I wondered if—

"Loose javelins!" called Rascha, and the sky darkened again. I waited a moment, then threw, instantly forgot that I wanted to see where my javelin ended up, and transferred my sword once more to my right hand.

Someone screamed, and someone yelled, " 'Ware sorcery!" so I let Spellbreaker fall into my hand, and I noticed that there were an awful lot of horses writhing about on the ground. At first I thought someone had strung a trip-wire, then I realized that they were the result of the javelins, and then I wondered why I hadn't thought of stringing trip-wire myself, or, at any rate, why someone hadn't thought of it, and then some guy came bounding up out of the ditch in front of me so I stuck my sword through his neck and he went down.

There was shouting, screaming, and the clashing of blades, but it all became a sort of noiseless noise, and I remember having the illusion that I was in my own universe, with no directions except forward; anything to the sides was someone else's problem. It was odd, and it was also odd how much time I had to think, to observe, to plan, and to act. Someone else bounded up, off balance and sword flailing as if he'd been propelled by something behind him, and I remember being able to pick my target, wait for it to line up, and to hit it. Then a hand appeared, and I cut it, and then I intercepted some sort of spell with Spellbreaker without being aware of how I spotted it. Then two came over at once, and I gave one a good cut across the legs while the other struck at me. I slipped to the side while holding my rapier up at a sharp angle—I even remember calculating the angle to keep the blade from breaking—and when I'd deflected it I stuck him one in the stomach. He fell forward, so I let a dagger fall into my hand from my left sleeve, stuck it into his throat as he lay on his back, and recovered Spellbreaker from his chest, where I'd dropped it.

I wiped my brow, dragging Spellbreaker in front of my eyes; its gold links were small now; no doubt that meant something. I waited for the next man to try to get past me, but there wasn't one; the assault was over.

I stood there and looked myself over, until Loiosh said, *"Relax, Boss; not a scratch."*

"Okay."

Then I looked for my tent-mates. Virt was on her knees breathing heavily, but didn't seem to be bleeding. Napper had one hand on the earthworks, the other holding his sword, as he watched our retreating enemies, and I had the impression he was willing them to return. Aelburr was sitting on the ground, grinning, shaking his head, and cradling his left arm with his right. He caught me looking at him. "Son of a bitch," he said, but not angrily, more as if he were commenting on the weather. "Dislocated my fucking shoulder."

"Next time," said Virt, looking up suddenly. "Try cutting them instead of throwing them around. For one thing, that way they aren't in such a hurry to crawl back over."

"I'll keep that in mind," he said.

I looked an inquiry at Virt, but she didn't provide any details. She opened up her water flask and helped Aelburr drink some, and presently the surgeon arrived. I walked away a little, because I don't like watching surgeons, physickers, healers, or anyone else whose job it is to undo the sort of thing I'm so good at doing.

Rascha came by about then and directed those of us who didn't need treatment to pick up javelins and make sure they were unbroken, which was sufficiently mind-numbing to be relaxing after the battle.

We had not, it seemed, been in the worst part of the engagement; there were places where the carnage was much worse, and Jhereg—normal-sized ones—were circling overhead. Sometimes one would come a little too close and someone would hurl a stone or a javelin at it.

"Why is it, Loiosh, that they hate Jhereg so much but like you?"

"My winning personality, Boss?"

"Yeah, that must be it."

By the time I got back, the bodies were neatly stacked, and the seriously wounded were gone, and the walking wounded had, for the most part, been tended to. Napper had gotten over his battle-fury and was himself once more. "We should attack," he said disgustedly.

"Good thinking," said Virt. "They only outnumber us about three to two."

"Don't matter," said Napper.

"And we'd be leaving our protection, which is the only way we survived the attack."

"Don't matter."

"And they could probably bring a spear phalanx against us."

"Hmmm. Matters," said Napper.

"What," I asked, "is a spear phalanx?"

"A unit specially designed to wipe out units like us."

"Oh."

"Think of a solid wall of very big shields with ranks of spears sticking out of them, and those in back, who aren't even in danger, pushing the ones in front at you."

"I see. Well, no I don't, but I'm convinced I don't want to."

"I've been through one of those," said Virt. "I didn't much care for it. I probably wouldn't be here if we hadn't had help."

"What sort of help?"

"They don't like getting hit from the flank while they're engaged in front. The especially don't like it when it's heavy cavalry."

"Do we have heavy cavalry?"

"Probably. I'd still rather skip that fight."

"Okay," I agreed. "I won't order it."

"Thanks," she said. "Which reminds me. That business last night."

"What about it?"

"Are you—"

I was saved from having to evade another question by the juice-drum, which told us to form our line again.

"Here they come again," said Rascha.

"Bugger," I said.

Napper stood and bounded back to the earthworks, his eyes shining.

"More mounted infantry," said Rascha. "Ready javelins."

You don't need to hear about the second assault, or the third. We survived, and more died. Virt picked up a gouge on her left leg that didn't amount to much, and I got a bruise on my forehead that knocked me down and would probably have been fatal if I hadn't been rushing my opponent; she caught me perfectly, but it was the flat of the blade. Things got hazy for a bit, and I don't know what became of her, but then it was over, and, while we were awaiting the fourth assault we got word to retreat. Napper didn't like it, but I was delighted.

Rascha came by and gave me a new cap, since I'd lost mine in the last assault, and Virt, limping along next to me, said that the bandage around my forehead made me look like a real warrior. I made scatological culinary recommendations.

"Loiosh, I just want you to know, for the sake of my familiar having complete information, that my feet hurt."

"I think you're cheating, Boss. Everyone else has to either carry on without complaint or be known as a complainer. You get to complain without anyone knowing it."

"Because I had the foresight to show up with a ready-made listener to complaints."

"That's a new job for me. Do I get a raise?"

"Sure, Loiosh. Your salary just doubled."

"Heh."

We didn't start the march until fairly late in the day, so we stopped blessedly early, posted the extra pickets, and settled in to a hasty but well-organized camp. I suppose the art of setting up camp has a whole lot of theory behind it, too. Maybe that was what Crown was so good at; I don't know.

I had the second picket duty, which gave me the dubious pleasure of sleeping a little less than four hours, standing guard for four, and then sleeping another hour and a half before having to get up. We weren't attacked during the night, which I wondered at. In fact, I wondered why we never launched attacks during the night. I wondered if it was some sort of agreement among Dragons, the way the Jhereg won't have you assassinated in your own home or in front of your family.

Turned out I was wrong, it was all a matter of generalship and the art of war, about which I know nothing now and at the time knew even less. You see, I somewhere got the idea that good generalship would have a lot in common with running the organization and that there would be a great deal of similarity between battle tactics and, say, planning an assassination. I found out later that I was wrong. Oh, in very general terms, sure there are some similarities, but not in any useful way. I was speaking with Sethra Lavode about the Wall of Baritt's Tomb and the campaign leading up to it. I said, "You have this reputation, you know. I mean, as being a great general. You were Warlord I don't know how many times, and—"

"What about it?"

I had to cast about for words. It's hard to tell the most powerful sorcerer and perhaps greatest general in history that you weren't impressed with how she did her job. She might take it wrong. After mumbling a bit, I finally said, "I don't know. It's just that the whole time I was marching and waiting and sneaking around and fighting and marching again I kept waiting for you to make some brilliant maneuver, or some great stroke, or pull some trick, or something."

"How many tricks do you use in your work?"

"Huh? I'll use a trick any time I think I can get away with it."

"So will I," said Sethra Lavode.

"But you usually don't?"

"Tricks, feints, sneak attacks, night attacks, they all work better if they're on a smaller scale. A unit, maybe a company, that's about it. Once you have anything larger, the chances for miscommunication and mistake become too great. And there's always more of a chance for error on attack than defending even in the most simple operations, so if you add something tricky it gets much worse. That's one reason I prefer to defend whenever possible."

"So that's why we kept holding positions and then retreating after we'd won?"

"Those skirmishes you're talking about—"

"Skirmishes?"

"All right, Vlad. Those battles, then, that you won, you couldn't have actually won if you had remained. Fornia wouldn't have attacked if he hadn't been pretty sure he could overrun those positions eventually. We had to keep drawing him after us."

"Well, I suppose that counts as a trick, then."

"Maybe. Except, of course, that he knew very well what I was doing."

"Then why did he do what we wanted?"

"Because it was what he wanted, too. He wanted to try to get past our advance positions so he could divide our forces, which would have put me in a very uncomfortable position. It was a race, if you like. I needed to hold him off long enough for all of our forces to be in position; he needed to break through and separate us so we couldn't combine. And then, of course, the big, decisive engagement. However much planning you do, you don't really know until the armies meet and have it out. Even if your position looks perfect on paper, or even if it looks utterly untenable, you don't know until someone calls for an attack and the fight happens."

"Okay," I said. I tried to phrase my next question, then gave up just as she figured it out.

"The reason," she said, "that I have been successful is that I pay attention to details. The fewer details you miss, the greater your chances of winning."

"Well," I said. "That much *is* rather like assassination. Or so I've heard."

"I don't doubt it. It means keeping open lines of retreat and communications, and always knowing how you're going to feed and water the troops, and where they'll be camping, and what sort of ground they'll be crossing at every point, and the nature of your officers and where their strengths and weaknesses are, and how much dependence to place on which intelligence reports, and how far to push a particular victory, and how to salvage as much as possible from a given defeat, and so on and on and on. The details—the little things that lead to your peace, instead of the enemy's."

"Lead to peace?"

"Peace is the goal of war. Didn't you know that?"

"Uh . . ."

"Come, Vlad. Until there is peace, you haven't won. That is, you haven't accomplished your goals. On the other hand, it is worth remembering that, until there is peace, you also haven't lost."

"I guess I hadn't looked at it that way."

"You have never had to."

"Yeah, I suppose."

"The other reason I've been successful, I think, is that I'm very aggressive. And of course, my reputation helps. They think of me as being a great general, which makes the enemy afraid to be aggressive, which makes me a great general." She laughed a little. "But my usual approach is to give the enemy every chance to make a mistake, and then I punish him when he does, and the biggest mistake may be not to be aggressive enough, which is one mistake I never make."

"Aggressive on defense?"

"Certainly, Vlad. After all, it's always the defender who starts the war."

"Excuse me? Then it was Fornia who started the war with Morrolan?"

"Yes, indeed. That made him the defender, and that was why so much of my effort was involved in bringing him over to the attack."

I shook my head. "I don't see how it is that the defender starts the war."

"It isn't that complicated. The attacker doesn't want war. The attacker wants to conquer. If the defender would simply allow him to do so there would be no war."

"Uh . . . Sethra, I think there's something wrong with your logic."

"No," she said. "There isn't. It's counterintuitive, but it isn't wrong."

I thought all that over, remembering the battles and the retreats and the marches, and I said, "Assassination is easier. Or so I've heard."

She smiled and made no answer.

But that, as I said, was months later. At the time I just sat in camp along with everyone else, stood picket duty, marched, and griped. I think of that period as "the long march," although it was made clear to me that it wasn't long by anyone's standards except mine. I don't know exactly where we marched—I keep meaning to find a map and trace the route—but we usually had the Eastern River on our left, and we always had the Eastern Mountains on our right, and we kept going north; and then one day we turned around for no apparent reason and headed back south, almost exactly retracing our steps. No one except me, it seemed, found that infuriating, but I was annoyed enough to make up for the rest of them. My comments on the subject met with shrugs and puzzled looks until I stopped talking about it.

The weather for the most part stayed dry and cold. The cold wasn't too bad, because marching kept me warm, but I learned that dry wasn't all that much better than raining, because we were now passing through an area that hadn't seen any rain in some time, and so whenever we were on a road, which was most of the time, the troops in front kicked up dust that we had to eat all day—even worse than before. Dust so thick you walked with your cap down and tried to keep your mouth closed, but you couldn't because your nose was plugged up. A few of my comrades had handkerchiefs over their mouths and noses; I tried that, but breathing became difficult so I stopped. Periodically someone would conjure up a cross breeze just to give us some relief, and even I took my turn at it, but we couldn't keep it going all day without a major weather-working, which was expressly forbidden by the Captain—something about interfering with "stated objectives of the Brigade."

Excitement, what there was of it, came in the form of raids from the enemy, usually directed at the supply trains that came along several miles behind us. We would hear about them because we'd suddenly be ordered to halt, we'd have to take battle positions, and then we'd wait, and then we'd be ordered back in line and we'd set off marching again.

Then, one day, we made a sharp turn, put our backs to the river, and headed toward the mountains. There began to be a feeling of urgency, or maybe *purpose* is a better word, but I'm not sure where it came from. It grew colder as we climbed still higher, and the Eastern Mountains loomed ever larger. One peak in particular seemed to be our destination; a very tall, reddish-looking mountain with, it appeared, nothing whatsoever growing on its side. One evening, before the light failed, we stopped a few miles away from it, and I saw just how steep it was; it seemed to rise straight up from the ground, its top lost in the overcast.

The funny thing was, I didn't recognize it until the next day, when, after only a two-hour march we reached its foot, and Loiosh dived into my cloak with a psychic squeal, and then I looked around and said, "I'll be damned."

"Then don't get killed," said Virt. "But what is it this time?"

"I know where we are."

"That's good. Where are we?"

"That piece of rock," I said, "is Baritt's Tomb."

She nodded and looked around the area: a few hills here and there, and off to the southwest a flat plain covered with rocks and low grass, then a tall hill beyond. I could suddenly imagine warriors on each of those hills, and others charging across the plain.

"Good ground for fighting," she said.

13

Just a few short minutes before, the approaching battle had been terrifying. Now it was also loud. I felt this awful sense of urgency, that I should be doing something *now*, but I just stood there, and so did Fornia. It did accomplish one thing—which was to give myself time to think. What was Fornia accomplishing by doing nothing? Why was he letting me, an enemy, just stand there like that?

Was he delaying, too? If so, why? The only thing he could want was for the battle to close in on him, and what would that get him? I would have given whole worlds to know what he had in mind. I wished—

I did a quick check. Yes, indeed, there was a teleport block in place. But. Maybe.

Time. I needed time. I needed time to find out why Fornia needed time. Well, okay, so maybe he'd be willing to give it to me.

"What are you going to do when they get here?" I ventured.

"You'll see," he told me.

"Do you expect me to just wait here?"

"Do as you wish."

"*Kragar!*"

"*Vlad?*"

"*Kragar, I need Daymar. Now.*"

"*Daymar?*"

"*Now.*"

"Uh . . . how do I—?"

"I'll give you my location, you pass it on to Daymar, and warn him there's a teleport block up."

"How can he get past a teleport block?"

"Damned if I know. But he said—"

"Yeah, he might at that. I take it this is urgent."

"You might put it that way, yes."

"I'll see what I can do."

"Hurry."

Yeah, Daymar. He might be able to help me. I didn't terribly enjoy calling on him; I hadn't much enjoyed what he'd done last time we'd met. That had been . . . what? Two weeks ago? Less? Impossible. In that time I'd fought in three engagements, marched halfway around the world through rain, mud, and dust, and come to here, to this place: the Wall of Baritt's Tomb.

There had been nothing, at first, to indicate that stopping there was any different from any of our other temporary halts, except for the obvious one that we had halted early in the day. But there was no rush to put up defenses, and no indications we'd been given a position we would be holding against an attack. I found out later that this was because the original plan had been for us to be part of a major attack against one side of Fornia's army, but that this had changed when Sethra, at the last minute, had learned how Fornia had deployed his forces.

"Deployed." That's a military word. I learned it from Sethra. I'll have to make sure to use it on Kragar sometime, just to see his reaction.

Virt and Aelburr scraped out a fire-pit while Napper and I pitched the tent. "No wood around here," said Aelburr.

"So we freeze?" I said.

They ignored me. Virt said, "The wagons should be across in a couple of hours."

I looked at Napper. "Coal," he explained.

I felt stupid and didn't say anything.

We went through the rituals of setting up camp, but I kept looking up at that mountain, the flat slab extending up until it became lost in the overcast. Occasionally the giant Jhereg would swoop down and Loiosh would dive into my cloak. The Wall had been dedicated to Baritt's memory, and as long as it stood it would bring him to mind whenever it was seen or even mentioned. I thought back to meeting him. Would someone by now have mentioned the Wall? Would he care? It seemed a shame, not to mention ironic, for him not to know that there was a monument to his memory.

On the other hand, I hadn't much liked him.

Three hours later we had a fire going and water heating. Aelburr made something called Soldier's Stew, which involved crumbling a lot of biscuits into boiling water along with the rest of our rations, and molasses, and it should have been disgusting, but he added some basil, mushrooms, toeroot, and nutmeg that he'd picked up somewhere, and the thing was all right; we sang his praises the rest of the day.

We did picket duty early in the evening, and so were able to get a good night's sleep, and the picket assignments indicated no enemy nearby. The next day some of the company drew out a squareball field, wrapped a bunch of rope around a rock to use as the ball, and played a good rousing game while the rest of us stood around and yelled encouragement and obscenities. The injuries weren't nearly as bad as a full-scale battle would have been but were bad enough to get us yelled at by Crown and cursed by the company physicker. I did, however, resolve never to get into a fair fight with Dortmond. That was okay, I had no intention of ever having a fair fight with anyone. There was more S'yang Stones that night, and someone pulled out a reed-pipe and a bunch of them sang bad songs off key, and Aelburr made more Soldier's Stew.

At one point, I found Rascha, Virt, Dunn, and Aelburr standing looking out over the flat field nestled between the hills.

"That's where they'll be," Rascha was saying. "They'll spread out between those hills, Dorian's and Smoker's, command both of them, and try to hold us off from there."

"If we fight here," said Aelburr.

"Well, yes," said Rascha. "But the sergeant hasn't given any indication that we're going anywhere."

"I think it'll be here," said Virt. "What I don't understand is why we haven't taken positions on those hills ourselves."

"You're the expert," said Rascha. "What do you think?"

"I think the only thing that could keep the Captain's grubby paws off those hills is orders from above."

"Good thinking," said Rascha.

"You've heard that?" put in Dunn. "We've had specific orders about them?"

"Only a rumor, but that's what I've heard."

"But why?"

Rascha looked at Virt and gave a bow. Virt said, "To entice an attack. Same reason we haven't built up any defenses. Sethra wants them to attack us, and she's making it as attractive as possible."

I said, "Will they fall for it?"

"It isn't a matter of falling for it," said Virt. "They'll know how we're laid out. If we're offering battle on favorable terms, they'll take it."

"But then they wouldn't be favorable terms for us."

"It isn't that simple," said Virt.

"Then don't try to explain it to me," I said. I wandered away. It was too pleasant a day to think about fighting. There was a breeze whipping south along the mountain that brought cool air, but it wasn't yet cold, and it was dry, and not even terribly dusty. I came upon Dortmond, who was sitting back in his chair, feet stretched out, smoking a pipe. He opened one eye and said, "Well, it's the Easterner who fights like a Dragon. Wine?"

"Sure."

He pulled a beautifully carved wooden goblet from a canvas

bag at his feet, filled it from a bottle next to his hand, and passed it to me. I tasted it. It wasn't wine, it was brandy; even better as far as I was concerned.

"To the soldier's life," he said.

I didn't care to drink to that, but I did care to drink, so I raised my glass and swallowed.

"How did you get this stuff?"

"The victualer is a friend of mine, and a few of the provisioners owe me some favors, and there's always a little spare room in some of the supply wagons."

I drank the brandy. Loiosh, who had been flying about collecting scraps of food, found me and landed on my shoulder. Dortmond eyed him. I said, "Do you believe he's good luck, too?"

"Sure. Why not? We've had good luck during the whole campaign, haven't we?"

"Have we?"

"Well, are you alive?"

"Haven't checked lately."

He refrained from the obvious wisecracks and poured me more brandy, still calling it "wine." He said, "I think the campaign has been pretty lucky, all in all." He reached into the canvas bag once more, removed a loaf of bread and a large chunk of cheese. He broke off some of each and passed them over to me. It was a smokey meiren cheese, very sharp and good. The bread was stale but not moldy, and much, much better than biscuit. He broke off some more cheese, held it up, and Loiosh flew over and took it from him in one claw, holding it almost delicately while feeding himself. I watched him eat: nibble, chew, swallow, wipe mouth on wing. He was rather more civilized than I.

"Luck," said Dortmond.

"*I feel sick, Loiosh.*"

"*Good cheese, Boss.*"

I said, "So tell me, what are you going to do after the campaign is over?"

"Me?" said Dortmond. "I'm going to go fight another one."

"Why, for heaven's sake?"

"Because," he said, "I like it."

"You're not looking for promotion?"

"No. I like it where I am."

"And if you get knocked on the head in one of these battles?"

He closed one eye, tilted his head, and said, "You're a cheerful son of a bitch, aren't you?"

"Just curious."

He shrugged. "All right. Well, you have to die sometime."

"Yeah, I've heard that before. It doesn't strike me as a good reason to rush into it."

"Have some more cheese."

I did. A little later a woman I didn't know came over and joined us. He gave her some cheese and brandy; I took the hint and made myself scarce. Back by our own tent I met Napper, who scowled, I suppose just on principle, and said, "Are we going on any more of your expeditions?"

"Did you enjoy it?"

"Yes."

"I don't know. Maybe. Hey, Napper."

"Yeah?"

"Do you ever wonder what it's all about?"

"What, the war? Why, do you know?"

"Yeah, sort of."

"What, then?"

"Fornia stole something Morrolan wanted."

"Oh. Seems reasonable. We should go steal it back."

"I doubt it will be that simple."

"You're probably right." I thought, but didn't say, *Besides, that would end the war, and you'd hate that.* Then I thought, *Yeah, it would end the war. Maybe I should do that.*

"*Sure, Boss. It'll be easy.*"

"*Well, but it might be possible.*"

"How?"

"If we get to a decisive battle, Fornia will be there, and if Fornia is there, the sword will be there."

"Sure, just walk up and take it."

"I don't know, Loiosh. Maybe—"

"Maybe you'll get yourself killed, Boss."

"Everyone's got to die sometime."

"Heh."

"And it'll probably be safer than standing to battle."

I had him on that one; he shut up.

We were joined by Dunn, Tibbs, Virt, Aelburr, and Rascha, and the bunch of us sat around and I listened as they told stories, most of them funny and not terribly complimentary toward officers, about various campaigns they'd been on. Rascha announced light picket duty again, which I went off and did, then I went to bed once more.

It was one of the most pleasant days I've ever had.

The next morning we watched as a cavalry troop rode in and set up camp near ours, and, shortly thereafter, we saw the movement of more of our infantry. I recognized Aliera riding a light-colored, spotted horse alongside the infantry column; I wondered if she knew how much those who marched beside her hated the dust she was kicking up. They made camp to the west of us.

Things changed with the new arrivals. Nothing drastic, yet it was unmistakable. There was a bit more snap to everyone's motion, and a little more saluting here and there, as if to look good in front of the conscripts. There was no fraternizing between corps, either.

Late in the afternoon, word spread through the camp that Sethra Lavode had arrived; Aelburr claimed to have seen her. Shortly after the evening "meal" a young-looking Dragonlord I didn't recognize arrived at our tent and said I was to follow him.

Virt shot me a look. I shrugged, collected Loiosh from one of his scavenging expeditions, and followed.

We went through the camp and into the camp of the conscripts. I tried to spot the differences between their camp and ours, but there just wasn't all that much; except, of course, that these were mostly Teckla rather than Dragons and there were certainly a great many more of them. But they had the same sort of campstools we were using, and the bits of conversation I caught seemed about the same, the expressions on their faces were no different from those in our camp. Make of that what you will.

At the far edge was a large pavilion tent, and it was to there my nameless escort directed me. I clapped and heard Sethra's voice telling me to enter. I did and was directed to a chair between Morrolan and Aliera—not a terribly comfortable position, by the way—with Sethra and the Necromancer sitting across from me. I had obviously interrupted some sort of discussion: Aliera had a look as if she were about to froth and spit; Sethra's brow was furrowed; and Morrolan kept making glances at his cousin as if she were an unidentified creature that had appeared in his soup. The Necromancer seemed only barely present; I wondered where her thoughts were while suspecting I was glad not to know.

"Well, Vlad," said Morrolan after I was sitting and drinking bad wine. "How are you enjoying the life of a soldier?"

I shrugged. "Loiosh likes it more than I do."

"I've heard," said Morrolan, "that he has been adopted by your company as mascot."

"Yeah. He's insufferably smug about it."

"Hey now, Boss. That's not fair."

"Truth isn't, Loiosh."

Sethra said, "You've done some good work, I am told."

"Sure," I said. "For what it's worth."

"I think it was worth something," said Morrolan.

"Maybe," I said. "I don't know. I don't have enough of an

idea of how our little company fits in with everything else that's been happening."

"You saved some lives in your company," said Morrolan.

"Okay," I said. "But none of those battles were decisive."

"The next one will be," said Sethra.

I digested that. "You're ready, then?"

"I hope so," said Sethra. "But, more important, Fornia is. He has to make a stand somewhere, and this location has symbolic importance. He won't be able to pass it up."

"Symbolic importance," I repeated.

Sethra gave me a half smile. "Don't start," she said. "It also has a great deal of strategic importance; as far as he can tell, we're backed up against the mountain, and—"

"As far as he can tell?"

"We have lines of retreat, Vlad. Northward. Let me worry about that part of it."

"Sorry."

"In any case, this will be a good place for him to win a battle. He'll fight here. He has to. From here, I can push straight into the heart of his realm. Besides, if he can hold us for a few days, he has another division coming up."

"He does?"

"He sent his third division all the way around the other side of Chengri to cut me off from my base of supplies."

"That doesn't sound good."

"Well, if we're stuck here for three or four days it won't be good. You'll start getting hungry. But I don't plan on being stuck that long; I plan on pushing through him while I have the advantage of numbers. He knows that. He'll fight here."

"I believe you," I said. "What exactly do you want of me?"

"What we want," said Morrolan, "or, rather, what I want, is exactly what you said you wouldn't do, way back when this all started. I want you to get that sword from Fornia."

"Funny about that," I said. "I'd just been thinking the same thing."

"I still don't like it," said Aliera, evidently continuing a discussion I'd missed the beginning of. "If we're going to do that, why not go all the way? Hire a thief and just be done with it."

"For one thing," said Sethra, "we don't know any thieves."

"Vlad can put us in touch with one."

"And for another," said Morrolan, "that wouldn't accomplish what I want. I don't just want the sword. I have a perfectly good sword." Here he touched the hilt of Blackwand. "I want it taken from him."

"You want him humiliated," said Aliera.

"Call it defeated," said Morrolan. "And defeated at every level. Both militarily and by losing the very item that caused the war."

"If you defeat him," I said, just to be argumentative, "won't he have to give it up?"

"Military defeat," said Sethra, "is not an all-or-nothing proposition. I believe we can hand his army a major defeat. That doesn't mean he'll be powerless, and it doesn't mean he can be compelled to surrender all of his forces. To do that would require a far greater campaign than this one, more costly in every way, riskier, and with the danger of Imperial intervention."

"We've been talking it over for some time," said Morrolan. "And we cannot leave him in possession of the artifact, so we must take it. Once we've taken it, we cannot leave him unbloodied, or he'll try to take it back. So we have to get it from him and, at the same time, bloody his nose."

"And you want me to do the getting."

"If you'd like."

"I'd like. How do you suggest I go about it? I suspect sneaking into his tent at night is going to be trickier than the other stuff I've been doing, and, really, I'm not a thief by profession or training."

"No," said Morrolan. "And that wouldn't do what we want anyway. We need it removed from him during the battle."

"Excuse me? Why?"

"Because I don't know any way to get it after the battle. He isn't going to leave himself vulnerable; he'll retreat, probably return home, and at that point we *would* have to hire a thief to get it."

"That may not be a bad idea," I said.

"I don't employ thieves," said Morrolan.

"Didn't you just ask me to steal something?"

"To remove it from him in the middle of a battle, yes. We do not countenance assassination either, but making targets of senior officers while in combat is not only proper but recommended."

"Too nice a distinction for me, Morrolan. I'm just a hardworking Jhereg. But what about before the battle?"

"If you do that, there won't *be* a battle, Vlad. He'll pull back, re-form, and launch his own campaign to get it back from me, maybe years from now."

I shook my head. "How am I supposed to go after the thing while we're fighting? How will I even find him, much less the whole question of getting to him."

Sethra spoke up. "For one thing, we're going to position your company in such a way that you'll be as close as possible to his command center."

I wondered how Virt would feel if she knew how her general was deciding on the order of battle. I resolved not to tell her.

I said, "I still don't see how I'm supposed to get out of a pitched battle, all the way to their command post, find Fornia, and extract the weapon from him."

Aliera said, "I don't either. I think the whole idea is idiotic."

"As for getting the weapon from him," said Morrolan. "As I said a moment ago, making targets of senior officers is an accepted tactic."

"Oh. So now you want me to kill him?"

"If necessary."

I shook my head. "If I'd wanted to kill him, Morrolan, I would simply have done so. Days ago. It isn't clear to me—"

"You won't be alone," he put in.

"I won't?"

"If you require assistance, we can supply you with as many subordinates as you wish."

"That," I said, "may make a difference."

"Boss, are you nuts?"

"Some people think so, Loiosh."

"Add me to the list. You can't—"

"Maybe I can, Loiosh." Aloud I said, "How much time do I have to think it over?"

"I don't know," said Sethra. "Fornia is bringing up troops all the time. Of course, so are we, and faster. Right now, delay works in our favor, so I would expect them to begin the attack soon."

"What does 'soon' mean?"

"Probably tomorrow morning."

"Yeah, that's soon."

"Tell me your decision through Captain Cropper," said Morrolan. "Just give him the message to give to me, don't reach me psychically; I want this going through proper channels."

"Why, for the love of the Gods?"

"Because that's how it's done."

"All right," I said. I stood up. "Have a good council."

"Do you need a guide back?" said Morrolan.

"No, thanks."

I left the tent. It had become dark and cold; I should have brought a cloak. Loiosh guided me back, and I was glad to find the fire; it felt like home.

"Well," said Virt. "Did you see her?"

"Sethra? Yes."

"And?"

"There will most likely be a battle tomorrow. A big one."

"Did you get another mission?" said Napper.

"An interesting question," I said. "I'm not certain."

"Well, if you need anyone—"

"Noted. Thanks."

Virt said, "Battle tomorrow, hm?"

"So it seems."

"We don't have any bulwarks built up."

"Yes."

"So either we're spearheading an attack or we're bait."

"Or both," I said. "I suspect both."

Virt shook her head. Aelburr sat there stirring the fire and not talking.

Virt said, "So, what's she like?"

"I don't know," I said. "I've never met any other vampires to compare her to. Excuse me, I'm going to take a walk."

"Don't go too far," said Virt. "We're in imminent, and up for picket duty in half an hour."

"Half an hour," I repeated. "I'll be there."

I stayed within the pickets and walked around the perimeter of the camp. I tried to focus on the decision I had to make, but the fact is I've never been good at just thinking about things, so I didn't get anywhere except around in a circle; my thoughts kept drifting over my recent experiences: fights, and marches, and sitting around fires. I didn't come to any conclusions about those, either, and then half an hour was up and I returned to our tent, where I collected Aelburr, Napper, and my heavy cloak, and we went off to picket duty, where we were not allowed to speak, which pleased me.

Picket duty passed without incident, and I passed the time without reaching any conclusions. Then I went to bed and got a few hours of sleep. The next day we were woken up appallingly early, even for the army, and ordered to move our camp a hundred yards closer to the Wall and a little north to the top of a small hill. Virt said, "The other option, of course, was that there was no point in having us erect defenses for a position we weren't expected to hold."

She seemed much cheered by the idea until Aelburr said, "Then why aren't we putting up defenses here?"

"Maybe we'll move again," she said, straining her eyes to the north, where we could make out plenty of activity but couldn't identify it yet.

Virt pointed to the hollow to our left and said, "Two spear phalanxes."

"Which means?"

"It means we aren't defending a flank. That's good, if you value a long life."

"Then I'm glad."

"On the other hand, if we're attacking, we may be sent against their flank."

So we finally got breakfast. I chewed a couple of biscuits, washed them down with water, and followed the company colors until I found the Captain, staring at the enemy through a telescope and talking to Crown. He looked at me when I approached and said, "Yes?"

"Morrolan asked me a question last night. He said I was to give you the answer to relay back to him."

He stared down at me and scowled, evidently not entirely pleased with being a messenger for a Jhereg. "Very well," he said. "What is it?"

"Tell him I said yes."

The Captain opened his mouth, closed it, nodded abruptly, turned to Crown, and said, "See to it the Lord Morrolan gets the message."

"Yes, sir," said Crown. He saluted and set off to find a messenger. The Captain returned his attention to the enemy. Just because I felt like it, I saluted before returning to my squadron.

14

UPS AND DOWNS

I kept thinking that I could put it all together if I were smarter. Whatever Fornia was up to should have been subject to deduction, but I couldn't figure it out. Of course, I was aware that figuring it out might not turn out to be useful; just because you know what someone is doing doesn't necessarily mean you can stop him. That was Sethra's attitude; her approach to this battle was straightforward, and fundamentally without deception, and it seemed to be working—at least to judge by the fact that a press of Morrolan's troops, including himself and Aliera, were pushing their way toward Fornia's command position.

On the other hand, the Eastern mercenaries, though retreating, had not yet broken. Nothing was yet decided, except that a large number of people had died here, and more were going to.

As I studied Fornia's face, I saw him concentrate briefly, and an instant later a mass of cavalry appeared in a long row over the lip of the hill behind us, about a hundred yards distant.

I watched, suddenly and temporarily oblivious to my own situation. The column rode down the hill, in no apparent hurry. I tried to estimate their numbers, but I'm not very good at that. At least several hundred, though, maybe a thousand, and as they drew closer I saw they carried spears.

As they came closer they spread out into a single line, and I couldn't help but admire the way they went about it; neat and precise, they formed up to charge into Morrolan's forces. I risked a glance at Morrolan, and saw him, now a bit back from the fighting, talking to someone and pointing at them.

"Watch closely," said Fornia. "Now it gets interesting."

I kept watching, and saw, behind the cavalry, a mass of infantry reach the top of the hill and begin marching down.

In military terms, Fornia had "committed his reserves." In my terms, things were going to get even uglier. I'd have done something if there had been anything to do. I admit I even gave another thought to trying to take Fornia down, but his personal guard had failed to be distracted by the battle; they were still watching me.

The decisive moment was approaching; not the best time for me to be indecisive.

Fornia said, "Are you prepared to hear my terms, then?"

"No," I said. "I don't have the authority to accept them."

He chuckled. "That doesn't make you the ideal negotiator, then."

"The negotiator will be arriving shortly, if you'd lower your teleport blocks—"

He laughed. "Don't count on that, Jhereg."

"It isn't a trick," I said.

"Oh, I believe that. It's much too crude to be a trick. But I have no intention of opening myself up to accidents. If your negotiator wants to show up, he can do it the hard way."

I was trying to formulate a response when Daymar appeared, either blasting through the teleport block or coming in around it; I don't know enough about either sorcery or psychics to tell you how he did it. But there he was, floating, cross-legged, about six inches off the ground.

"All right," I told Fornia. "The hard way, then."

There was an instant where I wasn't certain if they were going to strike us both down, but they were well trained, and they waited for the order. The order didn't come.

I suddenly felt Daymar's presence in my mind. It was shock-

ing, and not entirely pleasant. For one thing, I'm not used to
people I hardly know being able to communicate with me psychically; for another, well, imagine being gently picked up by a
relative stranger who you can tell could crush your body with
one hand if he wanted to. Sure, I said *gently*, but he's still a
stranger, and he could still crush you. As I said, I did not terribly care for the sensation.

"*What do you want?*" he asked in a sort of psychic whisper—
as if he were being very careful not to burn my brain out.

I said, "*That fellow, him. That's Fornia.*"

"*Well?*"

"*I want to know what he's up to.*"

"*Certainly,*" he said, as if I'd asked him to pass me the tray of
sweetmeats. Just how good was he, I wondered. I mean, his mind
was strong, and he'd clearly trained it, but was he good enough
to pull the information I wanted out of Fornia's mind? Well,
he'd pulled information out of Kragar's mind.

Thinking of Kragar makes me, in retrospect, realize just how
far away from my own world I was. He had picked exactly the
wrong moment to get in touch with me, and then I never heard
back from him until I thought of it, days later, when we were positioned to make a charge or await one in front of the Wall. I had
suddenly thought of it, then, and gotten in touch with him.

"*Kragar? It's me.*"

"*Howdy, Vlad. How's the army life?*"

"*You should know.*"

"*I tried to warn you.*"

"*For the most part I hate it,*" I told him, "*but then people try to
kill me and I really hate it.*"

"*It wasn't the trying to kill me part I didn't like, it was all the
rest of it.*"

"*I can sympathize with that. What was it you wanted?*"

"*A guy wants to open up a new game in our territory.*"

"*A guy? What guy?*"

"Don't know him. Jhereg, seems small time. He's willing to give us our usual cut, and he's willing to provide his own protection, but I didn't know if that would be too many games for the area."

"That was a while ago; what did you do?"

"I told him to go ahead."

"And?"

"Seems all right so far."

"Okay. Good. Anything else?"

"No, everything's quiet."

"Wish I could say the same."

"Oh?"

"Building up to a big battle here."

"I assume you're staying out of the battles."

"Not exactly."

"What? You're fighting? In the line?"

"I haven't always been able to avoid it."

"Do something conspicuous and you might make corporal."

"Let Loiosh make the wisecracks, Kragar. He's better at them."

"Sure, Vlad. Anything else?"

"No, I'll talk to you later."

I stared out at the place where the enemy gathered. It suddenly occurred to me that if Kragar had done something conspicuous no one would have noticed. That might explain some things that I'd never ask him about. As good an explanation as any.

I found Napper was watching me. I guess I don't always hide it well when I'm communicating with someone psychically.

"If your lips didn't move, Boss, it would—"

"Shut up, Loiosh."

"Well?" said Napper. "We got something to do?"

I shook my head and went back to watching the enemy gather across the field. There were now banners on most of the other hills, including the ones Virt had said we should have taken when we got here.

Someone came walking down the line passing out biscuits

and cheese. I had several of the biscuits, ate the cheese, and drank some water. I turned back to Napper to ask him why he was so damned eager to get killed when there came the rattle of the juice-drum again, another call I didn't recognize. I knew, however, that I wasn't going to like it, because Napper broke into a grin.

"What's that one?" I said.

" 'Time to Be Alive,' " he said. "It means to form up for a charge."

" 'Time to Be Alive,' " I repeated. "Is that someone's idea of irony?"

He didn't answer.

Rascha came along and placed us where she wanted us— elbow to elbow, hardly room to move. I realized that this was the first time I would be taking part in a charge; everything I'd done up to that point involved standing there and keeping the enemy from overrunning us; from our success, I was not encouraged about being on the other side. Napper was on my left, Aelburr on my right.

The Captain came out in front of our line, riding a dark-colored horse that seemed much too small for him; his feet didn't reach the ground, but it seemed like they could if he just stretched a little. The effect was vaguely comical. He spoke in a loud voice that carried easily, though he didn't seem to be shouting.

"We will," he announced, "be attacking light infantry, very much like ourselves. They have no bulwarks nor ditches, and they number significantly fewer than ourselves; however, we will, as you see, be attacking uphill. We will go at a brisk march, charging the last hundred yards. We will take the hill and hold it until relieved." No one commented on the fact that yesterday we could have taken the hill by walking up it and planting our colors.

He continued, "I will expect you to maintain formation until we meet their line. We will have additional support from the sorcerers corps, especially defensive. If we keep our lines dressed and strike quickly, I do not anticipate any difficulty. That is all. Attend to your squad leaders."

He rode off to the far end of the line, drawing his sword as he did so. It seemed like a functional sword; maybe he'd use it. I hadn't recalled seeing him in any of the action hitherto. But I might not have noticed.

Crown took a position in the middle, just ahead of us. He, too, was holding his sword. I realized my pulse had quickened. I said to Virt, "Do they have javelins?"

"Probably," she said. "Almost certainly." Then, "Do javelins worry you?"

"Not at all," I said. "I'm looking forward to trying to catch one in my teeth."

"That's what we need: fighting spirit."

I assumed she was being ironic, but I couldn't tell for certain. Crown gave a signal, and the colors moved out. The rest of us followed.

"War," Sethra Lavode once explained to me, "consists of missed opportunities alternating with narrow escapes, and it usually ends when someone, somewhere, fails to commit a timely error." If I'd had that discussion with her before the Wall of Baritt's Tomb, it might have done me some good. Or, I don't know, maybe some harm; in any case, I wouldn't have been as surprised by what happened.

We went forward, straight into an unmoving mass of warriors. They stood shoulder to shoulder about halfway up the hill. The hill, by the way, had a long and gentle slope, deceptively gentle. It looked like it might be possible to run up it without being winded well before you reached the enemy position. This turned out not to be the case. I was already breathing heavily before we broke into a run, and so were Virt and Aelburr. We kept getting closer, and I kept wondering how I was supposed to fight in this condition. And at the same time I was both dreading and longing for the signal to charge.

And then they launched their javelins at us.

When we had thrown, it had seemed as if we had launched a single, vast, sheet of metal at the enemy. Now I was on the other side, and it seemed just like that. Then, I had wondered how the enemy kept coming at us; I still wondered. Now, after it is all over, I still wonder.

But I kept moving.

Then Crown waved his sword, and the colors surged forward, and I heard Rascha's voice, somewhere to my left: "Charge!" I couldn't go any faster up the hill, but everyone around me was able to, so I did too, and the effort distracted me from noticing what effect, if any, the javelins had had on our forces. Then they launched a second barrage, and this time I noticed: Virt stumbled and went down, and I remember thinking that I wished it were possible to stop and help her, and I still don't know why it wasn't, but I kept running. There was a horrid yelling, and I realized that I was making some of the noise myself.

There was a third barrage of javelins, which did some damage, to judge by the screams around me, and then a fourth, during which one went screaming past my ear and made Loiosh yelp psychically, and then we met the enemy.

The noise is what I remember most about that first instant, a screeching, groaning thunder that filled my skull and became something greater than noise, that went beyond the pain from my ears. It encompassed the battle like a shroud, and everything that happened was twisted and dulled by the din—out of which it was impossible to isolate what was causing any of it; it was just one unending roar. And through it, I kept trying to go forward, and I couldn't.

Now look, I think I'm more than a match for just about any of the swordsmen you care to name. For one thing, I'm good with a blade, but more important than that, I fight in a way they aren't used to: We Easterners have our own ways of fighting that I can use to take advantage of the fact that I'm smaller and quicker than they are. This mostly involves staying out of the way of those big monster blades they use, not giving them a good target, and never putting myself into a position of setting my strength directly against theirs.

Okay, now that I've said that, you probably already see the problem. I was not out there fighting against another swordsman with the object of killing him or taking him out of combat; I was out there trying to get myself past a certain point along with several hundred others, and at no point did I really have the chance to settle in and actually fight someone. I ducked a lot, and scampered back and forth, and I'd occasionally make a half-hearted jab in the direction of one of the defenders, but there was just no way for my fighting advantages to be of help, whereas all of my disadvantages were multiplied.

It's nothing short of a miracle that I wasn't killed inside the first twenty seconds after we met their line. The very first instant someone brought a big old sword cutting down at my head, and I still don't know how I got out of the way. He certainly would have killed me if he had followed up on that first strike, but I guess he got distracted after that. For whatever reason, I picked myself up (no, I don't remember falling or dropping to the ground or whatever I did) and charged again, and someone came within a whisper of disemboweling me. I don't remember gasping for breath while this was going on, but I must have been. I just remember thinking in a strangely detached way, *That's two; the third will probably kill me.*

Then Loiosh said into my mind, *"To the left, Boss!"* which ac-complished two things. The first, and most immediate, was that it caused me to look to my left, where someone was drawing a bead on me with a sword swirling over his head. The second thing was that, somehow, it transformed me from a soldier into what I was. Or, to put it another way, it reminded me that I had more weapons than my sword—although that isn't accurate ei-ther, because I didn't exactly *remember,* because I never made a decision, but the next thing I knew I had put three shuriken into his chest, which slowed him down a bit, and while he was trying to decide how badly he was hurt, someone—I think it was Aelburr, though I'm not sure, cut his legs out from under him.

I went back to looking ahead of me, and when I attracted someone's attention I threw a knife at her, missing, but I guess making her decide to look elsewhere for entertainment.

How long did our assault last? Well, I saw in the log book where it was recorded at four minutes. To me it seemed longer and shorter. Longer because at the time it seemed to go on and on; I kept thinking that something had to break, but nothing did. Shorter because I can't account for most of it. I usually have good memories of fights because my mind is always working, keeping track of the movements that training has made instinctive and making notes for future reference, but in these battles it had been different, and in this one in particular I can only account for about a minute of the fight, and then we were retreating back to our own lines with Rascha shouting to maintain our line. I remember seeing our colors and telling myself, *Okay, we didn't take them, but we weren't broken.* I didn't know that the color bearer had gone down, and his replacement, too, but I suppose that didn't much matter; what did matter was that we retreated in order and looked threatening enough doing so that whoever was in charge of the company that had just repelled us decided not to counterattack.

Which is part of what I meant earlier when I spoke of mistakes. I am fairly sure they could have broken us if they had charged immediately. They had elevation working for them, and we were at least a little demoralized, but, probably because we looked like we were retreating in order, or maybe because we'd killed some officer, or maybe just because the enemy commander lacked backbone, they didn't attack.

It was only when we had retreated all the way back to the bottom of the hill and an additional hundred yards besides that I became aware that there was fighting going on around us. We had, it seems, been only one part of a major battle, which I should

have known but had never thought of until, motionless and re-
covering my breath, I noticed dust clouds from several of the
hills around us, and the movement of troops, and opposing banners awful close together.

I didn't watch, however, because I couldn't see much and
didn't want to anyway. I overheard various remarks about who
was winning where, but they didn't agree with each other so I
concluded that no one knew.

Presently Virt came up next to me, and it was only then that
I remembered she'd gone down. Aelburr said, "Good work,
slackard."

"Good move on their part," she said. "If they hadn't knocked
me down we'd have won."

"Yeah," he said. "You'd have taken the position by yourself."

"Damn right."

"What happened?" I said.

"The bastards missed my knee, that's what. Thigh wound,
about as clean as you could ask. I'd have kept going up the hill
but I felt like taking a nap."

"You and Napper," he said, which was when I realized that I
hadn't seen Napper since the fight, but then I noticed him almost at once, lying on his back just past Aelburr; as near as I
could tell he was sound asleep.

I tried to decide how I felt about that, but gave up and threw
myself onto the ground next to him.

"Behold the grim aftermath of battle," remarked Virt.

Loiosh tells me I caught a nap myself after that, and I can't
prove him wrong. In any case, the juice-drum brought me to
my feet with "Rubbing Elbows," the call to form a defensive
line. I looked around the battlefield, aware that I'd been resting
my eyes for a little while, and saw that the scene had changed;
our colors now occupied a hill we hadn't been on before, and I
could just barely make out fighting a long way to the right. They

were, I supposed, attacking our flank. (Well, no, they weren't, as it happened; it was some sort of complicated diversionary move to cover an envelopment on the other side that never happened, but I didn't find that out until much later.)

I asked Loiosh, who had been strangely silent since we charged, if he was all right.

"*Boss, we don't belong here.*"

"*I know. What's your point?*"

"*We should cut out.*"

"*Can't do it.*"

"*Why not?*"

"*For one thing, I've agreed to a job.*"

"*Do you see any way to do it?*"

"*Not at the moment, but—*" I said aloud, "Where do you suppose their command center is, Virt?"

She pointed to a hill about four hundred yards south of us. "I'd be there," she said. "It commands a good view, and it's hard to tell for sure, but I think it's pretty steep. It would be easy to defend, easy to retreat from, easy to advance from. I'd certainly have my sorcerers there, and probably my command post. Why?"

"Just curious," I said.

Napper gave me a look. "You got something?"

I shook my head and didn't answer.

Aelburr sat down with his head in his hands, his long knees drawn up. Farther down the line, Tibbs was in the same position. Virt, though still standing, had a look that matched their poses. Napper wasn't glowering; he was just staring at the ground in front of him.

I said, "We got beat, didn't we?"

Virt nodded. "We got beat," she said.

Napper glanced at me. "Maybe they'll come at us now," he said hopefully.

I agreed with him, but didn't feel hopeful, so I didn't say anything.

Presently Rascha came along the line. Virt said, "We're expecting guests?" She nodded. Virt said, "How bad did we hurt ourselves going up the hill?"

"Could have been worse," said Rascha.

"Which means?"

"Fourteen killed or missing, twenty-six wounded. It could have been worse," she repeated, and moved along the line.

"Sure," murmured Virt. "It could have been—"

"Why don't we have javelins?" said Aelburr, looking up suddenly.

Virt used the sort of language soldiers have traditionally used in such circumstances. I was impressed.

For someone who had never touched a javelin two weeks before, I certainly had become attached to them. I suppose charging through a storm of them and actually feeling what it was like on the other side had a lot to do with that. What was worse, however, was the feeling that, if things had broken down badly enough for our javelins to go missing, what else was liable to go wrong?

The answer was, something big went wrong, but fortunately it was in the enemy's camp: They failed to attack us. Another example of what Sethra was talking about, I suppose. I did ask about that, too, but Sethra didn't know why they failed to attack that day. As far as I was concerned, I watched them, tense and more than a little scared, for several hours. Around us the battle continued, but it was a day of missed chances and maneuvering, or so I've heard, and what I saw was a great deal of marching and almost continuous skirmishes, but no real battles except for our charge up that hill.

Lucky us.

A couple of hours later we were issued javelins, and a little after that we were issued more biscuits and cheese, and this time we each got a strip of salted kethna to chew on. By then we were entertaining hopes that they wouldn't attack and fears that we'd be ordered to go after them again. But we weren't.

Late in the afternoon, Rascha came by again. "They're shifting," she said.

"Leaving the hill?" said Virt.

"Now we can take it," said Aelburr.

"I assume they're being replaced. We'll find out tomorrow who we'll be facing."

"Tomorrow," said Aelburr.

"Tomorrow," I said. "I like that word. That's a good word. Tomorrow."

"But we have to stay alert for night attacks," she said. "Extra picket duty all around, and like that."

Napper moaned suddenly. "What is it?" said Virt.

He stared disgustedly at his javelins. "We have to set camp again."

"Life is rough," said Aelburr.

"Might as well get to it," said Virt.

We struggled to our feet.

"Tomorrow is going to be ugly," said Aelburr.

"I hope so," said Napper. "We going to take whatever that hill is called tomorrow?"

"Dorian's Hill," said Rascha. "And yes, I think we are." She moved off down the line. Loiosh and I kept our cynicism to ourselves.

INTERLUDE: COUNTERATTACK

The day after our visit with Aliera I sent a message to Sethra the Younger in care of Lord Morrolan.

"She'll be pleased," I told Cawti.

"There have been no promises," she said.

"Yes. But you know Aliera will agree. Eventually."

Cawti nodded.

That was the day before yesterday. Yesterday I finished telling my story, as far as I felt like going, and came home in time to prepare dinner for Cawti. I was planning to treat her to a three-fish three-pepper stew with leeks and white wine, because no woman who has tasted it can resist me. Oh, okay, maybe I'm stretching a point. But it is good. So I did my shopping (I enjoy shopping for food, and if I ever achieve real wealth, I think I'll continue to do so), returned home, started preparing the oysters (yes, yes, I know oysters aren't fish), and was interrupted by Loiosh telling me that someone was clapping at the door. I started to yell "Come in," when Loiosh said, *"It isn't Cawti."*

I opened the door and found myself staring up at Sethra the Younger. My mouth fell open. She looked down at me. I swallowed and said, "Would you care to come in and sit down? I'm afraid it falls short of your standards for a domicile."

"Save it," she said, stepping in. "I'm not here to criticize your decorations." She paused, looked around, then said, "Although I must admit I find your home surprisingly tasteful."

Tasteful? I have furniture that one could sit on, and floors that are clean, and walls that hold the place up. I have one shelf of knick knacks with sentimental value. Home is where I go when I sleep; the only room I've put much thought into is the kitchen. But okay. Maybe she meant she expected to find it a kethna's nest with peeling walls, bloodstains, and rusted weapons lying about, I don't know.

But I said, "Okay, why are you here?"

"Can't you guess?"

"No. If it was about the trade you want to arrange with Aliera, I'd have expected you to send for me."

"And would you have come if I had?"

"No," I said.

"I hadn't thought so." She unbuckled her sword belt, and I noticed its size at once. She carefully set it on a table, and then sat down. I gritted my teeth and brought out some wine. She said, "Perhaps we should send for Aliera and get this done."

"Actually," I said, "I had plans for the evening."

I could see her forming the words "Break them" and then changing her mind. After a moment she said, "Are they breakable?"

"Perhaps. If you can convince me—" There was another clap at the door.

"*Loiosh?*"

"*Yes.*"

"My plans for the evening," I said. I went over to the door and admitted Cawti.

She took in the scene at once; I saw her notice the sheathed sword on the table. I said, "It wasn't my plan. She wants to finish things tonight."

"Why not?" said Cawti.

"Why not indeed?" said Sethra the Younger.

I could have made some answers, but I decided the question was rhetorical. "All right," I said. "Then someone should reach Aliera. Who wants to do the honors?"

"Why don't you?" said Sethra the Younger.

"All right," I said, and composed my mind for the contact.

I reached Aliera more quickly than I'd have expected to. I guess I was getting to know her. I had mixed feelings about this.

"*What is it?*" she said without greeting, preamble, pleasantry, or anything else I hadn't expected.

"*Sethra the Younger is here.*"

"*There? Where is there?*"

"*My flat.*"

"*What does she want?*"

"*To conclude the transaction.*"

"*I haven't agreed to the transaction yet.*"

I said aloud, "She hasn't agreed to the transaction yet."

"Then let's talk about it," said Sethra.

"*Then she suggests you talk about it.*"

"*I—very well. Can you give me a picture?*"

I did so to the best of my ability. It got me enough into her head that I could tell what she thought about the best of my ability.

"*Very well,*" she said eventually. "*I'll be there directly.*"

"Well?" snapped Sethra the Younger.

"She'll be here."

She nodded.

We sat in uncomfortable silence for a few minutes; Cawti sat next to me and held my arm. Aliera clapped outside the door; I let her in.

Sethra the Younger stood up. They gave each other slight bows over mutual glares.

Sethra said, "You know the bargain I propose."

Aliera said, "You should never have received the weapon in the first place."

"Received it?" she said, and I remembered, then, that final encounter at Baritt's Tomb. It hadn't stayed with me because I hadn't known her then. She said, "I didn't receive it, Lady Aliera. I took it. I used it. I—"

"I remember. I was there."

"Yes, you were, weren't you?" She turned to me. "And so, I believe, were you."

"You could say that," I told her.

She nodded. "But, Lady Aliera, I believe the weapon should be yours. What is your opinion?"

"My opinion is that you want the sword of Kieron the Conqueror. My opinion is also that I'm no haggler."

"Well, then?"

"Then if you want it, come take it."

"I could do that," said Sethra the Younger, touching the hilt of the blade next to her.

"Not in my house, you don't," I said, but they weren't listening to me.

I concentrated hard and, very quickly, reached Morrolan.

"What is it, Vlad?"

"A favor."

"Oh?"

"Grab Blackwand and get your ass over here. Now."

He didn't ask why, or what was going on, or anything else. Whatever else you say about Dragons, they understand when it is time for action.

The same, of course, can be said for Aliera and Sethra the Younger. They had drawn their swords and were circling each other in the parlor.

I hoped they wouldn't destroy too much furniture.

15

SCRATCH ONE JERKIN

The instant after Daymar appeared was another moment when I felt like I was about to be snuffed out, but I wasn't. A little piece of my mind that likes to comment on what the rest of me is doing suggested that I was getting tired of almost getting cut to ribbons every few seconds, and then answered itself by pointing out that it was, at least, better than actually getting cut to ribbons.

"*You think he can do it, Loiosh?*"

"*Probably. But you need to give him enough time, Boss.*"

"*Any idea how much time is enough?*"

"*Not even a wild guess, Boss.*"

To Fornia I said, "This is Daymar, my associate. And, just to be clear about things: You're right. I'm not a negotiator. On the other hand, I was not sent here to kill you, and I have no intention of trying to. I only hope you'll be as reserved with regard to me."

He laughed a little. "Why should I be?"

"Curiosity. To find out what I'm doing here."

"I've never been all that curious. Any other reasons why I shouldn't do as Ori says?"

"Because you don't kill prisoners, and I surrender."

"*Boss!*"

"*Any other ideas?*"

He nodded. "That will do." He addressed his personal guard, then: "Search him carefully, and I especially want that gold chain in his hand. Bind him well and send him to the rear for quest—"

Someone whispered in his ear. He listened carefully, then put his telescope to his eye and studied the field somewhere over my left shoulder.

"Not quite yet," he said as three of his bodyguards moved toward me to carry out his orders, leaving me saying to myself, "Now what, smart guy?"

I guessed, from where Fornia was looking, that the subject of the message he'd just received was Dorian's Hill, where I had recently left the rest of my company in the middle of a battle, which I was certain was no more fun than it had been yesterday, when, after an entire day of fighting, I'd gotten myself good and properly nailed.

We had woken up yesterday morning to discover Dorian's Hill was deserted. Empty. Unoccupied. This provided the subject for that morning's breakfast conversation. There was constant chatter all around me, and I kept hearing the word "trap" find its way from the buzz and hum.

"What do you think, Boss?"

"The hill we spent yesterday trying to take is suddenly empty, and yet they think it might be a trap? What suspicious minds."

"I meant, do you think you'll be ordered to occupy it anyway?"

"Oh." I studied the hill in the morning light: green, harmless, a few shrubs on the top, only long grasses and a few sharp grey stones on the way up. The only sign of yesterday's action had been that the grasses were a bit tromped down. The hill was just sitting there. If it were human it would have been twiddling its thumbs, staring at the sky, and whistling. *"Probably,"* I told Loiosh.

At least they didn't keep us waiting. We were given breakfast, and within a few minutes after eating we were formed up, and the Captain rode out in front of us. He turned and faced the line, and said, "We will occupy the hill and immediately begin preparing to defend it. To that end, the engineers will accompany us. We can expect to be required to defend it at once."

"No shit," said Napper under his breath.

The Captain was done talking; Crown stepped out and led us up the hill. It was much easier this time. The walk wasn't even tiring.

"It's going to be a fight once we get there."

"I imagine so," said Napper.

"No, I mean they'll have something special waiting. Sorcery, or some traps they put up there. Something."

"Don't matter," said Napper. It was hard to argue with him, so we just walked for a while.

"It's just us," said Virt as we neared the top.

"Excuse me?"

"We're by ourselves up here. Just the company."

"And the engineers," said Aelburr.

"And the engineers."

"Oh," I said. "Not enough, huh?"

"Not enough," said Virt.

Aelburr said, "Trap within a trap?"

"Maybe," said Virt. "Which makes us bait."

"Grand," I said.

"Don't matter," said Napper.

In a way, it was irritating to just stroll up the hill that had caused us such agony the day before, but I didn't say anything about it because I knew what Napper would say, and if he said it again I was going to have to kill him.

We reached the top, and before we had even caught our breath Crown called out, "Form a perimeter, begin constructing earthworks. Engineers to the fore."

They passed out shovels and instructions, and we dug ditches and piled dirt for about half an hour, during which time javelins were distributed. We stopped working when the fog rolled in. Thick fog, blanketing the entire hill; it came up with only seconds of warning.

"I wonder if it's magical," said Virt as we scrambled for our weapons. That was irony, by the way.

Crown's voice cut through everything: "It's safe to breathe," he said, scaring me all over again, because it hadn't occurred to me it might not be.

"Form your line and stand ready!"

A whole lot of swords were drawn from a whole lot of scabbards.

"Where's our line?" I said.

"Right here, I suppose," said Virt.

I recognized a voice that cursed from my left. "What is it, Napper?"

"Tripped in the bloody ditch."

"Hurt?"

"No."

"Can't bring up a wind," said someone. "They've got it blocked."

I let Spellbreaker fall into my hand and searched for something to use it on, failed to find anything, and wrapped it around my wrist again.

That was the moment when I realized that I was surrounded by an elite corps and was grateful for it. They had to have been as terrified as I was; a single, isolated company, having walked into what we all knew was a trap, and now we were blind; yet there was no sign of fear from anyone around me. They just waited, coolly, swords in hand.

Well, I certainly wasn't going to be the first to panic.

The silence itself was terrifying, until I realized that, without anyone's having said a word, everyone was listening intently. An obvious thing to do, which I would have thought of myself if I hadn't been scared half out of my wits. I mentally cursed. Being frightened wasn't new to me, but letting it interfere with my efficiency *was* new, and very bad. What would Loiosh say?

Loiosh . . .

"Loiosh, can you—"

"On my way, Boss."

He left my shoulder soundlessly. I can usually hear the flap of his wings, but he is capable of flying silently when he needs to. I'm like that, too, now that I think of it. The air was still and there was no sound but that of a few random birds squawking overhead; why is it mountain birds always have horrid voices? Presently Loiosh reported. I said, "Corporal!"

"Quiet," said someone.

"Bug off," I suggested. "Corporal!"

"What is it?" she whispered in my ear.

"Relax," I said in a normal voice. "They aren't within earshot on this side."

"How—?"

"There are about fifty of them on the west side of the hill, coming up quietly. Right now they're between sixty and seventy yards below the ditch. More of them are at the bottom of the hill on the southeast side, waiting."

"How—?"

"Loiosh," I said.

"I see."

She clapped me on the back and moved off. If Loiosh had been popular before, I reflected, now he'd be a hero. And impossible to live with.

Presently the hero returned to my shoulder.

"Good work," I told him.

"Thanks, Boss. Just proves you don't need opposable thumbs to be a hero."

I had nothing to add to this observation, so I added my voice to the silence, wondering if Rascha was going to make any use of the information. I'd about decided she wasn't when I heard the command, "Loose javelins!" from somewhere behind me.

The javelins flew without noise. It was eerie. Then, very faintly, we heard a brief scream from far away, quickly cut off; at least one of the javelins had struck home.

"Loose javelins!" came again. This time I recognized Crown's voice.

Someone else screamed—maybe there were two. It was

strange and terrible, unable to see five feet in front of me, Virt and Aelburr indistinct shapes at my side, trying to guess what was happening from the sounds.

I never did find out exactly, but you can probably guess as well as I can. Nothing more happened for about ten very, very long minutes, where most of my activity involved reminding myself not to grip my sword so tightly my hand cramped. For excitement, I'd switch the sword to my left hand, wipe my right hand on my jerkin, and switch it back.

And then, finally, a breeze came up, and, in an instant, the fog blew away like so much smoke and it was daylight again, and there was no enemy in sight closer than the foot of the hill, and I felt like a fool for having been so frightened. I imagine they called off the attack when our javelins fell into them, assuming our sorcerers had penetrated the fog. But whatever, Rascha came by and ordered us back to digging ditches and piling dirt, which work lasted maybe two minutes before the enemy began moving up the hill in force.

"Here we go," said Virt needlessly.

Aelburr began whistling, then broke off abruptly. The look on Napper's face was familiar by now.

For the record, I didn't have any sympathetic thoughts about an enemy's going through what we'd gone through the day before; I was just pleased to be on the other end. We released javelins five times as they made their way up, and I could see we did some damage. By the time they reached us, I think they were having doubts about the whole idea, so when Sethra sent a company that, I learned later, was called Tuvin's Volunteers up the hill to attack them from behind, they broke before they even got there. I never bloodied my sword during that battle; the whole affair was slick, sweet, and easy, and it would have been perfect if it had decided anything, but the enemy broke back down the hill, skirted around Tuvin's people, and made it back to their own lines, where we watched another company come up to reinforce them.

Tuvin's company was pulled back to threaten the same maneuver rather than joining us to reinforce our position, so we watched and waited. Those who had been injured by our javelins crawled off the field as best they could or were captured by Tuvin's company. A few of them, of course, wouldn't be moving again ever, and they remained where they were.

They gave us about twenty minutes before they began moving up the hill again, a whole lot of them even with the units they dispatched to hold off Tuvin.

We threw more javelins, and they came, and we held them off. This time my sword got bloody, but I had learned: A few of my surprises got bloody, too, and when it was over, and they went scampering down the hill, we were still intact, breathing hard, but with the feeling that it could have been worse. Napper suggested it would be next time, and Virt didn't disagree, only it wasn't, as far as I was concerned, because the third attack that day came from the southeast, and I was facing the southwest, so all I did was stand there, listening to the yelling, the screaming, and the crashing sounds from seventy yards to my left, and waited to be sent in if needed, but presently it was over. We took a few casualties, but they took more, and then we got a breather.

The top of the hill had plenty of room to set up camp, which we did, while keeping an eye on the enemy below. When it was done I took a stroll around the hill. I looked to the north, where I could see the camp of our reserves, stretching all the way from the stream to the Wall. Between us and the Wall, to the northeast, was a smaller hill—"Beggar's Hill," I learned—which was occupied by two companies whose names I never learned. We held the north, and from there we were brought barrels of water and biscuits and salted kethna, and more javelins. The best part of receiving the supplies was that it drove home the fact that we weren't cut off, and where supplies could come, troops could, too, if they were needed. Where it was easy to feel isolated, this was no small reassurance. Good for morale, as Virt would put it.

To the west was the stream, a little spinoff from the Eastern River. It ran straight south until it emptied into Khaavren's Sea, some three hundred miles away. To the southwest were a couple of smaller hills, occupied by the enemy, and from there they were mustering to attack us again.

Earlier there had been fighting to the west, all over the fields between our hill and the ones they occupied, but now everything was quiet. Three hundred miles is too far away to smell the sea, so I'm certain the very faint tang was more in my mind than in my nose, but the wind was coming from the south. I don't know.

"Watching them muster?" said Virt.

"Yes. More of them, this time."

"We getting reinforced?"

"Don't know."

We watched some more.

"A lot more of them this time," I remarked.

"Well," she said, "if I were the enemy commander, and our assault had failed three times, and I wanted to make a fourth, I don't think I'd attack with fewer men. But that's just me."

"Shut up, Loiosh."

"I beg your pardon?"

"Never mind. Private joke."

Aelburr came up next to us. "Our side again," he said. "Napper felt left out last time."

"Wouldn't want that," said Virt.

The enemy began moving up. The juice-drum explained that it would be best if we formed a defensive line. I chose not to argue with the juice-drum.

They came slowly up the gentle part of the slope. Very slowly. I strained my eyes until my vision began to blur, then said, *"Loiosh, are they carrying something odd?"*

"I've been watching, Boss. They're all carrying a stick or something, but I don't know exactly what it is. I'll go check."

But he didn't have to, because Virt's eyes were better than mine. "What by Deathgate are those things?"

"That's what I've been wondering," I said.

"You know, it makes me a bit nervous to see an enemy approaching carrying things I don't recognize. It makes me—wait. I recognize them now. Rascha!"

The corporal came over. "What is it?"

She gestured down the hill. "Javelin shooters."

"Bloody damn," said the corporal. Then called, "Sergeant!"

A moment later I heard Crown's voice say, "Drummer! Beat 'Kiss the Ground.' "

"*That sounds entertaining, Boss,*" said Loiosh as the drum started up with a call I hadn't heard before.

I turned to ask Virt what it meant, but Virt, and everyone else, was busy lying down on the ground. I made a quick deduction and joined them. When the drum stopped, I said, "Javelin shooters? I don't like the sound of that."

"No. You won't like the effect, either."

"What—?"

"Here they come!" yelled Rascha, and a mass of javelins flew over our heads, save for a few that landed, point first, in the ground near us. Down the line someone began cursing, very creatively, in a low, even, conversational tone of voice. One of the javelins had fallen about two feet from my right hand, and was sticking out of the ground; it was much smaller than the ones we were throwing, and had feathers near the back, and, at the very end, the wood had a small notch.

"Take a length of green, bendable wood," said Virt. "Put a string to it, and you can use it to shoot those things a long distance. Longer, even uphill, than we can throw our javelins downhill."

"A shield would be nice to have along about now," remarked Aelburr.

"We just going to stand here and take it?" I asked.

"I doubt it. Most likely—"

She was interrupted by the juice-drum. "I recognize that one," I said.

" 'Time to Be Alive,' " said Virt. "We're going to charge them."

"Oh, good," I said.

"Any other ideas?" she said, standing up but remaining hunched over.

I waited for the order to charge. If I got myself killed doing this, not only would it be annoying to me, but Morrolan would be irritated that I risked myself this way instead of doing my job. There just wasn't any good reason to be here. I glanced over at Aelburr and found that he was looking at me. I managed part of a smile and turned my eyes back to the enemy.

Crown walked in front of us, about ten feet down the hill, appearing utterly unconcerned by the javelins falling around him. He waved his sword.

"Give them a good yell as you go," he said. And added, "Charge!"

Well, it was better than just lying there waiting to get a hole punched in me.

So I charged down the hill, sword in hand, and then I was back in my tent with a familiar face looking down at me.

"We were sent help," said Virt. "Otherwise I don't think we'd have made it."

"What sort of help?"

"A platoon of cavalry from one side, three companies of heavy infantry from the other."

"We grind them up?" I asked.

"No, but we escaped."

"Everyone all right?"

"Aelburr took a scrape in the shoulder, but no one got it as bad as you. And Napper had himself a fine old time."

"Oh?"

"He laid about in grand style. I think he took out six of them all by himself."

"Maybe he'll get a decoration."

"Yeah, and we both know what he'd say about that, don't we?"

I grunted.

She said, "How are you doing?"

"I feel fine."

"Yeah, well, they've got you pretty doped up."

"Do they? Really? I feel normal."

"You wouldn't say that if you could see your eyes rolling around."

Now that she mentioned it, I was having a bit of trouble focusing. I said, "My back feels wet. I'm not still bleeding, am I?"

"No blood. They got this gunk all over your back, for the burns."

"Burns? From what?"

Loiosh butted in at that point, saying, "Boss? You okay? You've been out cold forever."

"I think I'm all right. What happened?"

"I don't remember. You got hit by something. A spell. I must not have seen it coming."

"That's two of us, I imagine."

I said, "Where am I?"

"In camp. Top of Dorian's Hill."

"Did we delay their attack?"

"What?"

"The expedition. Burning up their biscuits. Did it—"

"That was days ago, Vlad."

"Oh. My head is scrambled."

Virt said, "You got caught by some spell, straight in the back. You don't remember?"

"I don't remember anything. Well—"

"Well what?"

"I don't remember anything that actually happened. I think."

"You think?"

"Was there a little girl on the battlefield? You know, a child?"

"No, I think I can safely say there wasn't."

"Then I can safely say I don't remember anything about the battle."

"That's probably just as well, then."

I tried to fill in the intervening time. Presently I said, "So their trap didn't work."

"So far, at least. And if Sethra or Brigade or whoever was planning a countertrap, that didn't work either. We're expecting a night attack, though."

"Don't wake me up for it."

"I won't."

"I was kidding."

"I wasn't. You're out of it tonight. Physicker's orders. He also says, by the way, that you're to stay on your stomach all night. I hope you can sleep that way."

"I always enjoy the chance to learn a new skill," I told her.

"As for fighting," she said, "we'll see how you're doing tomorrow."

"If there is a tomorrow."

"Oh, there will be. Somewhere. Now excuse me. The others want to know how you're doing."

"I'm touched."

"If you need help, you can . . ."

Her voice trailed off. What had she been about to say? See the physicker? Then why didn't she complete the sentence? Because the physicker wouldn't be able to do anything more than he'd done? Just how bad was I hurt, anyway?

"Just how bad am I hurt, anyway?"

"You'll live," she said.

"That's good to know. What else can you tell me?"

"Nothing."

"Okay. Well, thanks for coming by."

"You're welcome."

She left me alone.

"*What happened, Loiosh?*"

"*I don't know any more than you, Boss. Whatever got you, I caught a bit of it myself. I don't remember.*"

"*Are you all right?*"

"*I think so.*"

"*I don't like it that I got hit in the back, though. I mean, was I running?*"

"*Maybe, but I don't think you're smart enough for that. More likely you got turned around during the fight. Or—*" He broke off.

"*Or what?*" I said.

"*Well, it's possible it was our own people. I mean, if they were counterattacking, reinforcing us, and using spells . . .*"

"*Right.*"

Over the next several months, by the way, I started to remember more and more of it. I eventually got a pretty clear memory of getting hit: the feeling of having my muscles contract almost to the point of breaking my own arms and legs; the feeling that my eyes were trying to pop out of my head; the peculiar sensation of every hair on my body suddenly standing up; and watching the battle progress around me as I slowly fell over. But I still have no memory at all of what led up to it—the time between the beginning of the charge and the point where I was hit is completely gone.

All of which is to say that if you want war stories to tell your grandchildren, don't get hit by sorcery.

There, you ask for a story and you get useful advice out of the deal.

At the time, however, I remembered none of it, and that was scary, too. "*Wish I knew how bad I was hurt, Loiosh.*"

"*What good would it do to know?*"

"*I'm scared anyway. It would be nice to know if I had cause to be.*"

"*Well, Boss, if we can judge by what remains of your jerkin, your back got hurt pretty bad.*"

I thought that over and decided I didn't care for it, and I suppose I fell asleep for a while, but I didn't sleep well; I had all sorts of odd dreams.

16

A WALK IN THE PARK

"*Got it,*" said Daymar into my mind and into the silence of Fornia, his honor guard, and his sorcerers all staring at me and waiting for me to do something. Relative silence, I should say; there was still a battle moving toward me. Had Daymar actually succeeded? Pulled the information out of Fornia's mind, just like that? Well, I had to believe it.

"*Let's have it, then,*" I said.

"Wait!" said Fornia to those of his honor guard who were moving forward to search me. They stopped and looked at him, while he stared at Daymar, then at me, then back at Daymar. He had evidently felt Daymar invade his mind and he had evidently taken it personally. I wondered if that had pushed him over the edge—if he would now order us killed out of hand. Hell, I would have.

The trouble was, that wouldn't help him any, and would undo the good fortune—from his perspective—of my having arrived here, because, of course, my being here would likely draw Morrolan; so the Easterner's showing up, while puzzling, and thus worrisome, had fit in so well with his plan to have a face-to-face meeting with Morrolan in the middle of the battle and engage him so he could—Oh, *that's* what was going on.

"Good work, Daymar," I said aloud. And to Fornia I said, "You don't know exactly what it is, either. And you're only guessing about how to bring it out. That was a possibility that hadn't occurred to me."

Ori stared back and forth between me and Fornia, and the other sorcerers and the bodyguards also seemed uncertain about what had just happened and what to do about it. Fornia said, "I suspect killing you here will draw him to me anyway; I think I no longer need you alive."

Now, that was unfortunate for me.

I said, "Remember, I surrendered."

"Spies can be executed."

"I'm in uniform," I said, remembering from somewhere that that might matter.

"Then you'll look properly military when—" He broke off, staring over my shoulder.

"Boss, don't look now, but we've got company."

"Who?"

"Napper."

"What?"

In spite of his warning, I looked. And there, about fifty yards away, was Napper, sauntering up the hill, come, no doubt, to get in on the action. Did this change anything? Well, yeah, it did change one thing—it put my back to Ori, and that caused a panic that, I suppose, was inevitable after what I'd been through the day before, so I spun back and almost set off a melee right there. I can't believe, with Napper showing up right then, that Fornia would have done anything except have us killed at once if there hadn't been sudden cries from the honor guard—Morrolan's band was on the verge of breaking through—thus giving him other things to think about than this pesky Easterner and his odd friends.

He addressed those of his guard who had been about to bind and search me, and said, "Guard them, all of them. Kill them the instant they do anything suspicious," then he turned back to his war.

That was good. Twice in two days would have been uncalled-for, even if I lived through it.

I almost hadn't lived through it the first time. I even dreamed that I didn't. I half remember several of the dreams, but in one that I remember most of I was sent over Deathgate Falls, and in the Halls of Judgment (which looked a lot different in my dream than they did when I'd actually been there) the Gods all thought it was the greatest joke in the world that I was asking to be admitted, and in the confusion of the dream I tried to explain that I deserved to be admitted as a Dragon, and they just couldn't stop laughing. It sounds funny to tell, but I woke up in the middle of the night in a sweat, breathing hard, and shaking.

I got out of bed because I suddenly couldn't stand to be lying still. I walked out into the quiet of the camp; the mountain air was cold on my chest, but felt good on my back, which was hot, like I had a localized fever.

"Where are you going, Boss?"

"I'm not sure. I need to walk."

"The physicker's tent is this way."

"I've gotten plenty of physic."

I slipped past the pickets, almost out of habit. "Am I going the right way, Loiosh?"

"What do you mean, Boss? You're not heading toward the enemy, but you're going downhill."

"That's what I meant. I wouldn't want to present myself to the enemy just yet."

"Then where are we going? Are we finally getting out of here like sensible people?"

"I'm not sure."

"Because if we are, you've forgotten a few things."

I made my way down into the darkness, my eyes straining to pick out a path from the bits of light from distant campfires. Loiosh landed on my shoulder.

"Ouch."

"Sorry, Boss. You should have a jerkin on."

He was probably right. I had no jerkin, no cloak, no boots, no sword, Spellbreaker was back next to my bed, and the only weapons I carried were two paper-thin throwing knives concealed in the seams of my trousers. I hadn't been out of doors this naked since I joined the Jhereg, and there was something exhilaratingly spooky about it. It was a cleaner fear than what I'd felt in battle, and the pain of stepping on rocks with my bare feet was clean, too, and so was the cold. I hadn't realized how much I needed to feel clean.

I slipped past another line of pickets, effortlessly, and for a while I entertained the illusion that I was the wind itself, that I didn't feel the cold, rather I *was* the cold, and none could see where I went, but they would feel me pass by a prickling of the hairs on their necks. I was naked but invisible, helpless but omnipotent, and I was lost in the world I all but owned. Certainly, it was false; in the streets of Adrilankha I owned the world, but this was a desert filled with soldiers; the feeling was different, and illusory, but it was there. I made no sound, and, had anyone been looking, I don't think he'd have seen more than my breath in the night air. My awareness of those around me came, above all, from the faint sounds of breathing, and I knew that Loiosh, as silent as I, was above me in the night, in the wind.

A single bush, like a sentry, waves to say with a laugh that it, at least, sees me, and I wave back though my arm doesn't move; a pebble between my toes is a burden which I reject, so it rolls away in search of its own reason for being; my time is filled with empty space, and my space with empty time, and my legs can't move so I must float float float through the armies of the world, clashing forever on the battlefield of my mind where all is in motion and nothing moves and the Cycle looms overhead, and at its top is the Dragon, glaring, plotting, scheming, protecting its young by devouring the souls who are cast loose to roam the night and come to me for protection that I cannot give, for I am in no place but everywhere, and there is no end to the night that is me.

How long I walked, or where, I don't know; nor do I know how far my mind wandered on a journey of its own, but somewhere in the night real thoughts returned, and practical matters impinged on my consciousness and brought me a few steps closer to home.

I found that I was thinking, for example, about just how big Morrolan's army was. My own unit—I couldn't help thinking of it that way—was one company out of scores in one brigade out of dozens. I passed tent after tent, all the same, all full of Dragons and Dzur and Teckla who would be going out the next day to cut and hack at Dragons and Dzur and Teckla on the other side. I walked through the camps as one might travel in a dream, apart from it all, and it came to me that the power I held as a Jhereg was nothing to the power of a Dragonlord, who could, on a whim, command so many to do so much. If I had such power, how would I use it? And what would it do to me? Did that explain why Morrolan was the way he was? There are stories that, in his youth during the Interregnum, he had entire villages put to the sword in sacrifice to the Demon Goddess that she might grant him knowledge of the Elder Sorcery. If the stories were true, did I now understand why? Was it that, having such power, he used it merely because he could? And would I be the same way, given the chance?

I came to the river and turned north, walking by still more camps, and supplies, and pickets to whom I was invisible. That was my own power, and I was using it, I suppose, because I could, and maybe there was my answer. To my right were several large pavilions, some with lights showing within. Perhaps Morrolan and Sethra were meeting even now to plan the destiny of the thousands assembled here—because they could.

And what of Virt, and Napper, and Aelburr? They were all volunteers, professional soldiers, who fought—why? Because if they died bravely they would receive high status in the Paths of the Dead? Or have a chance to be reincarnated as a commander who could lead others into the sorts of battles that led to their own deaths? That didn't account for it, but I couldn't get any closer.

None of my answers satisfied me.

I stepped out into the river, just a few feet, and felt the bitter current against my legs and the sand between my toes. I stood there, alone amongst thousands, and only then became aware that my knees were trembling, and that I felt light-headed, and that my arms were without strength. Whatever the sorcery had done to my mind, which was, apparently, a great deal, it had also taken a lot out of me physically. I wondered if I'd be able to fight the next day. I began to shiver uncontrollably, but I stayed where I was. It would be wonderfully ironic if I passed out from weakness and drowned in two feet of water.

"You have any answers, Loiosh?"

"To what, Boss?"

"To why Dragons are the way they are."

"That's easy, Boss: They can't help it."

Well, there was maybe something to that, but it was hardly satisfying. When I thought about it, the differences in character among Morrolan and Aliera and Virt and Napper, to pick four, were greater than the similarities. What was the common thread? Put that way, the answer was obvious: Once having decided on a course, motivated by greed, or by anger, or by the highest moral outrage, they attacked with a ruthlessness that would excite envy—or disgust—in a hardened Jhereg operative. I tried to decide if this were inherently a bad thing, and I could come to no conclusion. Fortunately, no conclusion was demanded of me.

I did, however, come to two other conclusions. The first being that, if one were forced into the service of a Dragonlord, one was better off serving a Dragonlord who was better at being ruthless than the other Dragonlord. The second being that the river was bloody damned cold, and that it was surpassing stupid for me to be standing in it when I hardly had the strength to remain upright.

"I bid you a pleasant evening, Lord Taltos."

The voice came out of nowhere, but I must have subconsciously known there was someone around, because it didn't startle me.

"Who is it?"

I turned around. At first I couldn't see her, but then she came up to the edge of the water and nodded to me, and then I recognized her. It took me a moment to reconstruct where I had met her before, but it came back to me at last.

"You're the Necromancer," I said.

"What are you doing?" she asked me.

I considered the question carefully, then said, "Dreamwalking, I think."

Her head tilted. She was very, very thin, wispy, and her skin was so pale it almost glowed against the darkness and against the black of her garments. "I didn't know Easterners did that," she said.

"Neither did I."

"I sense that you've been injured."

I turned enough to show her my back, then faced her again.

"I understand," she said.

"Excuse me?"

"I understand why you're dreamwalking."

"Ah. But I'm really here, aren't I?"

"How do you mean that?"

Crap. Even while dreamwalking there was only so much mysticism I could take. I said, "I mean that if I drop dead I'll be really dead, and my body will be found here in the morning."

"No."

"No?"

"No. Your body will actually float downriver from here, at least as far as the next bend. If you climb up on the shore—"

I laughed, probably more than it was worth.

"You did that on purpose, didn't you?"

"Did what?" she said.

"Made me laugh. Brought me back."

"Oh. Well, yes. You may have to fight tomorrow."

"Not the way I'm feeling now."

"Oh? Oh, of course. You were hit hard, weren't you? Come here for a moment."

I did, walking up to the bank until only my ankles were in the river, and she reached out and cradled my face in her hands. Her hands were very, very cold, and I tried not to think about what was touching me. I looked into her eyes, and it seemed she was a long way away, speaking to me from another world. I got the sense that speech for her required effort; she didn't think in words the way I did, she probably thought in—no, I didn't want to consider what forms her thoughts might take; I probably couldn't understand them anyway.

She closed her eyes for a moment, opened them, and said, "Go back to your camp and sleep, dream-walker. You'll feel better in the morning."

"Right," I said. "And I'll think this was all a dream."

"Maybe. Maybe it is."

"We've been through that."

"Go back to your tent, Easterner. Go to sleep. Dream of bearded women."

"Excuse me? No, never mind. Don't explain. I don't want to know."

Now that I was myself again, the wind was really cold, especially on my wet legs. And the rocks hurt my bare feet. And I had to work to slip past several sets of pickets, more of them than I remembered from getting there.

"Well, she was pretty weird."

"Who was, Boss?"

"I hope," I said after a moment, *"that you're joking, Loiosh."*

"Ummmm."

"I've just had a conversation with the Necromancer, Loiosh. A real conversation. Out loud and everything. You really didn't see her?"

"Boss, I didn't see her, I didn't hear her, and I didn't hear you talk-

ing. You just walked out into the river, stood there for a while, and walked back."

"Grand," I said. "Just grand. I get myself into the army, stand up in battles I have no business in, get nailed in the back by sorcery, accept an impossible assignment to be carried out in the middle of it all, and then, just to top things off, I have to go have a mystical fucking experience. This is just great."

"Whatever it was, Boss, I think it helped. You're sounding like yourself."

"Oh, thank you so much, Loiosh."

I made it back to the camp, and to my tent, and to my cot, and I remembered to lie down on my stomach, and it was only then that I realized that whatever weakness I'd felt before was, if not gone, at least diminished. I tried to make sense of it, but I must have fallen asleep, because then it was morning, and I got up to the sound of the drum before I remembered that I probably wouldn't have had to. Rascha was outside the tent when I emerged, bare-chested and blinking.

"You all right?" she said.

In spite of everything, I managed to give her a straight answer. "A bit wobbly on my feet, and my back itches, and I could use about another forty or fifty hours of sleep, but yeah, I'm okay."

"Think you can take a spot on the line?"

"Sure."

"Good. We had some casualties."

"Did they attack last night?"

She looked at me. "Just before dawn. Glad we didn't wake you up."

"I think you could have burned the tent down without waking me up."

"Today, I think."

"Hmmm?"

"I think today will settle things."

"Oh. That's good."

"Yes. And our end of it shouldn't be too bad. All we have to do is hold this hill. Unless, of course, the powers-that-be change their minds and have us do something else."

"Holding the hill might be rough enough," I said.

"Maybe. Go get some food in you."

"Good idea," I said.

I went back inside and grabbed my jerkin and inspected it. I found that it no longer had a back—just a big hole, about a foot in diameter, with ugly burn marks around the edges. I started to feel queasy again.

"Boss—"

"Yeah. Impressive, isn't it?"

"What are you going to do for a jerkin?"

"I brought a spare."

"Oh. Good thinking."

I put it on and my back started itching. I filled the ribs and sleeves and the collar from my old shirt, then put a light cloak over it, and made sure that I was properly packed. I ate three biscuits and drank a lot of water, then got myself shaved and cleaned up as best I could.

My knees felt very shaky by then, and I wasn't looking forward to taking a spot on the line. If I'd remembered what I had promised Morrolan I'd do I might have panicked, but my brain was still a bit scrambled and that didn't occur to me until later. The experiences of the night before came back in pieces, and I kept wanting to think of the whole thing as a dream, but I couldn't convince myself, and then I made the mistake of asking Loiosh, who confirmed that at least some of it had actually happened.

When I returned to the tent, I found Rascha sitting with Virt and Aelburr. I sat with them, and soon after that Crown came along. "Morning, soldiers," he said cheerfully. "Today we take them."

Rascha nodded. "What do you think of the earthworks on the southwest side? They got pretty messed up last night."

He nodded. "It wouldn't hurt to build them up again."

Dunn came over then. He said, "Sergeant, I'd like—"

"No," said Crown. "Mora's taking the colors. If she goes down, then you're up. So stick by her. And keep her alive, if you can. You can answer to Dortmond if she shines."

"Yes, Sergeant. Thank you, Sergeant."

Dunn walked away. I shook my head. "I just don't get it."

Crown looked me up and down. "No, you wouldn't, would you?" He walked off.

"I think," I said, "that I've just been insulted."

"Don't let it keep you up nights," said Virt.

From farther down the line someone called out, "Here they come," and we walked up to the remains of the earthworks and waited for the assault to begin.

They came, and we held them off, and they came, and we held them off. The whole time Loiosh remained on my shoulder, maybe for whatever effect it might have on anyone who faced me. I kept asking him why he didn't get to somewhere safe, but I didn't get a satisfactory answer, just questions to which I couldn't give a satisfactory answer. My legs kept wanting to buckle—residual effects from getting hit the day before, but I never quite collapsed at the wrong time. If the Necromancer had actually done something, well, it must have worked.

After the second attack, Virt said, "Have you noticed that every time they attack they've been knocking away at the earthworks?"

"Uh . . . you're right."

"And that they attack with more troops each time?"

"Right again," I said. "You're on a roll. Don't stop now."

"They're forming up for another charge," she said.

Rascha came by and said, "Up to the line again. Where's Aelburr?"

"I'll sit this one out, I think," he said.

That was when we noticed that he was flat on his back, bleeding from two distinct chest wounds and another on his right leg.

"Physic!" came the call, from Rascha and Virt at the same time.

As the physicker approached, Virt said, "We're awfully cut up. Do we have anyone left to plug the holes?"

"No," said Rascha. "We've got holes everywhere. About twelve percent casualties. And, from the looks of things, I don't think we can expect any support from Brigade."

"Oh," said Virt.

"Time for someone to think of something clever," I suggested, at which moment the juice-drum gave the call to prepare for a charge. I said, "That wasn't the sort of clever I was thinking of."

Virt said, "This should be interesting."

"Interesting?" I said. "We're too weak to defend, so we attack? That isn't sound military practice, is it?"

"No," said Virt.

"Well good," I said. "See? I've learned something."

"I'm sure it will do you a lot of good next time you enlist." She paused. "It's been done before, though. And it isn't that bad an idea. One time, at Kipper Bay, we—" She broke off abruptly and pointed. "I'll tell you the story later," she said optimistically.

They were coming up the hill, and there was something horribly determined about how they came. I didn't like it at all. We prepared to go down the hill. I liked that even less. At least we had elevation on our side.

One way or the other, we were going to settle it right now.

"*Well,*" said Loiosh. "*Here you are.*"

"*No shit,*" I said.

17

I turned back toward Fornia and stood there next to Daymar as
Napper approached from behind me to my left, and the whole
bloody war approached from behind me to my right.

Napper got there first. He came up next to me, holding a
short, heavy sword that was streaked with red. I glanced over at
him, and his eyes were shining, and he wore a delighted smile all
over his face. I said, "Napper, meet Daymar. Daymar, Napper.
And that is the Count of Fornia. Anyone bring wine? Cheese? I
could manage some biscuits."

The three who had been assigned to watch us didn't think
I was very funny, but neither did they construe my remarks
as suspicious enough to cut us down. "Your weapons," said one
of them.

"Daymar, can you break through the block and get us out of here?"

"No," he explained gently. *"They strengthened the block after I
broke through it."*

"Pity," I said.

"If I can get about half an hour—"

He might as well have asked for half a year. *"Yeah, well, I'll let
you know."*

"Weapons," repeated the soldier. "Now."

"What's the plan, Vlad?" said Napper, loud enough for everyone to hear.

"The good news is that we're negotiating," I told him. "The
bad news is that I surrendered."

"You what?"

"On the other hand, if he plans to kill me, I'll have to say the surrender is off. In the meantime, you'd best give the nice man your sword. I would, too, but I don't have one."

"Carefully," added the guard. "Unbuckle the belt and let it fall."

He looked fairly tough. So did the others. I didn't like Napper's chances against all three of them. One was between us and Fornia, the others flanked us. Napper began to comply, with exaggerated slowness.

"I don't suppose, Daymar, you know what they're doing?"

"No," said Daymar. *"He has me blocked."* Daymar sounded hurt.

Orders came barking out from somewhere in the group, and swords were drawn. I drew in my breath, terrified all over again, but the honor guard and the sorcerers turned to face the approaching battle. For an instant, with all the movement, I had a clear shot at Fornia, but then it was gone before I could have taken it even if I'd been so inclined.

There was an odd, unreal quality to the whole thing that lingers in my memory even now. I stood with Daymar on one side of me and Napper on the other, with the whole war, or at least a crucial part of it, rushing down on me, with Fornia amidst his honor guard and sorcerers turning away from us as if we were suddenly no part of their world and certainly no threat to them.

Well, okay, we *were* no threat to them.

I knew what Fornia was doing, I knew why he was doing it, I knew where it would lead; and there wasn't anything I could do about it.

There's a certain frustration that players of S'yang Stones get when their best shots fail and their opponents keep getting lucky breaks. I've seen it, and I've had it happen to me. You start just throwing your stones, even the flat ones, almost at random, as if you want to punish yourself for your bad luck by playing badly. I was feeling the same thing right now.

Was I making a bad play out of frustration, or was I really

getting the odds I needed, now that the battle was loud and everyone had their backs to us?

I threw a shuriken into the throat of the man in front of us, the one who was threatening Napper, and then planted a knife in the throat of the one to my left; I heard Napper draw his sword, and by the time I turned around the third of the guards was dead and Napper was finishing off the one I'd started on. I caught of glimpse of Daymar staring, wide-eyed.

Better yet, Fornia hadn't noticed, nor had any of his group.

Napper said, "What's the plan?"

That almost made me laugh. A little demon in my head wanted me to say "Kill them all," but I resisted temptation.

"Boss, does this situation seem a little absurd to you?"

"Absurd? Well, among other things, yes."

Then Morrolan's band reached Fornia's honor guard, and the game was being played in earnest.

I saw Aliera, now dismounted, standing next to Morrolan; around them were several others I didn't recognize, and behind them—where she came from I couldn't say—behind them, mounted, was Sethra Lavode, holding the weapon I knew to be Iceflame. They were all of them heading straight for Fornia, who was waiting with the patience of a gambler who has staked everything he has on one throw and knows, now that the coins are spinning, that all he can do is wait and see which way they land.

My task was simple, put that way: just reach my hand out and scoop up the coins before they stopped spinning. And somehow contrive not to have my hand cut off.

Now *that* was a thought.

Good. I had a thought. All I had to do was combine thought with opportunity and I'd have something else: a chance.

I tried to make contact with Morrolan, but either I didn't know him well enough or he was concentrating on his mayhem too hard, or both. Probably both. I knew Aliera even less, but it was a worth a try—

And at that moment Fornia's honor guard fell back toward us as a body, struck by Morrolan's attack—or, more exactly, the remnants of the Eastern cavalry that was being pushed into Fornia's honor guard—and the three of us had to scramble or be trampled down.

"The plan," I told Napper, "is not to get killed."

"We could attack from behind."

"And get maybe two each at the most before they wiped us out. I don't think so."

Now, you must understand that, as we were speaking, we were also running to get away from the retreating honor guard. This left me facing the northeast, the highest part of the hill. I touched Napper's arm and said, "Look. What's that?"

He stopped in his tracks, watching another mass of humanity head toward us. "That's the hammer," he said. He gestured back over his shoulder and said, "And that's the anvil."

"Well, we had to expect him to have reinforcements handy once Morrolan started breaking through."

"That makes me feel better," said Napper.

Daymar, who had been silent this entire time, said, "I think I am perhaps no longer useful here."

"Does that mean you can teleport now?"

"Not exactly. I was thinking of a different method."

I thought of Morrolan's window and an idea began to form. I said, "Tell me about it."

He stared at me with a puzzled expression and said, "I was thinking about running."

"Oh," I said. "I hadn't thought of that."

The battle continued pressing toward us, and the approaching company looked to be light infantry.

"Do you think Morrolan will reach Fornia before the reinforcements arrive?" said Napper.

"If Fornia has his way, he will."

"Beg pardon?"

"I have to do something," I said.

"Like what?"

"Something clever."

We backed up a little farther. "Clever," said Napper, "will only get you so far."

I didn't answer, because things had gotten even louder, and that just wasn't the right moment to be philosophical. The light infantry was closing on us quickly, and on the other side Easterners were dying, and to the smells of battle that I've already refused to describe once we can add the distinctive and equally unpleasant smell of dead and dying horses.

What Napper said was reasonable, though: Fornia's plan wasn't "clever" in the usual sense; rather it was a bold, calculated gamble, like redoubling the bet when the pattern is in your opponent's favor but one perfect throw could give you the game and you're down to your last flat stone.

"Napper," I said aloud. "I think it's time to die valiantly. What do you think?"

"Yes!" he said.

"How 'bout you, Daymar? Want to join us?"

"In what?"

"We're going to attack, of course."

"Oh. Very well," he said.

"He's not armed," pointed out Napper.

"I most certainly am," said Daymar, sounding slightly offended.

Well, he wasn't carrying a blade, but I believed him.

"All right," I said. "That one, with his hair in a queue, is Ori. He is preparing a split-second teleport as part of Fornia's plan to, well, never mind. The important thing is to kill him. Killing Fornia will be harder, because he is surrounded by his honor guard, but it isn't as important either. It is Ori who has to die."

"All right," said Napper.

"Very well," said Daymar.

"Any questions?"

There were none.

"Charge," I said conversationally.

We walked forward at an even pace. I had evidently drawn a dagger at some point, and I held it in my right hand. Spell-breaker was in my left, swinging in circles. It had grown longer somehow, to almost three feet, I think, and the links were bigger; its swing covered my whole body, and Daymar on my right and Napper on my left.

Napper said, "Should we give them a yell as we go in?"

"No," I said. "We should say nothing. No more talking."

"You're going to strike them in the back, without warning?"

"Yes."

"I don't—"

"You volunteered for this. We're doing it my way. If you don't like it, take off. In either case, keep quiet."

"Yes, sir," said Napper. It didn't occur to me until later to wonder if he was being ironic. Thinking about it, I don't believe he was.

Yes. Battles are decided, Sethra told me, when timing and momentum and courage all come together and, at just the right moment, someone fails to make a critical mistake and doesn't manage to miss a vital opportunity. An opportunity that, perhaps, no one quite realized was there, because it is just all too confusing to have a complete grasp of everything that is happening. I was right in the middle of it, and I still don't know enough about who was doing what to give a complete picture. But I have my incomplete picture; I have to be satisfied with that, and you will, too.

As we approached, I reached out for Daymar, who was astonishingly easy to make contact with, and I said, *"What is Ori doing?"*

"Which one is Ori again?"

"That one."

"Oh. I don't know what he's doing exactly. They're still blocking me. But he's concentrating on a spell of some kind."

"Doing one, or preparing to do it?"

"*Oh, he's preparing to do it. He's—what's the word? Poised. Yes, that's the word. He's poised to do a spell.*"

We hadn't stopped walking forward, and by this time we were ten feet behind the sorcerers, who were just behind Fornia and his honor guard. Ori was facing away from me.

I walked up and stuck my knife squarely into his back.

He screamed, and everyone turned around and looked at me as Ori spasmed and dropped to his knees. I couldn't see the expression on Ori's face, but I wasn't terribly interested in it, either. Fornia, however, stared at me wide-eyed.

"I hope," I said, "I haven't interfered with your plans."

"Kill him," said Fornia. "Kill all three of them."

And likely they would have, too; except that, at that moment, Morrolan broke through the final line of Eastern cavalry, and, amid the cries of people and horses, they charged Fornia's honor guard.

Fornia was thrust back toward me, which might have made it an excellent chance to kill him but I couldn't because I had to get out of the way of the large, very plain, unadorned Morganti greatsword he was swinging at my head. I did so, falling to the ground and rolling. I continued to roll away, not knowing exactly where Fornia and the Morganti blade were, and making the calm, rational decision that I needed to get away from them both, and besides, it was all I could do in the midst of my panic.

"*Boss! Boss! You can stand up now!*"

It's always embarrassing to panic in front of Loiosh. I stood up, and for just an instant, no one was around me and nothing horrible was happening in my immediate vicinity.

Then I spotted Fornia, about twenty feet away. He held both hands on the hilt of the sword, holding it at about waist height. Napper, his back to me, stood facing Fornia. Neither of them moved. It took me a second to realize that I could see a few inches of the point of the Morganti greatsword sticking out of Napper's back.

Napper dropped his sword, which fell, point first, very slowly, then stuck in the ground and swayed back and forth, also slowly. Nothing else moved in the entire world; Fornia and Napper were like twin sculptures, and would hold that pose until the world dissolved into the dreamstuff of the Gods, as my people say it will someday. But even then, the essence of Napper would never come back, and the shadowy remembrances of him in the minds of people like me, his comrades, would be all that would ever again exist of him.

And still they both stood, mutually transfixed.

Then Fornia looked at me, Napper unceremoniously fell to the ground, and the world started up again.

My moment of panic was over, replaced by a kind of hollowness that isn't all that bad a way to feel in such circumstances; at least it didn't keep me from observing, anticipating, and acting. I threw a couple of knives at Fornia just to let him know to keep his distance and began working my way toward Morrolan. At this point, the light infantry finally reached us. They flowed past me—I guess they figured that, being an Easterner, I had to be one of their cavalrymen—and Fornia was momentarily lost from sight.

I tried to spot Morrolan, but, ironically, now that he was within a knife-throw I couldn't see him. I kept looking.

Thinking back on it, this was what I had always imagined a battle to be like: constantly dodging, moving, trying to look in every direction at once, and never really sure of what I ought to be doing. The actual battles I had been in had certainly had elements of confusion, but at least I always knew what I had to do, and I could always concentrate on one direction. I guess the difference was that there were no actual lines here: Everyone was mixed up with everyone else, the entire thing being broken up into an endless, chaotic series of one-on-one or two-on-one fights. I could just imagine how often those who were actually participating had to stop and check caps or sashes to make sure they weren't about to strike down someone on their own side. Probably a few people got hit because they took too long to be sure, and almost certainly a few people got hit because the guy in front of them didn't take long enough.

At length I spotted Morrolan, just a glimpse of him through a temporary part in the sea of struggling humanity, and I moved toward him. If, by the way, you're wondering what became of Daymar, I still don't know. Maybe he was around the entire time, mixing it up with the enemy in his own way and doing what damage he could, but I suspect he took to his heels right around the time Fornia was destroying Napper. Can't say as I blame him much.

I skipped around a few fights, shuffled, dodged, and tried to spot Morrolan again. On the way, I passed by Napper's lifeless and souless body, and had another, very brief, moment of panic until Loiosh said, *"He's not here, Boss. Not in sight, at least."* I kept going.

I wrapped Spellbreaker around my left wrist again and grabbed Napper's sword from where it stuck out of the ground, even though it was too heavy for me, and moved toward where I'd seen Morrolan, hoping that I could trust Loiosh's perceptions and that Fornia wasn't about to appear swinging at the back of my head.

But no, Fornia wasn't coming after me just now, he was coming after Morrolan. And Morrolan seemed pretty pleased about it. They faced each other in a spot that sensible people had stayed away from, circling each other, and both apparently delighted by the encounter. Just beyond Morrolan I saw Aliera and a couple of other officers I didn't recognize, and they also seemed quite happy with this state of affairs.

In fact, everyone was happy about it except me, and I wouldn't have minded either except that I knew what Fornia was up to. The fact that I'd killed Ori had certainly messed with part of his plan, but he was going merrily on with the rest of it, I suppose trusting himself to find a way out when it was over. Or maybe not caring if he found a way out; he was, after all, a Dragon.

"No way around it, Loiosh."

"Boss—"

"I know. But I hate letting people get away with things. It offends me when they think they've put one over on me. It's a pride thing."

"You've been hanging around Dragons too long."

"Lieutenant Loiosh—First Jhereg Assassins—Charge."

"Whatever."

It was less of a charge than a stroll, but I carried it out, hardly planned and barely thought about, as neatly as any assassination I'd ever done, and under the circumstances that is no small thing. I did my calculations during the half dozen paces that separated us: I still didn't want to kill him, and didn't want to get close enough to that weapon to be so much as scratched by bad luck should he spasm; but I couldn't let him fight Morrolan with that weapon. I held Napper's big, heavy sword with both hands and toyed with it a bit. I wished I'd had more time to get a feel for the thing.

I came up directly behind Fornia. Morrolan spotted me, although I was awfully close before he did; he probably doesn't know how I did that, or maybe he just thinks he was concentrating too hard on Fornia. But the look on Morrolan's face warned Fornia, who took a step backward and started to turn, and when he was part of the way around I stepped in and swung Napper's sword down in a long overhead arc such as no Eastern fencer would ever execute and I put everything I had into it, knowing that if I missed I was dead and worse, but that it would likely take all my strength.

I struck him just above the wrists, and his scream was instantaneous and a joy to my ears. The force of the blow left my own weapon embedded in the ground, but I was done with it anyway. Before I could think about what I was doing—because, I assure you, thinking would have done me no good at all—I picked up the Morganti greatsword by the pommel, and ignoring the hands still wrapped tightly around it, I tossed it in Morrolan's general direction, being careful not to throw it actually *at* him, because I knew he might take that wrong.

Fornia sobbed.

His honor guard closed on me, and I did something I had been wanting to do for several weeks: I turned and *ran*.

My plan at that point was to run as fast as I could and as far as I could and not stop until I reached Adrilankha, and if I happened to be going in the wrong direction, well, okay, so maybe I'd make a bit of a detour; they say the world is round, after all.

As I dashed by, I saw someone stoop to pick up the Morganti sword that Fornia had recently held—I didn't even notice at the time which side had recovered the thing—and that gave me even more reason to run. Adrilankha, here I come.

I didn't actually make it that far—it was more like fifty feet before I was stopped. The command, "Hold it!" was so sharp and so, well, commanding, that I found I had obeyed before I actually thought about it. I turned around and found I was looking up at Sethra Lavode, atop a horse that, with my equine expertise, I can assure you was dark colored and very big. It looked at Loiosh and tossed its head, snorting like Morrolan had on one or two occasions. Loiosh didn't dignify it with an answer.

Sethra said, "Where are you going, soldier?"

"Uh . . . I think you have me confused with someone else," I said.

"I doubt it," said Sethra. "In any case, there's no reason to run now; the battle is nearly over."

I looked at where I'd just come from, turned back to Sethra, and said, "You're kidding, right?"

"I'm not kidding. Your unit routed the enemy from Dorian's Hill and drove them almost right up to the Wall. That would have been Fornia's moment to bring up his reserves, except that he was busy just then and didn't get around to it. Besides, Morrolan informs me that Fornia is dead now, anyway, and we have the weapon that caused all the trouble, so there isn't all that much to fight about. I expect a general surrender within the next few minutes, as soon as they can find someone with sufficient authority to surrender to us."

I looked again. "If you say so," I said.

Sethra seemed amused. "It's over, Vlad. Trust me. I've done this sort of thing before. You should have run earlier, when it would have done some good."

"I know, I know."

"Now you might as well wait here, with me."

"You're not going to send me back into battle as punishment for desertion?"

"The punishment for desertion is beheading. Being sent into battle is a reward."

"You mean that, don't you?"

She looked serious for a moment, and said, "Yes."

She was right, though. I don't mean about being sent into battle, I mean about the whole thing being pretty much over. Within half an hour the fighting had stopped, there were banners piled up all over the field, and Sethra, Aliera, and Morrolan were all involved in negotiations with their previous enemies. The war was over. If I chose to, I could convince myself that I had had a major part in winning it. I would have preferred to forget the whole thing, but that was harder.

We eventually formed a camp on the hill where we'd lately fought with Fornia, his sorcerers, and his honor guard. Most of the honor guard had fallen to Blackwand and to Kieron's greatsword (Aliera's actions in the battle were much discussed, although I hadn't actually seen much of her). I sat far away from the action, but eventually Virt found me. She had a brand-new scar on her face and a noticeable limp.

"Hey there," she said. "So you bugged out, huh?" She sounded more bantering than hostile.

"Yeah," I said. "I bugged out."

"I've heard about it. Probably not accurately, but I've heard. Good show."

"Thanks."

"And I've heard about Napper. We're going to have services

for him this evening. Aelburr and I would like you to help us anoint him."

"What's the point? There's nothing left for Deathgate."

"I think you know what the point is."

I took a deep breath, then I nodded. "All right. I'll be there."

She moved on. A little later, Rascha came by. She said, "Good work, soldier."

"Thanks," I said.

"I also convey congratulations from Crown, and from the Captain."

"Thank them for me."

She started to say more, then snapped a salute and walked off. A little later Sethra walked by again. She said, "You should know that Cropper has recommended you for a Dragonshead Medal. I declined on your behalf, with thanks, but I thought you should know."

"Thanks," I said. "And thanks."

How did she know me so well? I suppose that's part of being a general, or maybe part of being Sethra Lavode. I knew that in a few days or weeks the idea of being recommended for a medal by a Dragon warrior would be pretty funny, but right now a ceremony would be nothing more than an irritation. They'd be giving out a lot of medals this evening, and I didn't have much interest in hanging around to watch, much less participating. I just wanted to go home.

I said, "Will Napper receive one?"

"Yes."

"Good."

She wandered away, and a little later Aliera came up and stood over me. I looked up at her, and then away. When she didn't speak, and the silence was becoming uncomfortable, I said, "I understand you did a lot of killing today. Congratulations. Did Morrolan get the weapon?"

"No."

I looked up. "No? What happened to it?"

"It was picked up by the officer at whose feet it landed when you threw it. She claimed it as battlefield spoil. Hard to argue with."

"Oh."

"Morrolan was wondering why you jumped in when you did."

"Fornia had a plan; I wished to stop it. Besides, I told him I'd get the damned thing."

"Wasn't Morrolan well on his way to stopping Fornia's plan anyway?"

"No, he was well on his way to helping Fornia carry it out."

"I don't understand."

"As Napper used to say, it don't matter."

"No? Well, maybe not. But tell me: Do you understand us a little better now than you did when you signed up?"

"No."

"I think you do," she said.

I didn't answer, and presently she walked away. At least she didn't salute.

Later that night I met up with Cropper Company and helped anoint the bodies for Deathgate. There were thirty-four dead, and many more in various stages of recovery. Dunn was among the dead, having fallen carrying the unit colors, just as he wanted. I had the awful feeling that some of the company were jealous of him. No one, of course, was jealous of Napper. And, pointlessly, Virt and Aelburr and I rubbed the oil onto him so his body would remain whole until he went over the Falls, where his body would eventually rot anyway. Then came the ceremonies for the dead, and the awarding of decorations, and then we were done, and back to our tents.

Virt and Aelburr and I sat around and watched the fire burn down. I said to Virt, "You got what you wanted, didn't you?"

"Yes," she said. "And so did you."

"Yes," I said. "I did."

"Was it worth it?"

"Yes. Just barely, but yes."

"That's how I feel."

"Sometimes winning is painful, but it's always better than losing."

"Hear, hear," said Aelburr.

The teleport blocks were down, and I could have returned to Adrilankha that night, but I told myself that I was in no mood to have my insides scrambled, so I spent one more night in the tent, and it was only the next morning, when confronted with salted kethna, bad coffee, and biscuits that I said good-bye to Virt and Aelburr, suggested they come visit me sometime, and teleported back to my own street, where I found a place that served decent food and I ordered klava, hot muffins, boiled goose eggs, and a thick slab of bacon, with onions.

I lingered over breakfast, then headed back home for a nap. I figured I'd earned a day off. Tomorrow I'd go back to making crime; it was so much kinder than war.

Epilogue: Trophies

When it was over, my dining room table was suitable for firewood, and the upholstery on two of my chairs was suitable for rags, but my favorite chair had escaped with only a slight nick in one leg, and my carpet had no blood on it. Sethra the Younger lay next to the window box, half conscious, her eyes rolling about in her head.

Morrolan, who had broken up the fight, much to Aliera's disgust, stood between them and addressed me: "You knew all along, didn't you?"

"Excuse me?"

"I mean, back during the battle. You knew."

"I only knew what Fornia had in mind, and I didn't find that out until the end."

"Why didn't you tell me?"

"My job was to get the weapon. I got it. I didn't much care who ended up with it."

"But you knew—"

"Yes, dammit, I knew. And now you know. There was a Great Weapon concealed inside that blade Fornia had taken from Baritt, just as you suspected. I assume it was Baritt who concealed it, and that he did it for reasons of his own. Fornia was able to find it, but didn't know how to release it from its concealment. His idea was that if it clashed with another Great Weapon, it would emerge. I tried it tonight. It worked."

"And Fornia," said Aliera before Morrolan could compose a

response, "set up his battle so that he would cross blades with a Great Weapon, either Blackwand or Iceflame. He could," she added reflectively, "have just challenged Morrolan to a duel and gotten the same result."

"He probably would have," said Morrolan reflectively. "But I launched a war, and he was never one to turn down a challenge like that."

The weapon in question lay on the floor midway between Aliera and where Sethra the Younger sprawled. All around it were pieces of the greatsword in which it had been hidden. With its concealment gone, it appeared as a dull, black short sword. No one touched it.

"You could say thank you," said Morrolan suddenly.

Aliera said, "For what?"

"For saving your life, cousin. Do you think you could have gone up against a Great Weapon?"

"Yes. Besides, Cawti was going to stick a knife in her back."

Morrolan looked at Cawti, who was leaning against the wall with her arms folded. She dimpled and dropped Morrolan a curtsy. I was surprised that Aliera had noticed. Aliera added, "And Loiosh was going to attack her, too, I think. She never really had a chance. If you hadn't butted in—"

"If Morrolan hadn't butted in," I said, "we wouldn't have discovered the Great Weapon, which I take to be—what did they call it, Morrolan?"

"It is called Pathfinder."

"Well named," said Aliera. "It found its way to me, eventually."

"To you?" said Morrolan.

Aliera stepped forward, bent over, and picked it up, transferring Kieron's greatsword to her left hand. "Yes," she said.

"And what do you suppose Sethra the Younger will say about that?"

Aliera unbuckled the sheath she wore on her back and tossed

it onto the floor near Sethra. Then she put Kieron's sword next to it. "She'll say we have a bargain," said Aliera.

"You know, Vlad," said Morrolan, "I've suspected for years now that there were things you never told me about the Wall of Baritt's Tomb."

"There were things I didn't want to think about," I said. "Some of it I still don't want to think about, and some of it I still don't remember clearly. But you told me to get that sword—you didn't, by the way, tell me anything about how to go about it or what to do when I'd gotten it—so I went and got the sword. And—as I say, that's all I remember."

"That's all you remember, is it?"

"My memory sometimes plays tricks on me, Morrolan. Just a couple of days ago, I suddenly remembered a few things about our trip to Deathgate that I'd forgotten up until then. Maybe, someday, I'll remember more about this."

"You expect me to believe that?"

"You have to believe it; you're in my house. Next time I'm at Castle Black you can call me a liar if you want." His lips twitched. I added, "And with everything you knew but didn't tell me, you have no cause to come down on me about not telling you everything."

"Hmmm. I may concede on that point," he said. "I'll have to think about it."

"Do that," I said. "In the meantime, why don't you get your things, including that"— I pointed to Sethra the Younger— "and leave me alone. I'm sure she wants to go plan the invasion of the East, and Aliera wants to play with her new toy, and you, well, maybe you'll want to go start another war or something."

"Vlad—"

"Never mind, Morrolan. I just want to relax now."

"I'll send someone over to clean up the mess."

"No, I can get it. I'll see you . . . sometime."

He nodded.

They gathered up Sethra and headed for the door. Aliera carried Pathfinder. Morrolan started to say something at the door, then shrugged and walked out. What they did after that I neither know nor care about; the Wall of Baritt's Tomb was finally over for me, except for the final telling. And at the cost of a table and a couple of chairs I considered it a pretty good deal.

I sat down in my favorite chair, and, because the others were destroyed, Cawti sat in my lap. I leaned my head back and closed my eyes.

"That," I said, "is what the Dragons call negotiating."

"Mmmm," she said. "What now?"

"As I said, I'll clean the place up tomorrow. Eventually I have to go put this whole thing behind me by having a last session with an odd metal box, and then—what day is it?"

"Farmday."

"Right. Valabar's won't be too busy. Thinking about all those months of bad food has made me want something good, and I'm in just the mood to have someone else cook it and bring it to me and then wash the dishes."

"My treat," she said.

"Mine. I'm finishing a job and getting paid."

"All right. When are you going to go talk to the box?" She leaned her head on my shoulder. Her hair smelled of sandalwood and was very soft.

"Soon," I said. "But not instantly."

Loiosh flew over and landed on my shoulder. I didn't much want to move, but it would be good to have the whole thing finished. I opened my eyes and looked at the wreckage of my flat, thought back on my days in the army, and stroked Cawti's hair.

If just surviving can be counted as a win, I was way ahead of the game.

BIO

What would you like to know about me, assuming that you care? My full name is Steven Karl Zoltán Brust. I was born in 1955, so I'm forty-two at the time of this writing, and I have a big bald spot which I cover up with a hat, but I was wearing the hat before I developed the bald spot so it doesn't really count. I live in Minneapolis, Minnesota, except that I spent this last winter in Arizona, and if you don't know why, you haven't spent a winter in Minnesota.

I play drums, guitar, banjo, and Middle Eastern percussion, and I've written some songs, and I have produced a solo record called *A Rose for Iconoclastes*; if you want information on the record you can get it by sending E-mail to UncleHugo@aol.com, and if you don't understand the title you need to read more Roger Zelazny.

In addition to the abovementioned Zelazny, my heroes are: Alexandre Dumas, Mark Twain, Leon Trotsky, Dorothy Parker, Mickey Hart, and Mike Caro. If you don't recognize one or more of these names, it doesn't make you a bad person.

I have a Strapping Son named Corwin and three Charming Daughters named Aliera, Carolyn, and Toni. I live with my Lovely Associate, Liz Cooper, in a beautiful house in a crummy neighborhood. I have a dog named Miska and a double-yellow-headed Amazon parrot named John Henry Holliday, and if you don't know his nickname you should see Val Kilmer in *Tombstone*.

Liz has a cat named Rogue and an African Grey parrot named Loiosh, and if you don't know where the name "Loiosh" comes from, why are you even reading this bio?

My favorite games are Texas Hold 'Em and Stud hi-lo/8. If you don't know what those are, I'd be glad to teach you.

Steven Brust
Lake Havasu City, Arizona
February 1998